The girl grinned, her teeth so white they were almost blue. . . . She had fangs like a viper, the tips red with blood. . . .

"I know everything, my love," she said. "Everything. I can free you from the pain," she said, her lips now against his ear.

A feeling of warmth flooded through him, releasing all tension from muscle and sinew, his will completely replaced with desire. Peregrine was not a religious man, but now he was convinced that the Angel of Death existed, an exquisite creature whose embrace no man or woman would want to resist. He closed his eyes and waited for the bliss of death to cleanse him forever of misery and hate. . . .

By Michael Romkey
Published by Ballantine Books:

I, VAMPIRE
THE VAMPIRE PAPERS
THE VAMPIRE PRINCESS
THE VAMPIRE VIRUS
VAMPIRE HUNTER
THE LONDON VAMPIRE PANIC
THE VAMPIRE'S VIOLIN

Books published by The Random House Publishing Group
are available at quantity discounts on bulk purchases for
premium, educational, fund-raising, and special sales use.
For details, please call 1-800-733-3000.

AMERICAN GOTHIC

A Vampire Story

MICHAEL ROMKEY

BALLANTINE BOOKS • NEW YORK

This is a work of fiction. Names, characters, places, and incidents are the products of the author's imagination or are used fictitiously. Any resemblance to actual events, locales, or persons, living or dead, is entirely coincidental.

A Del Rey® Book
Published by The Random House Publishing Group
Copyright © 2004 by Michael Romkey

www.delreydigital.com

ISBN 0-345-45210-0

Manufactured in the United States of America

First Edition: April 2004

OPM   10   9   8   7   6   5   4   3   2   1

For Carol,
with love

PART ONE

NEW ORLEANS
1863

1

Desire

THE FRENCH DOORS at the rear of the parlor stood open, letting cool night air spill into the house. Outside in the garden, the shadowy outlines of orchids and ferns came to life with each breath of wind, starveling forms animated in darkness. There was an exotic genus of flower in the garden that opened its blossoms only to the moon. Nathaniel Peregrine had not been in the South long enough to know it by name, but he could sometimes smell its perfume, when the scent was not hidden beneath the cloying sweetness of the incenselike smoke that permeated the house.

Peregrine's long frame was stretched out on a divan. Beside him asleep was a young woman in a gown made of burgundy velvet. With eyes half closed, he watched the air slip through the trembling specters in the garden. The breeze combed small, brittle music from the bamboo wind chimes, a sound like the delicate clicking of finger bones strung together with black thread. Peregrine seemed to have no more presence than did the wind; he felt insubstantial, a puff of smoke, an outline drawn in fog, a ghost who continued to haunt his body though his real life had ended in September of the previous year.

His eyelids, too heavy to resist gravity, fell closed again.

The house seemed to float upward with the wind, rising and falling with each whisper of air. He pictured it crossing the river, picking up speed as it left the city behind, like a ship when wind fills the sails, sending it flying through parting seas. Over the bayous, toward the Gulf of Mexico, where it would lose momentum with the dying breeze and drop into the dark waters, sinking beneath the waves. There, the house and its habitués would settle slowly into a lightless abyss beyond the touch of sun and seasons, a safe black nothingness where the pain of living could no longer find them.

The breeze turned, renewing the quiet, almost imperceptible clicking of the wind chimes, counting tears one by one.

Click, click, click, click, click . . .

Peregrine opened his eyes wide and his head came up from the silk pillow, which was embroidered with an image of a dragon chasing its own tail. The house—square, stolid, built of red brick—remained firmly anchored to its stone foundation in the middle of a street a few blocks from the Mississippi River on the upstream end of the French Quarter.

Nothing had changed.

Horrible as it was to realize, nothing had changed.

Before the war, planters divided their days between Garden District mansions and the plantation great houses where slaves tended fields of cotton stretching from ivory-pillared porches to the horizon. New Orleans was a treasure city, the capital of an antebellum aristocracy built upon the lash. Ships from Europe came into port to trade for cotton. The wharves were lined with warehouses that groaned with riches. Traders, captains, and ship owners became as wealthy as the landed gentry.

An ancient Indian prophecy warned the city to beware of death by water, and so it twice came, in 1812 with the British, and a half century later, in 1863. Union forces attacked the Crescent City from two directions during the Civil War. First came the sea blockade, severing the vein that carried the city's golden lifeblood. But the city did not fall until an assault was thrown down the river. Now soldiers wearing uniforms of midnight blue patrolled the streets, and the city's inhabitants were subjected to the marshal law of a Yankee general who had no love for the South.

Outside the city, in the countryside of nearby parishes, the great houses that had not been burned were mostly occupied by Union officers. The slaves had run away, the cotton confiscated or left to rot in the fields. And New Orleans, Pearl of the Mississippi Delta, was transformed into a purgatory of shattered family dynasties and lost fortunes.

A match flared in the dim room. Someone muttered a few indistinct words punctuated with a dry cough.

Peregrine lifted his hand a few inches. Yu, the opium den's keeper, came to him and knelt on the floor to prepare another pipe. The woman beside Peregrine stirred, awakened by the smell of smoke. She looked up at Peregrine until he finished and passed her the pipe.

Evangeline McAllister had already known hardship in her young life. Her fiancé, one of Jeb Stuart's officers, had been killed at Bull Run. Her home was destroyed in the siege of Vicksburg, her father shot dead trying to stop Union soldiers from setting fire to his shops. She had come to New Orleans to stay with a maiden aunt, but the old woman had died, too, carried away by influenza, leaving the girl penniless and in the sort of straits that lead young women to desperate measures.

Peregrine put his head back against the pillow and closed his eyes, listening to the sound of Evangeline drawing the sickly-sweet blue smoke up the opium pipe's silver stem.

The wind returned in a silent rush as the narcotic seemed to take hold of him by the base of the brain, pulling him down into its dream, smothering him with a warm blanket of forgetfulness. The house opened itself to the night, unfolding like a giant puzzle box. There were invisible fingers under Peregrine, lifting him gently into the sky. He floated over the city, waiting for the wind to blow over him again, extinguishing this last bit of consciousness, and with it the everlasting grief.

Peregrine awoke with the sense that time had passed. The garden was dark, so it was still night, although it could have been the next night for all he knew. It was a little like waking up after the Battle of Antietam, coming out of a coma to find he was not in the afterlife but in an army field hospital. The doctors did not expect him to live and gave him generous quantities of opium to ease the suffering. The drugs helped to ease his physical pain, and with it the real source of his misery, which had nothing to do with the rebel bullets the doctors had dug out of his shoulder, chest, and leg. But Peregrine did not die, and in the months of convalescence, the poppy became a constant companion for the newly promoted brigadier general.

How many pipes had Peregrine taken that night with Evangeline?

Yu would give him an accurate reckoning. The opium den keeper was a scrupulous businessman, never asking for more or accepting less than his due, never admitting a customer whose account was in arrears.

Peregrine debated with himself briefly before deciding

to have one last pipe before returning to his boarding-house. He looked around again, but the Chinaman was nowhere to be found. Peregrine closed his eyes and was instantly asleep. When he next opened his eyes, he felt the presence of someone bending over him. He expected it to be Yu, but instead there was a girl hovering so close to Evangeline it seemed she was about to kiss the woman as she floated inside the dragon's dream. The girl bowed over them had the sort of face that causes men to forget what they're saying in midsentence and stare open-mouthed. Her face was as perfectly drawn as a doll's, her skin white as porcelain and nearly translucent, the color made all the more striking by the vivid red of her lips. She was far too young to be in an opium den.

"Hello," Peregrine said. He wanted to tell her an angel had no business in such a place, but he did not have the will to make himself speak further.

The girl's large green eyes turned up to his in a slow movement of such languor that Peregrine felt desire stir deep inside of him. It was only by degrees that Peregrine realized the girl's hand was upon Evangeline's breast, which had been freed from the low-cut bodice of her dress. Evangeline's skin was golden in the candlelight but for its small raised circle of rose-colored flesh.

The girl held Peregrine's stare until his body caught up with his mind enough for him to draw back from the two women. She smiled to see the shame he felt at awaking to such an intimate moment.

The girl turned her attention back to Evangeline, bury-ing her face in the soft flesh of her neck. Evangeline moaned and drew the other woman near. Then her eyes flew open with a sharp, reflexive movement, as if with a stab of pain. But the unnatural passion seemed to take full possession of her in the next moment. Another low moan escaped her lips, and the pupils disappeared beneath the upper lids of her hooded eyes.

The bizarre tableau attracted as well as repulsed Peregrine, and disgusted as he was, he could not make himself look away, as if driven by the power of an irresistible attraction to witness the unspeakable.

The girl brushed back a tendril of jet black hair that had fallen across her face, and she glanced up at him as if to judge his reaction. She seemed completely unashamed, and indeed, he saw a sparkle of wicked delight in her eyes, though whether from her debasement or Peregrine's he did not know.

New Orleans was a decadent place, he thought, a wretched whirlpool of depravity, where the innocent were sucked into degradation, women abandoned, children ruined. Sin had accumulated in the old port city as thick and viscous as river mud.

Peregrine saw a fluid motion of color at Evangeline's neck as the young girl broke off the embrace and pushed herself up on one arm, her eyes never leaving Peregrine's. Difficult as it was to break away from those mesmerizing eyes, it was impossible for him to keep from staring at the twin puncture wounds in Evangeline's neck. Two rivulets of blood trickled from where the young woman's mouth had been on the neck. Evangeline's eyes stared at the ceiling, sightless. Peregrine knew the look well enough. She was dead.

"What manner of fiend . . ."

The girl grinned back at him, her teeth so white they were almost blue, parting her lips so that he could see how she had done the thing. She had fangs like a viper, the tips red with the blood she'd drunk from the living fountain, now dead between them.

Peregrine squeezed his eyes shut. It wasn't real. The

beautiful demon was the work of the poppy. She laughed merrily when he opened his eyes again and realized that all was as it had been. He could hear madness in her laughter.

Peregrine tried to push her away but felt what little strength the opium had left him run out like water from an overturned cup. He sank back against the divan, helpless to resist the creature who was so strangely filling his soul with equal measures of dread and desire.

"I see so much suffering in your broken heart," she said, the words an intimate whisper intended for Peregrine's ears alone. "Your poor family."

She waited for him to gather himself enough to speak. "How did you know?"

The new kindness in her eyes drained the alarm from Peregrine. He had never seen her before that night, but for some unknown reason he had the sense that they had known each other for a very long time. He felt close to her, as if they had shared many long discussions and he had told her the innermost secrets of his mind. For whatever reason, he began to trust her. He could see the caring in her eyes, like the limitless compassion of a Madonna.

"I know everything, my love," she said. "Everything."

She put her hand against his face. Her skin was warm, nearly feverish, but dry. Somehow he could feel her pulse through her fingertips. Their two hearts were beating as one.

"I can free you from the pain," she said, her lips now against his ear.

A feeling of warmth flooded through him, releasing all tension from muscle and sinew, his will replaced completely with desire. Peregrine was not a religious man, but now he was convinced that the Angel of Death existed, an exquisite creature whose embrace no man or woman would want to resist. He closed his eyes and waited for the bliss of death to cleanse him forever of misery and hate.

There was a commotion in the front of the house. Peregrine had the impression of men coming noisily into the parlor as if searching for something, but he did not open his eyes, not wanting to break the spell. Surely the Angel of Death could not be distracted by the trifling interruptions of helpless mortals.

"There he is, me boys!" cried a voice thick with a familiar Irish brogue.

A strong hand gripped Peregrine by the upper arm.

"Come on, sir, let's get ye home."

Peregrine opened his eyes, knowing he would find himself facing Captain Seamus O'Rourke, his aide. And so it was. The beautiful angel was nowhere to be seen, his opportunity for release from earthly care snatched cruelly away at the last possible moment.

O'Rourke's expression changed as his eyes settled on Evangeline.

"Damn me, Peregrine, what have you done? The wench is dead!"

"My God, Captain," one of the soldiers cried out. "They're all dead!"

2

A Man of Qualities

DURING THE CIVIL War, the St. Charles was New Orleans's finest hotel, a sprawling complex with beds for a thousand people, occupying an entire city block. Newspaper advertisements called it "a city within four walls, where prosperous guests and contented employees alike benefit from its splendid environments. Scientifically constructed, embodying the utmost in sanitation, ventilation, safety, and conveniences."

General Benjamin F. Butler was a man who appreciated conveniences. The city's new military governor seized the St. Charles to serve as his headquarters.

On any given morning, including Sundays, the St. Charles lobby was a seething mass of human odds and ends, the bad company that assembles, like infection in an untreated wound, where calamity creates the opportunity for profit. Politicians, soldiers, traders, government men, and carpetbaggers jostled cheek by jowl in the noisy room. They smoked, chewed, joked, and played cards, passing time as each awaited an appointment, preferment, order, or contract. The wealth of the Deep South was up for grabs, and the sovereign power administering the division of spoils was doing business out of the St. Charles Hotel.

The pair of privates detailed to escort Nathaniel

Peregrine trailed him into the hotel. Peregrine surveyed the claustrophobic scene, his mouth set in a grim line.

On a bench beside the front desk, a doctor examined a soldier's wounded eye. The bandage, filthy and crusted with dried blood, was on the floor at the soldier's feet. Peregrine spotted O'Rourke's sandy-haired head on the far side of the lobby. The captain sat in an elevated chair, having his boots shined. Seeming to sense Peregrine's arrival, O'Rourke looked over the top of the newspaper held in his hands, which were red-knuckled, a fighter's hands. He climbed down from his perch, flipped the little black boy with the boot brush a penny, and began to shoulder his way through the crowd.

"Cigar, General?"

Peregrine shook his head at the florid-faced man in a beaver top hat who had stepped in front of him. But the man in the top hat ignored the refusal, pushing a cigar into Peregrine's breast pocket. "For later, then," he said, and offered his card. "Mordecai Johnstone, purveyor of the finest-quality army-issue provisions."

"I'm not a quartermaster, Mr. Jones," Peregrine said, handing back the card. "I don't have anything to do with buying supplies."

"I'm just here to make friends, General," Johnstone said, touching his hat as Peregrine stepped around him. "Hang me for a toad, sir, but I'm the sort of fellow who just plain likes people."

"Perhaps we shall be friends then," Peregrine said, walking away, his escorts close behind.

O'Rourke saluted as he came up. "That'll be all, boys," he said, dismissing the privates.

"Am I under arrest, Captain?" Peregrine asked.

"No, General."

"I ought to be."

"Begging your pardon, sir, but there is no crime in a gentleman indulging himself in a bit of sport from time to time."

"Like hell."

"There are allowances to be made, General. Your grievous wounds. The tragedy of your family, sir."

Peregrine looked away.

"We are all fate's playthings, sir," Captain O'Rourke said.

"That's a reassuring thought, Seamus."

"Begging your pardon, General. General Butler is expecting you."

"I don't want to keep him waiting," Peregrine said. "I'm in enough trouble as it is."

"Aye," Captain O'Rourke said. "Luck to ye, sir."

Butler did not look up as Peregrine stood at attention before what had until recently been the hotel manager's desk.

The military governor was a bullet-headed man, with small, sad eyes looking out from between heavy lids, with deep bags below. He wore his hair long on the sides and in back, a fringe around a bald pate, a droopy mustache disguising a weak mouth. Before the war, Butler had been a criminal lawyer and legislator in Massachusetts. He was a political general, lacking either McClellan's style or Sherman's dash, his army commission the handiwork of supporters in Washington. Peregrine would have predicted—correctly, as it would turn out later during the inept Bermuda Hundred campaign—that Butler would prove a poor leader of men in battle. Operators like Butler were better suited for duty in the rear echelon than upon the killing fields of Virginia. Butler made no secret of his plans to run again for office after the war, trading up his general's stars for a governorship.

"Nathaniel," he said at last, signing his name to a paper with a flourish. He did not return Peregrine's salute but handed him the document he had just finished composing.

General Order Number 28 was being issued, the document declared, in response to the uncivilized manner in which the women of New Orleans treated Union soldiers.

Peregrine read: *Hereafter when any female shall by word, gesture, or movement insult or show contempt for any officer or soldier of the United States, she shall be regarded and held liable to be treated as a woman of the town plying her trade.*

"What do you think the rebs will say about that?"

"It will offend their Southern sense of chivalry to have you ordering Union soldiers to treat their women like common prostitutes if they insult us," Peregrine said.

"To hell with Southern chivalry. Do you know what they call me behind my back, Nathaniel? 'Spoons' Butler. Of all the infernal cheek. *Spoons!* The gossips say I confiscated the silver from the Crescent City's homes and churches to line my own pockets. You know that I gave no such order. If liberties were taken, then it's no more than what the traitors deserved. The eight hundred thousand dollars I confiscated from the Dutch consulate—tongues are wagging over that, of course—was being held in escrow to purchase rebel war supplies. You know I'm not averse to taking stern measures when they are warranted. The fellow I hanged for hauling down the Union flag at the Mint, for example. How do these people expect me to react to such a provocation?"

Butler took the proclamation out of Peregrine's hands and bellowed for the lieutenant manning the desk outside the office. He handed him General Order Number 28 and ordered it be posted throughout the city without delay.

"They can hate me all they want," he said to Peregrine, "but they'll damned well obey me."

Butler came around his desk toward a pair of leather club chairs arranged on either side of a smoking stand. He lowered himself into a seat and indicated to Peregrine to accommodate himself in the other. Butler lit a cigar and puffed quietly for nearly a minute, meditating on the cloud of blue smoke swirling in the air. Peregrine studied a map of the city opposite his chair. The cigar Mordecai Johnstone had given him stayed in the pocket of his jacket. His head was beginning to ache. It was not a cigar he craved, but a pipe.

"That was a rum business last night at the Chinaman's," Butler said at last.

"Yes, sir. I want you to know that I didn't have anything to do with those people getting hurt."

"Of course you didn't. You're a Union officer, and a highly decorated one at that. The idea that you could sully your hands with crime is unthinkable."

Peregrine felt his face redden.

"Did you find and arrest that strange woman?"

"Woman?" Butler's eyes narrowed. "I don't know anything about a woman. The Chinaman is the one responsible for those foul deeds."

"Yu didn't hurt anybody."

"He damned well did. Five people he murdered, two of them defenseless women. And worse than that, he came this close to murdering my most-decorated brigadier general."

"I'm afraid a mistake has been made, General Butler."

"No mistake," Butler said, underlining each word with

a slashing movement of his cigar. "It's all in the report. You can read it, if you want. I have taken care that *your* name is not mentioned. Once his clients were rendered insensible with drugs, the Chinaman strangled them one by one. The motive, it seems, was theft."

"But they weren't strangled, sir," Peregrine argued. "The puncture wounds in their necks—"

"There were no wounds," Butler said, cutting him off. "None whatsoever. You're lucky you got out alive. If Captain O'Rourke hadn't come looking for you, your body would be in a pine box right now, on a train home for burial, killed by that murdering yellow bastard."

"My God," Peregrine said.

"Buck up, son," Butler said, misinterpreting Peregrine's frustration. "You've survived close scrapes before and will do so again. You need to save your luck to use against the real enemy, not some yellow-skinned, squint-eyed hophead."

"I saw the wounds, General Butler. Here—in the neck, a pair of punctures as if made by some beast's teeth."

"Nathaniel, stop. That is an order. There were no wounds. Ask O'Rourke."

Peregrine opened his mouth, but the look Butler gave him led him to shut it again, as Butler glared like a minor devil through a mephitic exhalation of blue smoke.

"You weren't in any condition, Nathaniel, to know what you did or didn't see last night. No doubt you also saw purple-spotted elephants dancing about. Not even a bourbon-drooling, cousin-marrying, backwoods Southern judge would consider the testimony of a witness who was insensate from the effects of smoking opium at the time of the crime. We gave the Chinaman a drumhead trial—which was more than he had coming, if you ask me—and hanged him at dawn. I've ordered all the hop joints in the city closed. This sort of thing will not happen again on Benjamin F. Butler's watch."

Butler reached inside his jacket as he spoke and withdrew a folded paper, which he unfolded with great drama.

"This is a telegram from the War Department. It says"—he paused a beat for effect—"that Halleck is putting you forward for the Congressional Medal of Honor for bravery at Antietam."

Peregrine's face began to burn again. "I don't deserve that."

"Stuff and nonsense, Nathaniel. If you hadn't held your men together when A. P. Hill finally attacked to pull Lee's chestnuts out of the fire, it would have turned into a rout. The Union can't afford many more battlefield fiascos if we're going to put down this damned insurrection. I suspect President Lincoln himself gave Halleck the idea about putting you forward for recognition. I understand you and the president are old friends."

"That's hardly the case. I don't even remember the president visiting me in the field hospital. I was out of my head from blood loss."

Butler turned sideways in his chair and regarded Peregrine closely, his small, shrewd eyes shining. "The Union needs heroes, Nathaniel. People imagined the war would be over in three months, and now here it is dragging into its third year. The authorities in New York are worried that there will be draft riots if Mr. Lincoln orders up any more conscripts, as he certainly must do."

Butler pushed his head forward on his neck, like a snapping turtle contemplating a minnow with unblinking eyes.

"You need to pull yourself together, Nathaniel. You're too valuable a man to the cause for me to have to hang you. Do I make myself clear?"

"Clear as a bell, sir."

Butler puffed thoughtfully on his cigar, his manner softening, the need to threaten past.

"I know you are grieving for your family, Nathaniel, but you need to swallow your grief before it consumes you. You are certain to ruin your health as well as your career if you continue on this path. It's time you did some hard thinking about your situation after the war, my boy. An educated and handsome young fellow, with a battlefield promotion to brigadier general and a chest loaded with gleaming medals, will have excellent prospects once we whip the rebs. This war isn't going to last forever, you know. We need to make the most of our opportunities. But a word to the wise, Nathaniel: Don't hitch your star to your friend Mr. Lincoln. He can't possibly win reelection in 1864. The way the war has gone, the voters are certain to send him back to Springfield to practice law."

"Have you considered my request for transfer to a battlefield unit, sir?"

"Ha ha!" Butler leaned over and slapped Peregrine's knee. "You *are* an ambitious young man. But you have not fully recovered from your wounds."

"I am fit enough."

Butler squinted at him through the smoke. "Your skin has an unhealthy pallor."

"Yes, from being penned up in this infernal city of traitors."

"Don't think your prospects to kill rebs will be limited by serving under me, Nathaniel. I'm promised a command in Virginia as soon as Banks can relieve me. If you remain on my staff, I can promise you all the fighting you can stand."

"Begging your pardon, General, but I am anxious to get back into the field as soon as possible. Sitting in this rebel city with little to meaningfully occupy my time is doing me no good."

"I will give the matter consideration," Butler said. "The War Department would have to agree. They won't be anxious to send one of our most decorated heroes back in harm's way."

"My job is killing rebels, sir."

"And you've proven you are very good at it. Now, Nathaniel, regarding the other unpleasant matter . . ."

Butler reached for the ashtray to unburden his cigar of a precariously long ash.

"You are hardly the first officer to develop an unhealthy friendship with the poppy while recovering from wounds. I am a worldly man. I understand that men must have their vices. But in a civil society, it is necessary for government to define the limits of what will be tolerated. We are a nation of laws, Nathaniel. That is why we will win this war. We have right on our side. We are doing the Lord's work, fighting to free the slaves from bondage, although what we will do with them after the war remains to be seen." His voice fell slightly. "Confidentially, I question whether it is healthy for the races to mingle. Perhaps the best answer is to repatriate the Africans to the Dark Continent."

"My wounds cause me little pain now," Peregrine said. "I no longer need the medicine. I can wean myself from it."

"I know you can, son. Get a grip on yourself and you'll pull through. You must put the past behind you and look to tomorrow. A man of your qualities has a very bright future indeed."

3

Saints Preserve Us

"WHAT DID YOU see last night at Yu's?" Peregrine asked.

"You were there, sir. You saw what I saw."

"The bite marks in their necks—you know Evangeline and the others weren't strangled?"

O'Rourke gave Peregrine a long look. "No, sir, I saw none o' that."

"Forget what Butler told you to tell people. Man-to-man, Seamus, what you saw."

"Aye, a grim scene it was. There will be more than one nightmare born of that, I'll wager. But I saw nothing to do with bite marks, sir, not that I looked any harder than I needed to be sure those poor people were dead."

The saloon keeper came to the end of the bar where Peregrine and O'Rourke were standing, bringing two glasses and a bottle.

" 'Tis a salutary thing, a glass of whiskey," O'Rourke said, raising his glass after the bartender had turned away. "It gives strength to the weak, sight to the blind, and comfort to the afflicted, the perfect medicine."

O'Rourke touched his glass to Peregrine's and they both drank. Whiskey would take some of the edge off the sickness rising in Peregrine's belly.

"I haven't thanked you," Peregrine said into his glass.

"Not to mention it, sir. As concerns to your safety, it

was your interview today with old Spoons that had me worried."

"General Butler was most accommodating."

"You deserve accommodations, sir."

"No, but that doesn't matter. It isn't expedient for Butler to cashier me. God save the United States Army from politicians."

"They have their place, sir."

"I asked General Butler again to transfer me to Virginia. He said he'd think about it, but he isn't going to help me. I'm more useful to him if he keeps me around as a symbol of Union fighting spirit."

"The men do look up to you, sir. If we had more general officers like you, we'd win more fights."

Peregrine took another swallow and shrugged.

"You're a hero, sir, like it or not."

"The only difference between me and any other soldier is that I have learned how pointless it is to fear the inevitable. The things you know about and can see—like some Alabama sharecropper in homespun gray pointing a squirrel rifle at you—aren't the worst things that can happen to you. The things we ought to be afraid of are the things we never think about until it's too late." Peregrine reached for the bottle. "We're all as good as dead anyway. The sooner it happens, the sooner it's finished."

"Permission to speak freely, sir?"

"Don't insult me with that kind of question, Seamus."

"I wouldn't have taken you for a cynic. It's unbecoming of an officer."

"I don't give a damn."

"You sound as if you've given up."

"Maybe I have."

"Then maybe you aren't that man I thought you were. Not if you're going to talk like a coward."

"Careful, Seamus."

"You said I could speak plainly."

"Just be careful."

O'Rourke grinned at his commander. "I can handle meself with my own two fists."

"So can I."

"That's more like it, sir," O'Rourke said, and laughed. "Let's have another drink."

"Let's."

O'Rourke freshened their glasses.

"To tell you the truth, General, I'm concerned. Your grief is eating you alive."

"I'd rather not discuss personal affairs, if it's all the same to you."

"Sometimes it helps to talk, sir."

"It never helps me."

"Well, then I'll do the talking, if it's all the same."

Peregrine didn't look up from his glass.

"The good Lord created us for noble purposes, sir, not to be broken beneath the weight of sorrows. I saw my share of troubles before coming to America. Three brothers put in early graves and many a friend, too. It was hard to leave home, the hardest thing I'd ever have to do, but there was nothing left for me in Erin but the gallows and an English rope."

"But you didn't forget."

"No, sir, forgetting is the one thing I could never do. But time has taken away the sting. We have to move on or our past destroys us. I will never forget, but still I've managed to move on."

"Leave it be, Seamus."

Peregrine poured another glass. The whiskey made it easier to forget some things, but not the important ones.

"So you saw no wounds in the neck of the woman I was

with last night?" he asked, giving it one last try. "Just here," he said, pointing with two fingers. "You've got to tell me the truth, Seamus. I need to know."

"May the devil take me if I've ever been less than completely truthful with you, General Peregrine."

"There was a beautiful young woman there, tiny of frame, with coal black hair, green eyes, and white skin, like a porcelain doll. She must have passed you as you came in. Young, hardly more than a girl."

"No, sir."

"Maybe you saw her on the street outside Yu's?"

"Sorry, sir, I saw no such female."

A muscle in Peregrine's face began to twitch. He turned away from O'Rourke and rubbed it with his fingers to make it stop. "Yu didn't strangle those people."

"General Butler hanged him for it right enough."

"It was the young woman I told you about. She killed them all. She would have killed me next, if you hadn't come busting in when you did."

"A wee girl strangled those people?"

"I told you: she bit them in the neck and sucked the lifeblood out of them, the way a spider kills a fly. She's no ordinary woman. She can't be. I don't know what exactly—something monstrous."

"Listen to yourself. Begging the general's pardon, but you're speaking pure madness."

Peregrine didn't disagree. He couldn't.

"You were out of your mind with the opium last night, General. You don't know what you saw. It must have been a dream."

"That's what General Butler said, but I know what I saw."

"Saints preserve us!" O'Rourke cried.

The bartender looked their way.

"If you continue talking like that," O'Rourke said in a furious whisper, "they will lock you away in an asylum, and it will be an unpleasant end for you. Maybe you did see something in that hop house. It's not for me to say, sir. It's a right queer world God created for us to live in. If there are angels and devils, then maybe there are comely banshees who sup on the blood of the living. But for the love of Mike, General, put this experience behind you, along with your grief for your own poor murdered family. Spoons has his eye on you. Who knows what he'll do if he senses you turning yourself into a liability to his political career. I'd rather have a division of rebels in front of me than a treacherous old snapping turtle like Ben Butler behind me, staring at my back with his goggle eye. You're balanced on the surface of a soap bubble, sir. If you aren't careful, it will burst, and you'll burst with it."

The people on the street gave wide berth to Peregrine's blue uniform with the brigadier general's gold star on each epaulet. The men, nearly every one a rebel at heart, looked away or stared past Peregrine, as though he were invisible. Butler's cold-blooded decision to hang William Mumford for taking down the federal flag at the Mint had been brutal, but it had curbed the outward defiance of New Orleans's conquered men.

An old woman with a bottle green parasol stepped out of a dress shop as Peregrine passed, looking up at him over the top of her pince-nez spectacles with surprise that quickly transformed to disgust.

"Nigger lover," she yelled after him.

Peregrine considered stopping to advise her about General Order Number 28, but he kept walking. She would find out about it soon enough without his help.

4

The French Quarter

HOW DO YOU make yourself forget? The subject was on Peregrine's mind as he walked back to the boarding-house, exchanged his uniform for civilian clothes, and went out again. He had intended to report to the infirmary, but he made it no farther than the nearest saloon, where he spent most of the afternoon drinking alone. After making a luncheon of pigs' feet washed down with beer, he decided to pay a visit to the public library to see what wisdom the world had to offer him on the science of forgetting.

Amid the stacks of books made musty by the humid air, Peregrine found no shortage of advice instructing the forgetful on how to remember. An absentminded person could carry a notepad to jot things down, always deposit the house key in the same drawer, and post written reminders in conspicuous places. Unfortunately, the wisdom on the question was entirely one-sided. The learned philosophers of the human intellect had much to say about remembering, but they remained perfectly mute on the subject of teaching oneself to forget.

Peregrine's own humble experiments in the science had proven disappointing. As soon as he had recovered enough from his wounds to accept official responsibility, he made a conscious effort to bury himself alive in work.

He restricted his waking attentions to the unending flow of reports and orders, the great tidal flood of paperwork that fuels an army, which is, away from the battlefield, little more than an elaborate bureaucracy. But this was distraction, not forgetting, and the pain would bite down on his heart the moment he dropped his guard.

He could not bear to look on the few tender mementos he had carried with him to war in a battered steamer trunk. After Antietam, he kept them locked away—the silver-framed photographs of his wife and children, the letters from his wife, the penknife she gave him on his last Christmas at home. Other reminders were harder to escape. A little girl's laughter; a boy rolling a hoop along the street; even the smell of vanilla, which conjured up the mental picture of his wife in the kitchen—these things and a thousand others afflicted Peregrine like scaldings. There were times when it was all he could do to keep from tearing his hair and screaming.

Seamus O'Rourke had said time would lessen the sting of his loss, but that had not been Peregrine's experience. The poison was too deep to be drawn out by degrees and discarded along with pages ripped from the calendar. Peregrine woke up every day to realize he remained trapped in a life he loathed, his family doomed to die again in his memories with each unwelcome sun. And worse were the nights. In his nightmares, his family screamed piteously for him to save them. But there was nothing he could do to help them—not then, not now.

Peregrine was covered in vomit when he awoke, unable to recollect much after leaving the library. The drug had made him sick. Laudanum did not agree with him unless he restricted himself to small doses. He peeled off the sticky shirt, struggling to keep from retching at the sour smell. He leaned over the washbasin. The water was cool and felt good against his face.

Maybe he had a fever.

The afternoon had slipped away into night. He found matches and lit a candle. His gold pocket watch was on the nightstand, between an empty flask and a corked bottle of milky liquid labeled PROFESSOR NEWTON'S FINEST TONIC *(Laudanum; Contains Narcotics; for Medicinal Use Only)*. He picked up his watch and had trouble opening it, as though he were wearing thick woolen mittens. It was six minutes to seven. Through the lace curtains, the street was a glistening ribbon in the light rain, a halo of mist around the lamp across the street.

Peregrine shuffled through the riotous disorder of his room—he kept it locked and refused to admit the housekeeper to make it up—until he found a gin bottle with something still in it. Three deep swallows steadied him enough to button a shirt without his fingers shaking. After he was dressed, he pulled a cape over his shoulders and went out, locking the door behind him. Laudanum be damned, a pipe of opium was what he needed.

Peregrine walked as if leaning into an invisible wind, traveling not quickly but deliberately through the French Quarter. Past the Ursuline convent to Royal Street, he turned right; two more blocks and he would turn again. Peregrine could have found his way to Yu's in his sleep. He came around the last corner, saw the golden sparkle of light on brass buttons, and halted, cursing under his breath. There were two sentries stationed outside Yu's door, bayonets fixed on their rifles. He had not really expected to find the dead man's establishment still open for business, yet he felt a childish disappointment at having his irrational wish denied. His fallback had been to break in and search until he found a ball of the sticky black tar opium, perhaps scraping residue from the insides of Yu's pipes to get enough to smoke. The sentries made that impossible, even though Peregrine knew that logically there was little chance that pipes or opium would still be found on the premises.

A woman in a hooded cape entered the street from the opposite end of the block, stopped as Peregrine had, and stared at the sentries. The soldiers noticed her immediately. The woman hesitated, twisting the long cords of her purse in her hands as she looked toward Yu's house. She stepped backward and was gone so quickly that she seemed to simply disappear.

Peregrine spun on his heel and hurried back the way he had come, turning at the first cross street and breaking into a run. When he came around the corner of the house at the end of the street, he saw her ahead of him in the middle of the next block, a small woman in a long cape with a hem shiny from the wet street even though the rain had stopped.

Peregrine waited until she was a block ahead of him and fell into step behind her, careful to maintain a safe distance. With a little luck, she would lead him to another opium den. It had been a mistake to confine his patronage to Yu. He knew that now, his supplier dead, his joints aching, and nowhere to turn for relief but the wretched laudanum.

At first the woman headed back toward the center of the Quarter, but then she took a seemingly random course up and down the streets. Still, she kept moving swiftly along, as if she knew exactly where she was going, a destination in mind despite her wandering. Perhaps there was some reason to delay her arrival by taking an indirect route.

Or maybe, Peregrine thought, it was to avoid being followed.

No sooner had this idea occurred to Peregrine than the woman stopped and looked back over her shoulder at him.

Peregrine nearly flung himself through the open door of a working-class tavern before their eyes could meet. There were only two customers standing at the bar, a thick man with battered ears and a flattened nose, and a broad-shouldered character in a patched coat with a zigzag scar bisecting his head, the thick welt of white tissue standing out against the pink skin of his bald skull. The bartender was the most reputable-looking member of the low crew, even with one milky blind eye and thin, bony elbows sticking out at angles from his body, as if he were about to dance a jig.

The three of them stopped talking the moment Peregrine entered. They scrutinized him carefully, as if estimating the amount of money he might have upon his person. Peregrine turned and nearly collided with a woman who must have been sitting or standing beside the door when he came in.

"Good evening, monsieur," she said, her words slurred. He took her in with a single glance—the teeth bad, the face painted garishly in a failed attempt to disguise the ravages of age.

"Would monsieur care to buy a lady a drink?"

But Peregrine was already past her. He expected the whore and the toughs to follow him onto the street, but they must have decided he was not worth the trouble it would take to rob him, at least not at that early hour of the night. Peregrine normally put a pistol in his pocket before going out on the street at night, for New Orleans was dangerous after dark, but when he patted the jacket beneath his cape, all he found was the outline of a glass bottle.

Peregrine's woman was nearly two blocks away now, walking quickly into the crowd surging out of St. Louis

Cathedral at the end of evening Mass. Peregrine tried to hurry, but his progress was blocked by exiting worshipers chattering happily to find the rain had ended.

He stopped and raised himself up on his toes to see over the hats and bonnets, despairing to be denied a glimpse of his quarry's receding figure. He pushed his way through the crowd as best he could, but it was no good. He had lost her.

Peregrine stood near the side of the great cathedral, chin on chest, arms slack, eyes staring at the wet ground a few feet ahead. He had been so intent upon following the woman in the hooded cape that he had failed to realize that he, too, was being followed.

5

Doubting Thomas

NATHANIEL PEREGRINE WANDERED into Jackson Square and sat heavily on a bench. St. Louis Cathedral loomed overhead, an overawing vertical presence against fast-moving gray clouds, like a judge looking down on the accused, prepared to pronounce judgment.

It was only now that the obvious occurred to him. Peregrine leaned forward and put his face in his hands. Although he had no way to really know, he was possessed with the certainty that the woman he had been following was the porcelain-skinned girl from the night before.

How could he have been so stupid?

And, all the more appalling, what if he had caught her? How perfectly he remembered what she had said to him. *I can free you from the pain.*

Except that she hadn't.

Somebody sat on the bench beside him. Peregrine jumped as if jolted by an electric current, looking up, expecting it to be her.

"Sir?"

"I am too old for a wet nurse, Captain," Peregrine said to his aide.

"I'm just looking out for your welfare, sir."

"You were following me."

"Yes, sir, I was. You went back to the opium den."

The set of Peregrine's jaw softened and he had to look away from O'Rourke. "I feel bad about Yu," he said, not wanting to confess to his subordinate the fear that he could not escape his need for the poppy's poison.

"That Chinaman was no choirboy, sir."

"He wasn't a murderer. He didn't deserve to hang."

"Rough justice is the way of the world, sir. Men don't always get it right. We have to trust in God for that."

"God," Peregrine said, looking up at the church through narrowing eyes. "Where is God when innocents die?"

"The fact that we don't understand His plan doesn't mean He doesn't have one for us, sir."

"God has abandoned us."

"You must not believe that, sir."

"Where is God in any of this?" Peregrine jabbed a finger toward a legless beggar across the square. The man, a former Confederate soldier, judging from his tattered jacket, held a tin cup up to passersby, begging for alms.

"You must not give in to despair, sir. Hold on to the hope that you will once again see your wife and children in heaven."

Peregrine felt as if he'd been struck a hard blow in the stomach; the breath caught in his throat, and he began to shake. He would have broken down if Seamus O'Rourke said another word, but the captain said nothing, perhaps thinking he had already said too much.

"I appreciate your concern, Seamus," Peregrine said finally. "I'll be all right. And I don't need a minder. General Butler has ordered all the hop houses in New Orleans closed, and I doubt there is a pipe to be found in the city. Butler is nothing if not efficient when it comes to exercising authority over the civilian population."

"Is there anything I can do to help, sir?"

"Do you have a supply of tar opium?"

O'Rourke's expression was shocked until he realized Peregrine was joking.

"The only thing that will help me is getting back into the fight, Seamus. A man can't think about his troubles looking down the throat of a rebel battery."

"Are you acquainted with Colonel Joseph Stroyan? He's on Butler's staff and an old mate of mine."

"Irish?"

"He's as Irish as Paddy's goat, sir. Joey knows where General Butler keeps his skeletons hidden—or as I should say, where Spoons keeps the spoons hidden, if I may be so bold. He might be able to help expedite your transfer papers, sir."

"Don't get yourself into trouble on my account, Seamus."

"Not to worry, sir. Joey is as smooth as good whiskey. He's a lad who can say little and imply much, if you get my meaning."

"Don't sell Butler short."

"Compared to the murdering English, old Spoons is harmless as a tomcat."

Peregrine offered his hand. "This means a lot to me. I won't forget it."

"It's a pleasure to be of service, sir."

"And one more thing."

"Sir?"

"Don't follow me again. That's a direct order."

Peregrine walked up the middle of the street, keeping pace with a mule and its drunken rider. The man slumped forward in the saddle, periodically wobbling violently from side to side yet managing to stay seated on his mount. A door across the street opened and a man in shirtsleeves came out and stumbled off toward Jackson Square.

Air, exercise, and the conversation with O'Rourke had cleared Peregrine's mind, and he found himself thinking hard about the differences between appearances and reality.

Two drunks came into the street to fight, but Peregrine hardly noticed the commotion. By the time he got to them, the brawl was over. The winner disappeared and the loser sat on the stone curb leaning forward on his knees, blood dripping from his nose and mouth into the gutter. The seam was ripped out of the shoulder of his jacket, cottonlike padding extruding from the wound.

Peregrine abruptly stopped and looked hard at the man, at the blood on his face, clothing, and even the street, crimson in the light of the streetlamp.

More often than not, appearance *was* reality, Peregrine thought. He did not have to dip his fingertips into the blood to know that what he saw was real. If he were to insist on submitting his perceptions to a formal series of tests and proofs—hardly practical—he would likely be forced to conclude that *nothing* was certain, and that all of experience was, like O'Rourke's conception of God, a matter of faith.

Peregrine knew what he had seen the previous night, Butler's report be damned. The opium he'd taken might have distorted his perceptions to some degree, but he had been conscious and aware.

He resumed his way up the street, his pace unhurried, walking now as one walks when one has no clear destination in mind.

Peregrine had no rational explanation for what he had seen. A beautiful young woman with teeth like a viper's, who drank the blood of the living, leaving corpses in her wake—such a creature did not fit into the scientific modern world of 1863. And yet Peregrine could not deny the evidence of his own senses. Which was the more logical: to believe something he had seen but could not explain; or to deny the possibility of what he had witnessed and knew to be true, but could not rationalize?

Peregrine wished he had asked to see General Butler's report about the opium den incident. Did the investigating officer *really* believe the victims had been strangled? Or did the report detail strange wounds in the dead that defied a simple explanation?

It was easy for Peregrine to imagine Butler either ignoring the report or falsifying its conclusions. Butler was not a man who appreciated uncertainty, especially when it might jeopardize his ambitions. Attributing the deaths to a Chinaman, and hanging him quickly to bring the matter to neat conclusion, would satisfy his taste for brisk administrative efficiency. On the other hand, fears about a monster preying on the French Quarter would threaten the sense Butler had cultivated that the conquered city was squarely under his thumb. Mysterious murders and rumors about supernatural beings might well lead to the sort of public hysteria that would call Butler's authority into question. Were their roles reversed, Peregrine might have been tempted to cover up the facts in the interest of expediency and maintaining control over the hostile populace.

But Peregrine had to know.

Either he was losing his mind, or there *were* wounds in the neck of Evangeline McAllister and the others.

There was one way to submit the matter to proof.

He turned right at the next cross street, setting off in search of a corpse.

*   *   *

The sound of a woman's sobbing came from the house on Chartres Street. Peregrine climbed the stairs, which were in need of paint, and went in the open door. From the foyer he could see the casket in the parlor. Chairs were arranged in a semicircle before the casket, each occupied by a woman. Peregrine was the only man present.

He came into the room, nodding as the women looked up with curiosity. That Evangeline's station had fallen further than he had imagined was evident from a cursory look at the painted ladies, whom he took to be the other residents of the house.

"You must be Major Dickinson," said one woman, rising and coming to greet him, her manner making it plain that she was the senior member of the household. The beauty in her face had faded but she held herself with authority. She might have been a popular courtesan in years gone by, the mistress of wealthy and powerful men.

"Yes," Peregrine replied, surprised at his easy duplicity.

"I am Mrs. Foster."

"Pleased to make your acquaintance, ma'am." He bowed. "I wish it were under better circumstances."

Mrs. Foster gave a solemn nod. "You've come to pay your last respects to Miss McAllister."

"I wonder if I might have a private moment with her?"

"I understand perfectly, Major. I'm sure she would have been glad you came. She thought very highly of you."

Mrs. Foster turned toward the hall. Without a word or sign, the others rose en masse and followed her from the room, Mrs. Foster sliding the pocket doors closed behind them.

Peregrine stood stiffly over the casket, wondering if he could force himself to do it. He had seen his share of men killed in battle—the maimed, the dismembered, some blown to bits so that there was nothing left but a tangle of greasy entrails spread out across the dirt. But somehow this was hard for Peregrine to look at: a lovely young woman in a long black dress, laid out for burial.

Without thinking about it, his fingers found the bottle in his pocket. He pulled out the cork and took a swallow of Professor Newton's Tonic.

The wooden coffin in which Evangeline McAllister lay was neither finished nor lined with satin, the cheapest means available for burying a body besides dumping it into the river or a nearby bayou. Her complexion, fair to begin with, had turned a ghastly shade of pale. He was lucky she did not look at all like Mary or he could not have borne it.

The elixir of laudanum and alcohol almost immediately took some of the edge off Peregrine's nerves. A feeling of release spread through him, like the unwinding of a twisted towel.

He leaned low over the body, breathing in the odor of rot that no quantity of cheap perfume could disguise. It was with a sinking feeling that he noted no sign of puncture wounds on the girl's neck, but then the black lace collar chastely covered most of it.

Peregrine did not think he could make himself touch her in death, but he had come too far to stop now. He carefully took the edge of the collar between his thumbs and forefingers and drew it slowly down, making sure he did not touch the cold, dead flesh.

Nothing. The neck betrayed not the slightest evidence of the twin holes he had seen oozing blood at Yu's.

Peregrine stood up, struggling against the panic trying to take hold of him, the chaos and confusion of madness.

"Think!" he whispered to himself.

How could what he was seeing be real? And if he could not trust his eyes, had they lied to him last night, or were they lying now?

He bent again over the coffin. Wounds in the dead do not heal themselves. When you were dead, you were dead, and there was no disguising it.

Or was there?

Peregrine vainly studied Evangeline's neck for signs of artifice. There was no other way: he would have to touch her.

He tentatively pressed his fingers to the body, like doubting Thomas probing the wounds in Jesus. It made him shudder to feel the cold, lifeless flesh. He began to gently knead the claylike skin, searching for wax and makeup used to disguise the wounds.

He found no wounds.

He *was* going mad.

A woman coughed discreetly behind him.

Peregrine spun around, horrified that he had been seen pawing the corpse. The pocket doors were open just far enough to admit a person. Mrs. Foster stood close behind him, looking up at him with—this, a surprise—great tenderness and sympathy.

"The stricken look on your face tells me that you cared for her very much, Major. You are the only one of Evangeline's gentleman friends to call and pay your last respects. It is not easy to be alone in the world."

"I know."

"Evangeline came from a fine family. They lost everything in the war. Her family has a crypt in the Lafayette Cemetery. The other girls and I would like to send her there to buried, if we can raise the necessary funds. That's what she would have wanted, to be with her family."

Peregrine was seized with the impulse to tell Mrs. Foster just how little he cared about the sacrifices of Southerners. If not for the rebellion, his own family would still be alive. The anger quickly passed. He had no animosity toward poor Evangeline. She was as much a victim of war as he.

"How much do you need?"

Mrs. Foster mentioned a figure.

Peregrine took the money from his wallet and put it into her open hand.

"That's very kind of you . . ."

Peregrine didn't wait to be thanked but lurched out the door. It was suddenly too much for him—the thought that he was going mad, Evangeline, his memories, and his grief. Peregrine had the bottle of laudanum to his lips before he was down the front stairs of the brothel.

6

The Quadroon Ballroom

NATHANIEL PEREGRINE PERCHED on the edge of his chair, a cake plate balanced on one knee and a teacup daintily held between thumb and forefinger. He was making polite small talk with Colonel Harry Kuehl's wife. How unusual it seemed, he said, to spend Christmas in New Orleans, without a prayer of snow. How true, Clara Kuehl agreed. And the temperature—she declared that Crescent City winters were seasonable as September back home in Connecticut!

In the two weeks that had elapsed since Peregrine's shattering visit to Evangeline's wake, he had stopped drinking and gradually reduced his intake of laudanum. His eyes were clearer than they had been in many a month. Seamus O'Rourke remarked daily about the improvement to his commander's color. Peregrine's appetite had recovered some, though he still had no taste for food and took little pleasure from eating.

Peregrine's room at the boardinghouse was no longer littered with empty liquor bottles. He had thrown all that out before surprising the housekeeper a week earlier by asking her to please begin making up his room each morning—and giving her a generous tip in recompense for the burden of having to catch up after so long a time without dusting or having the rugs beaten.

The night had become foggy by the time he left the Kuehls' holiday party. He decided against taking a carriage back to his room. A walk would be good after the noise and forced gaiety. It was an unusually quiet night, the fog absorbing the sound of the city and perhaps keeping people off the streets.

The brass tip of Peregrine's walking stick tapped against the bricked sidewalk, punctuating each alternate step with a brilliant click, while the silk liner of his cape whispered against his trouser legs.

He paused to light a cigar. As he cupped his hand around the wooden match, his eyes rested on the display inside the shop window barred against thieves in the decadent metropolis. Three new Colt pistols with walnut grips rested on a bed of red felt, looking as immaculate and precise as a surgeon's tools. Peregrine squinted against the smoke. There was a moth inside the display case, trapped when the shopkeeper had last opened the glass doors to arrange the weapons. The dead insect lay on the bed of red cloth, wings spread wide, freed of its brief, meaningless life of fluttering from one thing to the next.

The cigar tasted bitter in his mouth, though it was a good cigar, a gift from Harry Kuehl. Peregrine dropped the smoke and put his boot on it, twisting the foot back and forth, back and forth, extinguishing it completely.

A similar army-issue Colt revolver could be found in the bureau drawer back at the boardinghouse. In the right pocket of his trousers was the derringer he carried when he went about New Orleans. He did not need to touch his pocket to feel its weight against the front of his leg.

That was how it would finally end, Peregrine thought— a bullet from a rebel gun, or from one held in his own steady hand.

From the next block came the tinny rattle of dance music

played fast. A rough cheer went up from the crowd outside. Peregrine smiled mirthlessly and shook his head. There was so much vice in the city that he could scarcely go out after dark without happening upon at least one altercation.

The confrontation was entirely one-sided, he saw as he came closer. A big man in a bowler hat held the much smaller man from behind while his confederate struck the little man repeatedly with his fists, which were clothed in tight black leather gloves. Peregrine stepped into the street to skirt the onlookers. He had no interest in such affairs. There was a time when he would have stopped such a brutal thrashing, but what did he care if Southerners beat one another to death? It was all happening outside one of the city's more notorious haunts. Before the war, the place had been known as the Quadroon Ballroom—and it was still, for all Peregrine knew, though Butler had put a stop to the crude, and distinctly Southern, transaction for which the ballroom had become famous.

It was illegal for a white man in Louisiana to marry a woman of color, so a twisted social convention was devised to formalize intimate relations between wealthy Southern "gentlemen" and the most beautiful young café au lait women. Mulatto mothers would bring their free quadroon daughters to the ballroom and auction them to rich men not to serve as slaves but mistresses. The practice, known in the city as *plaçage,* was perversely ritualized, even to the degree that notarized contracts specified the money and property to be given the *femmes de couleur* to support them and any bastard children resulting from their arrangement. Butler had outlawed the rites of *plaçage,* yet the ballroom was still a locus for assignations between the races, as well as those attracted to debauched "entertainments," including common prostitutes.

The man doing the beating, a sharp-faced thug in a

gaudy double-breasted vest of purple silk, took a sap out of his jacket and struck their victim across the head. The man's body went instantly limp in the big man's arms.

A flash of color the hue of blood drew Peregrine's eyes to the gallery. There, among the people who had come out of the ballroom to enjoy the beating, was a woman in a striking scarlet gown. She was smaller than the other women, with a complexion so white and perfect that she might have been made of porcelain.

A chill of recognition shivered through Peregrine's body.

She was already watching him by the time he saw her. The corners of her mouth turned upward and her eyes glittered in the light of the gas lamps.

And then, without seeming to move at all, she somehow was no longer there in the crowd pressed up against the gallery banister.

Peregrine staggered slightly, but the streets of New Orleans were so filled with drunkards and degenerates after dark that no one paid attention as he caught himself with the help of his cane.

The fight ended, the revelers were now fast disappearing back into the Quadroon Ballroom.

Peregrine stood frozen in the street.

Part of him wanted to rush back to the boardinghouse and lock the door against the girl, against the madness threatening to smother him in a boiling chaos of delusion. But he also wanted to know if she was real, if he *had* seen what he thought he had seen in the opium den, or if he was indeed becoming insane.

The first course led to safety, the more dangerous path to knowledge.

Peregrine was unafraid to die.

And besides, he had to know.

*   *   *

"What you?"

"I'd like inside," Peregrine said to the hatchet-faced man in the silk vest, when he stepped sideways to block Peregrine's passage into the ballroom. "Is there an admission fee?"

"Private party." The man looked Peregrine up and down. "Beat it."

Peregrine shrugged, allowing his cloak to fall open. The man in the silk vest scowled, but seeing the blue uniform drained the certainty from his eyes.

"You are interfering with a federal officer on official business," Peregrine said. "I will have you arrested if you delay me."

"Official business in here?" the man in the vest said, gesturing with his thumb. "You've got to be joking."

Peregrine took a step closer, taking advantage of his height to make the shorter man look up at him. "Your employer may not particularly care if I have you clapped in irons, but he will take a dim view when I come back with a company of men and permanently close this public nuisance."

Peregrine smiled with half of his mouth.

"And I promise he'll know his notorious business would still be in operation, if not for you," he said.

The muscles worked in the man's jaw but his hands remained outside of the pockets where Peregrine had seen him put the sap.

"It's a *she*," the man in the silk vest said, referring to his employer. He stepped out of the doorway so Peregrine could enter. "Enjoy yourself, sir, on your *official business*."

Peregrine turned sideways as he went past the gatekeeper, not giving the man in the silk vest the opportunity to hit him over the head while his back was turned.

* * *

The Quadroon Ballroom was hot, smoky, loud, and jammed with people. On the stage, an orchestra of black musicians played "The Camptown Ladies" at a frenetic, nearly demented tempo. The trumpeter, a skeleton of a man with sweat streaming down his shaved head, jerked and writhed as he played, as if battling a seizure that threatened to make him heave his horn into the seething mass of dancers.

Peregrine found a vacant spot against a pillar to lean. The ballroom was stifling, but he kept the cloak wrapped tight around him; it would have been suicide to reveal himself to the crowd in a Union officer's uniform.

A high-pitched wail rose above the frenzy. Peregrine seemed to be the only one who noticed, the revelers in the ballroom too possessed by abandon to pay attention to a woman's scream.

Peregrine moved off toward the sound, but progress was nearly impossible in the jammed room.

"Excuse me," he said repeatedly. "Excuse me. Excuse me."

He had no opportunity to prepare himself against the assault that hit him from the blind side, slamming him through the open door of the cloakroom. Peregrine lost his cane as he was driven back against the rear wall. It was the big man in the bowler, the one who had held the man outside while the other man in the silk vest administered the beating. He held Peregrine against the wall with a massive forearm across Peregrine's chest. Peregrine's eyes followed his attacker's free hand as it went up in the air. His attacker was holding a sap filled with lead shot by the leather thong. A blow across the head would knock him unconscious, fracturing his skull, possibly killing him.

Peregrine pressed the derringer he'd held in his hand

since entering the Quadroon Ballroom against the big
man's coat. The big man sucked in his breath between his
teeth, and Peregrine reflexively pulled the trigger, not giving the other man the opportunity to split his head open.
There was a muffled crack, the man's coat and the close-
ness of their bodies smothering the gun's small report.

The big man sat down hard on the floor. The sap fell out
of his hands, which he put over his middle.

"Bad luck for you," Peregrine said.

Peregrine kicked the sap away in case the other man
made a move for it, but the big man just sat there, looking
down at the blood leaching between his fingers and shaking his head, as if he couldn't believe what had happened.
He groaned, closed his eyes, and sank slowly to his side until his cheek was pressed against the wooden floorboards.

He was dead.

Peregrine went to the door and looked out. One shot remained in the little two-barreled weapon. He saw no sign
of the man in the silk vest, or the lady he had come into
the ballroom to find. Peregrine's cane had disappeared.
The Quadroon Ballroom was not the sort of place where
property left unattended lasted for long.

The woman shrieked again, nearer now. There was an
alcove ahead on the right. The cry seemed to come from
within.

Slowly, tortuously, Peregrine shouldered his way
through the crowd. As he inched closer, he was able to see
into the smallish space, which had room within for only a
single table. The candle on the tabletop threw spears of
iridescent green light through two glasses of absinthe. A
woman was seated in one of the chairs, her skirt drawn up
far enough to reveal the garter and a shocking expanse of
naked leg. Above the garter was a black hand belonging to
an attractive woman with high cheekbones and almond

eyes that made her look almost Oriental. The other woman's head was tipped forward, a mass of chestnut curls hiding her face until the hand disappeared beneath the skirt and her head rolled back.

It was Mrs. Foster.

Peregrine lost what little hope he'd had that Mrs. Foster had used the gold he'd given her to bury Evangeline in the family crypt. It was far more likely that he'd financed a spree for the madam. Evangeline had probably ended up dumped into a pauper's grave, the sexton frantically shoveling in quicklime and dirt in a race to stay ahead of water seeping into the grave.

A scarlet gown materialized through the haze of smoke.

Mrs. Foster and Evangeline instantly forgotten, Peregrine strained against the bodies to follow as she paused in the far corner of the hall. She looked back just once before disappearing through the door, her eyes going straight to his, as if she knew he was watching her.

It was impossible! Peregrine thought. What could he do? She was so close, and yet there he was, trapped by the crowd. It was like the recurring nightmare he had in which he ran and ran to catch up with his family, but hard as he tried, they only got farther and farther away until at last they were gone.

Peregrine flung himself over a table and onto the dance floor. Ignoring the angry cries behind him, he dodged between the dancers and shoved his way toward the back of the ballroom.

The doorway opened to a corridor lined with rooms whose purpose was easily divined by the men and women queued up for their turn to purchase a few minutes of intimacy. At the end of the hallway, a door was closing behind a vanishing vertical line of scarlet.

Peregrine tried to run, stumbling past the plungers and

jezebels. Something caught his foot—he either was tripped or tripped himself—and he went sprawling, the derringer cartwheeling across the filthy floorboards and disappearing amid the forest of boots and shoes. Peregrine scrambled back to his feet, expecting to hear the gun discharge, but the people laughing at him, who might have been hit by the errant lead slug, were lucky that night. Without wasting time to look for his weapon, he crashed through the door and nearly fell down the steep wooden stairs leading to the rear alley.

The alley was empty but for a closed carriage moving quickly away, the driver whipping the horse into a full run.

7

The Garden District

PEREGRINE THREW MONEY at the driver, angry even though he knew there was no reason to blame the man for losing the other carriage in the traffic of St. Charles Avenue.

The woman who had killed Evangeline, and who had come close to killing Peregrine—assuming it wasn't all the creation of a bizarre fantasy—had gotten away from him again. Peregrine felt like a hapless wanderer, pursuing a will-o'-the-wisp through the night. Each time he got tantalizingly close to the deadly fairy, she would pull away and vanish. The chase was leading him deeper and deeper into a perilous swamp, even though the dangers might have been confined within his mind, which had suffered a series of terrible shocks since he'd marched off to war.

Peregrine wandered down St. Charles on foot.

"Matches, sir?"

He practically ran into the old black woman standing in the middle of the boardwalk. He hadn't even seen her.

"Buy my matches, sir."

He absently pushed back his coat to put his hand in his pocket. The wide-eyed stare made him realize his mistake, but by then it was too late.

"God bless Mr. Lincoln," the old woman said.

Peregrine nodded and shoved a handful of money at the

woman. He stepped around her, ignoring the box of matches in her hand.

"God bless you, sir," she cried after him. "And God bless the Union Army."

Peregrine cringed inwardly and drew the cloak around him as he walked away as fast as he could.

The Garden District was the quarter of New Orleans where wealth was most concentrated. The war had been hard on the South, but the Garden District showed few outward signs of hardship. The war had destroyed most small and midsized planters, but Peregrine suspected the people who lived in these pillared mansions set back from moss-draped oaks had been shrewd enough to put aside money against the eventuality that the Confederacy lost the war. The rich had a way of enduring. There was old money in places like New Orleans and Savannah that had outlasted the French, the Spanish, and the British. The old-money people would survive the present troubles as well, their gold hidden safely away in the bank vaults of Europe.

Walking quickly but with an almost desperate aimlessness, Peregrine left St. Charles and turned up Philip Street, hoping to find some clue or talisman that the woman who had become his quest had come this way. The houses on Philip Street were well lighted and decorated for the season. Holiday parties were being thrown here and there, like the one Peregrine had attended earlier in the evening, almost as if the city were still in control of the rebels and not under the martial law of an occupying army.

In the middle of the block, a carriage stood outside a Palladian mansion tucked behind a jungle of tropical foliage. It could have been the carriage that had carried the woman away from the Quadroon Ballroom, though Peregrine couldn't be certain. He crossed the street toward it. There was no driver in sight. A lead from the team's reins was wrapped around an iron hitching post cast in the shape of a horse's head set into the ground next to the curb.

The sound of a child singing came from the house. The breath caught in Peregrine's throat. The memories, the memories—how long could he endure, haunted by his terrible memories?

The horse whinnied when Peregrine put his hand on its back. The creature had been tied up long enough to cool off, so it couldn't have been the carriage he was seeking.

From inside the house, the singing continued. It made Peregrine's heart ache to hear the high-pitched voice sweetly mispronounce words. At least the child was not in jeopardy from *her*.

Peregrine continued up one street, turned, and continued again until his intuition took him down another street, wandering until his feet were tired and he stopped to rest. He realized without any special sense of concern that he was no longer certain of the way back to St. Charles Avenue.

An open buggy was coming toward him up the street, pulled by a horse driven by a black man with a wreath of gray hair. Hooves clapped against the cobblestones with a rhythm that gave Peregrine an odd feeling in the hollow of his stomach, a strange sensation of weightlessness. The driver tugged at the reins, stopping beside Peregrine. He continued to stare straight ahead. The buggy was empty.

"Excuse me," Peregrine said.

The driver kept his eyes forward as if in a trance.

A voice from within silently commanded Peregrine to get into the buggy. He resisted, thinking that there was no rational reason for such an impulse.

"Did she send you for me?" he said at last.

Still the driver did not respond. Perhaps he was deaf. The horse stamped and shook its head.

Peregrine put his hand on the door. He expected some
reaction as he opened it, but the ancient driver gave no
sign he was aware of Peregrine's existence. Peregrine
climbed in and sat back against the leather seat.

"I am ready," he said. "Take me to her."

The driver showed no sign that he had heard, yet he
snapped the reins, and the buggy began to move, taking
Peregrine further into the mystery.

The hour was approaching midnight and few were still
about.

They drove up and down streets threading through the
Garden District. If there was a destination, Peregrine
could not divine it. Their course seemed to be entirely
random, sometimes backtracking over the same streets
they'd traveled earlier. Peregrine settled back into the
comfortable leather and fell into a dreamy reverie, content
to watch the passing scene and wait for whatever the night
would bring him.

The Lafayette Cemetery passed by on the left, the
graveyard surrounded by a brick wall. Inside were the
aboveground crypts, a walled neighborhood within a
neighborhood where the residents were all dead.

After a long while—Peregrine could not be sure how
much time had elapsed—the carriage turned onto Chestnut Street and stopped in front of a house where a spirited
party was going on despite the increasing lateness of the
hour. Golden light filtered through the well-tended plants
and trees partly screening the house from the street. Peregrine made out a square Italianate villa, with four columns
upholding the gallery that divided the structure's two stories, three crowning dormers barely visible from the
street. Intricate ironwork prevented people from falling
from the gallery, the same pattern repeated in the fence

atop the low stone wall surrounding the property. Tall windows ran from floor to ceiling, each framed with black shutters that could be closed against the hurricanes that blew off the Gulf. Piano music spilled from the house, something by Beethoven, Peregrine thought as the music concluded to the sound of enthusiastic applause and a few cheers and cries of "bravo."

The elderly driver climbed down from his seat without bending his spine, his back stiff with age. He opened the carriage door for Peregrine.

"Thank you," Peregrine said.

Not the faintest flicker of acknowledgment passed across the old man's yellow eyes. The driver turned and climbed back into his seat, maintaining what might have been a religious vow of perpetual silence. As the carriage began to move away from Peregrine, a trill of female laughter came from within the house. There was something odd about the high-pitched laughter—a tone that was brittle and uncontrolled, hilarity bordering on the hysterical, mirth mingled with an equal measure of madness.

Peregrine knew it then: he had found her.

The iron gate closed behind him with a metallic rattle. Peregrine went up the stairs toward where a woman reclined in a wicker chaise longue on the porch near the entrance. She was young, curls of red hair framing a heart-shaped face. Her eyes were shut. She could have been asleep or dead. Peregrine thought about pushing back her hair to see her neck, but if he did and found wounds over her jugular vein, what would it really prove?

A servant in livery opened the door.

"Good evening," Peregrine said. The man looked past him. "Is your mistress at home?"

The other man made no answer. His eyes remained

fixed, as if staring at something over Peregrine's shoulder in the middle distance. He appeared to be mesmerized, like the carriage driver.

A maid in a black dress and spotless apron so heavily starched that it crackled helped Peregrine out of his cloak. She, too, was unresponsive when he thanked her as she disappeared with his coat.

The front parlor was filled with people talking gaily and drinking champagne. The men were in formal evening clothes, and the women wore elegant gowns with pearls around their necks and jeweled bracelets on their arms. Peregrine was the only one wearing a uniform.

The uniform!

Peregrine's heart began to pound. He stood perfectly still, waiting for the inevitable reaction while he wondered how he could have been so stupid. He was just too far inside the room to turn away and retreat without attracting notice. Moving only his eyes, he scanned the party from left to right. Either they were blind or the Union uniform was of no concern to them, though both possibilities seemed equally implausible. Still, it was impossible to imagine that he could walk into a Garden District party wearing the uniform of a federal general without drawing, at the very least, looks of cold disapproval, if not outrage, insults, and challenges to fight duels.

A woman directly in Peregrine's line of vision smiled at him, and the man she was talking to nodded. Peregrine tipped his head slightly in return.

Who were these people?

What kind of party was this?

With what he hoped looked to the others like a perfectly casual gesture, he brought his hand to the pocket where he carried the derringer, only to remember losing it on the filthy hallway floor in the Quadroon Ballroom.

A servant came through the room with a silver tray of glasses filled with champagne. Peregrine took a glass and drank, wishing it were whiskey.

Music resumed in the next parlor, the piano playing the overture to an opera Peregrine could not identify. The other people began to filter toward the sound. Peregrine followed, putting the empty glass on a drum table next to a couch where two women leaned against each other, their eyes closed. Peregrine saw at once that they were different from the other women at the party. Their dresses were cut from cheap fabric, the tailoring inferior and showing evidence of wear. The toes of their boots needed polish, while rouge, powder, and lipstick were far too liberally applied to their faces. They did not belong in the house on Chestnut Street any more than Peregrine did.

The women were dead, Peregrine realized with a lack of surprise that was in itself surprising.

No one paid him the least attention as he bent slightly forward from the waist for a closer look. A set of neat, almost fastidious bite marks disfigured each woman's neck. The skin around the bites had a purplish discoloration, a sign that mouths had suckled greedily from these mortal fountains. The tissue around each individual wound was raised and swollen, a ring encircling a red center glistening with blood that was still wet and, Peregrine guessed, as warm as it had been in life only a few minutes earlier.

8

Memento Mori

PEREGRINE PICKED UP a second glass of champagne as the others moved past him into the music room, and stood turned away from them, pretending to admire an English landscape painting on the wall.

The wounds in the dead girls' necks had already faded from what they had been barely a minute earlier. The torn skin was pulling itself together, the purplish discoloration fading. Some unknown mechanism—Peregrine refused to consider the possibility that supernatural powers were involved—was causing the corpses to heal themselves of the only outward evidence of the attacks that had killed them.

Peregrine felt himself almost physically lifted on a wave of relief as he realized that there was an explanation for it all that didn't involve madness—the bite marks he had seen in Evangeline's neck at the opium den, and then, later, the absence of those same fatal wounds when he examined her body as it lay in its casket. Through the work of some mysterious agency, the damage repaired itself even after life had ended, eliminating all visible proof of the cause of death.

"Clever," Peregrine said beneath his breath, "very clever indeed."

The pianist in the other room played a flourish, stopped,

and said something that made the people in the other room laugh. It occurred to Peregrine that he should flee; strange, but he felt no compelling reason to make his escape. He did not feel threatened, though it was not because there was no menace present. The two dead women on the couch beneath the Constable oil painting were proof enough of *that*. He thought it likely some, perhaps even most, of the guests at the macabre soirée belonged to the same secret race as the girl-woman who had been playing hide-and-seek with him, luring Peregrine away from the Quarter, away from the safety of crowds and the recourse to summon Union soldiers to assist him in his quest to find out what he had become mixed up in. Still, no one at the party had so much as looked at Peregrine sideways. Perhaps the others sensed, as had Peregrine, that he had been invited to the party—as the carriage sent to bring him clearly indicated—to meet with the porcelain-skinned lady and learn whatever dark meaning there was within the heart of this bloody mystery.

By choosing to enter the house on Chestnut Street—no one had made him do it—Peregrine had willingly crossed the invisible threshold separating the ordinary world from one where none of the usual laws applied. Here, he was in the midst of an intimate circle buried as far as one could hope to go in the ever-narrowing circles of New Orleans society, each more exclusive, more hidden, more jealous of its secrets than the previous. It went without saying that he already knew far more than it was safe for him to know about *them*. Even his casual association had taught him that these creatures, whatever they were, existed side by side with ordinary society, unknown and unsuspected by other people or the authorities. But appearances were deceptive. They might have looked like ordinary human beings, but they were different, beginning with a complete disregard for the value of human life, and including the most disturbing distinction of all: their desire, or perhaps their need, to drink the blood of the living. Ultimately, Peregrine thought, the two races had no more in common than do wolves and sheep.

Beginning to feel conspicuous, Peregrine joined the others in the music room, where the crowd had formed a semicircle around the piano. He stood in the back of the room as the music began again, the first part of the selection instrumental. The singer stood near the pianist, the only one in the room who was turned away from him in order to face the audience. She was German or Polish, Peregrine guessed, judging by her blond hair and strong, handsome features.

On a settee in the corner, a man and woman were embracing with an intimacy that was scandalous outside of a Crescent City brothel. Peregrine was looking away in embarrassment when he noticed the woman was the seemingly ubiquitous Mrs. Foster! She must have left the Quadroon Ballroom after him and come straight to Chestnut Street, the guest of one of the monsters, brought here to service their pleasure. But then something else occurred to Peregrine, an idea that made him frown. Perhaps the slatternly madam was one of *them*. The bouncer at the ballroom had said his employer was a woman. Maybe Mrs. Foster was the mistress of both houses of ill repute, though she seemed too low to exercise that much authority, even of the most perverse variety.

The singer opened her mouth and joined a crystalline soprano to the music pouring from the piano, making it impossible for Peregrine to keep his attention focused on Mrs. Foster. The lyrics were Italian, an aria from another opera Peregrine did not recognize.

A sharp gesture brought Peregrine's glance back to Mrs. Foster.

She had become suddenly, even dramatically rigid, as if she were in the grip of a grand mal seizure. Her fingers clutched empty air, and her legs were stuck out straight in the air. One slipper came off and fell to the carpeted floor, the sound hidden beneath the soaring music. All the while Mrs. Foster was held tight in the embrace of the long-haired man whose face was buried in her neck. Her eyes were open wide, her mouth contorted with animal passion.

It was an expression he had seen before, on Evangeline's face.

Peregrine could not stand silently by and watch as Mrs. Foster was slaughtered. He started to move toward them, but a small hand on his arm stopped him before he'd taken his first step.

"Don't."

Peregrine found himself looking down on a slim, olive-skinned woman with jet black hair and eyes as dark and shiny as black pearls. She was a gypsy, Peregrine thought, though his only evidence of that was the riding boots she wore beneath her long, sheathlike dress.

"You cannot stop it," she whispered in a low voice colored with an indeterminate accent that might have been Russian. "Do not try or you will only cause your own death."

She stepped around him and put her hand against the wall. The wooden panel started to move away from her the moment she touched it, and she was halfway gone before Peregrine realized she wanted him to follow her through the hidden door.

But Mrs. Foster—his honor would not let him turn his back on a woman in need.

The gypsy was still in the passage, her eyes intent upon him, waiting, when Peregrine decided to follow.

It was already too late for anyone to help Mrs. Foster.

The door closed with a dull click, merged into the wall of bookcases. Peregrine doubted he would be able to find it, assuming he had the opportunity to try.

The hidden library was windowless, the walls covered with bookshelves that extended from the floor to the ceiling fourteen feet above. A fire burned in the fireplace carved from marble, a baroque fantasia of cupids and filigree that probably was once part of a Florentine villa. The furniture was French—brocade chairs, parquet tables, an ornate chest. In the corner, sitting at an angle, was a big marble-topped table, each leg a carved lion's claw grasping a globe. A heavily carved wooden chair, imposing enough to have served as a throne in a bishop's palace, was pulled up to the table. Open on the blotter—as if the reader had been called away in the midst of study—was a large, leather-bound book. The printing on the page was in a language Peregrine did not recognize. Not Latin, Greek, or even Cyrillic, he thought. The alien script in the illuminated manuscript resembled Celtic or Norse runes. He stared down at the book. Perhaps this was the language of these creatures.

The woman standing by the fireplace watched him with an expression that seemed to indicate she knew his thoughts. She was an exotic creature. He had not noticed it before, but her eyes were like a cat's: large, wise, sensual, and predatory, in a quiet feline way.

"I should have stopped that," Peregrine said.

"There wasn't anything you could have done."

"I could have tried."

"Safian would have torn your throat out with his fingers

without looking up from his fun. He does not like being interrupted by underlings."

What sort of name was Safian? It sounded foreign and menacing, matching his appearance.

"I am no man's underling," Peregrine said.

"Safian is not a man."

"He looks like a man."

"In outward appearance, yes, but he has been something else for a long time."

"How long?" Peregrine said, pretending to scan the titles on the shelf nearest him. Some were in English, others in the weird language of these creatures.

Her eyes sparkled in the candlelight. "You're curious," she said.

"Yes, I am. That is why I am here. How long has Safian not been a man?"

"For centuries."

"How can that be possible?"

"You cannot begin to guess all the things that are possible," she said, and started slowly toward him.

Peregrine held himself still and upright as she walked slowly around him, looking at him the way one might appraise a horse at auction. She did not seem big or strong enough to be a threat to Peregrine, who had killed men in battle with his bare hands. Still, he knew she was a killer; he could feel it in his bones. But he wasn't afraid. Fear was an emotion he could no longer experience, perhaps because his reasons for living had themselves been dead this past year.

"If he's not a man, what is this Safian, besides old enough to be my grandfather's grandfather?"

"One of us, my child," she said from behind him.

"Us?"

"Yes," she said, turning the word into a purr.

She came around in front of him and looked up into his face as if interested in him in an unexpected way. "You are not afraid."

He did not deny it.

"You should be afraid."

"Perhaps."

"Most people who want to die are weak." She leaned close and put her cheek against him. He could feel her warmth through his tunic and shirt. She drew in a breath through her nose. "You do not have the stink of cowardice. Do you want to die?"

"I don't know how to answer your question. I no longer have any interest in life, but it might be more accurate to say I'm indifferent on the subject. The one thing I do want is to understand what this is all about—you, the others, the woman who introduced me to all of this."

She spun away from him, giving Peregrine the impression that she did not want him to see whatever was in her eyes.

"She is of no concern."

"She brought me here tonight, although I can't explain how she did it."

"She brings many here," the gypsy said, her new smile so bright that Peregrine thought it had to be false. "That is what she does, you know; she brings people here. She is like a flower drawing insects here to the nectar."

"Or is it just the reverse—she draws the nectar here to the insects?"

"You have a quick wit."

"Take me to meet her," Peregrine said.

The smile flickered but only just. "That would not be wise. You know what happens when the moth flies too near the flame."

She put her hand on his breast before he could speak. Desire came flooding into Peregrine then, catching him unawares, possessing him, setting him on fire from inside. How could she do this to him, with a touch of the hand?

Peregrine saw his yearning mirrored in the gypsy's gamine eyes, and though he knew it was only her hunger for his blood, he could not make himself resist. An inexplicable paralysis robbed him of control over his body, so that all he could do was stare down at that hand, smooth and white as the marble fireplace, the long fingers tapering to nails the color of blood. She wore a ring of an antique design, the gold setting holding a square-cut ruby. The jewel glowed with the same sensual fire burning within him.

"A lover gave it to me," her voice said, sounding very far away, as in a dream. "He is dead now. I keep it as a memento mori."

Her hand began to move across his chest, the caress making his heart race. She slipped her fingers inside the edge of his tunic and drew him to her, pulling them both backward until she was against the table. She released him long enough to raise herself up onto the marble surface. Peregrine found himself standing between her legs, looking down to see that she had raised her dress up to her hips.

Peregrine put one hand on her arm, the other around her back. He did not know what he was doing or why he was doing it, only that he had no control. They were face-to-face, eye to eye, Peregrine leaning forward until there was no more than a breath separating their lips.

A glitter of light at the edge of the gypsy's mouth became the serpent's teeth, appearing from beneath her upper lip.

Peregrine had not discovered what he'd come to the house on Chestnut Street to learn, but it no longer mattered to him. The bliss enveloped him, erasing all memories, cares, and intentions. He had long since ceased participating in life except insofar as it allowed him to pursue vengeance against the people who murdered his family. This final act severing him from the world would be but a formality, the formal ending to something that in actuality had been over a long time ago.

"What will you give me as a memento mori to remember you when you are dead?" she said in his ear.

Their lips touched briefly before she lowered her face into his shoulder. The ecstasy crashing into him seemed without limit. No wonder Evangeline and Mrs. Foster had gone to their deaths moaning with delight. Who could resist pleasure a million times more powerful than anything that came out of an opium pipe?

Her nimble fingers had opened his tunic and were drawing down the collar of his shirt, her lips parted against the skin of his throat. Peregrine closed his eyes, waiting for it, wanting it, anxious for her to possess him completely, and for the peaceful nothingness that would follow.

The ugly hiss destroyed the moment, breaking the spell as completely as a rock thrown through a windowpane. Peregrine felt himself thrown roughly back. Disoriented and staggering, he saw the gypsy push herself up from the table, her upturned face contorted with rage at an apparition on the ceiling she alone could see.

Peregrine's hands came up defensively, but she flew past him and was gone, leaving one bookcase turned out into the room at an angle. Through the opening, Peregrine saw the revelers still circled around the piano. Behind them, sprawled across the settee like a discarded doll missing a shoe, was Mrs. Foster's dead body.

9

Les Vampires

THE CORPSES HAD accumulated in the mansion during the brief time Peregrine was sequestered within the hidden library. No one seemed to notice him as he walked through the music room, stepping over the body of a young man stretched out between the two parlors. Behind him, the pianist began to play Mozart's *A Little Night Music.*

The foyer was deserted, without a doorman or servants to bring him his cloak—or to dissuade him from leaving. The double glass doors remained open, with only the screen outer doors separating him from escaping into the night.

Peregrine did not move. He stood there, shifting his weight from one foot to the other, trying to make up his mind. He was in a house of death, and he had no more illusions about being able to control his future if he stayed there, beyond seeing himself become one of the monsters' next victims.

But *she* was in the house. He knew it without knowing quite how he knew it. Surely she had brought him there for some reason. Peregrine did not think it could have been to kill him, or he would have been dead already, at her hand, or the gypsy's, or one of the other blood drinkers. Why engage him in such a living game of chess, moving and countermoving herself and her deadly chess pieces, unless she was building to something more than Peregrine being slaughtered—or allowed to walk out the door?

A cool breeze blew in through the screens, flowing past Peregrine as he stood rooted, like water dividing around a boulder in the stream. During the intermittent pauses between the phrases of Mozart from the farther room, Peregrine heard the faint sound of bamboo wind chimes. It reminded him of something, although he wasn't sure what. And then it came to him, the connection to chimes he'd heard that night in the opium den, a sound like the clicking of finger bones laced together with thread.

Peregrine tilted his head, straining to hear the sound. There was more than an overwhelming sense of remembrance or an unnerving moment of déjà vu. A chill of cold sweat broke out on Peregrine's neck as he realized he was hearing *exactly* the same sound he had heard at Yu's. He did not know how this could be, or if there really was a wind chime outside the house on Chestnut Street, or if it was all inside his mind. What he did know was that she was able to play tricks with the night, controlling events and perceptions with a power that seemed nothing short of wizardry.

Only a fool would contend with such a being without expecting to pay a severe price.

Peregrine began to take a step toward the door but stopped himself.

The other side of the coin was that only a fool would think he could step willingly into the black widow's web, then change his mind, turn around, and leave without paying the consequences.

Peregrine's eyes looked out through the screen. The Spanish moss moved gracefully back and forth in the night breeze, either beckoning him to come or mocking him for his predicament.

If he stayed, he died. If he left, he died. Peregrine was a

king in check. The mistake was in the earlier moves, now too late to recover from. All that was left was to see how long it took the endgame to play itself out. Escaping checkmate was not even remotely possible.

He saw a subtle change in the darkness outside the door, the shadows moving across one another. He thought it was just the moss swaying in the wind until the shadows coalesced into something solid. He heard the scrape of shoe leather against wood as the shadow turned, directing its attention away from the street to focus inside the house. Peregrine would not close his eyes for even a fraction of a second. There was someone out there, looking in at him through the door.

Another sliding footstep. A face took shape in the darkness, but it was not the woman. It was someone as big as Peregrine, perhaps bigger. A shock of black hair emerged in the reflected light, then an arching eyebrow and curling upper lip.

It was Safian.

That decided the matter for Peregrine. His reaction was purely tactical, like a general arriving on the field to find the advance blocked and his position untenable. Without the least expression of haste, he turned away from the door and started to climb the stairs, toward the upper regions of the mansion on Chestnut Street in search of the woman he had come there to find.

The broad staircase curved around like the shell of a nautilus, depositing Peregrine in a hallway running the length of the house. The doors along either side of the hall were closed except for the last door on the right, which stood ajar a few inches. A pair of ornate iron stands, whose design might have been copied from an Egyptian tomb, framed the door, shoulder-high oil lamps the only light in the hallway. The windows on either end of the hall were open, their gossamer draperies moving in the breeze with motions as sinuous as Turkish dancing girls. No sound of the gaiety below penetrated the house's second level. The Garden District mansions were built solid as tombs, with stout brick walls and floors made from thick planks of cypress or oak.

Someone had dropped a woman's white scarf in the middle of the hall. The breeze stirred the silk, fabric so fine that it seemed to have no more substance than a whiff of smoke. As he stood on the landing, the scarf lifted a few inches from the floor and fell back. It stretched itself, like a snake uncoiling after sleep, and edged toward Peregrine, as if possessing both will and purpose. He watched it rub itself against his foot the way a cat does when it wants to be scratched. His wife had once owned such a scarf, a memento of their honeymoon in St. Louis, traveling there on the newest steamboat in the Peregrine Mississippi & Ohio Line.

The scarf rose unsteadily and levitated in the air in front of his face, twisting and turning, until Peregrine's hand shot out and grabbed it. Or so he thought. He stared at his empty hand. The scarf was gone.

"Ohhhhh."

The moan came from the door on his left, the sound of pain and pleasure merging into one. The hair stood up on the back of his neck, like static electricity in the air a moment before lightning strikes.

Refusing to be diverted by whatever was going on inside that room, Peregrine walked straight to the door between the braziers at the end of the hall, a sixth sense telling him that was where he would find her. He put his hand on the knob. It was cast brass, cool to his skin. He ran his finger over the decorative metal raised along the outer edge of the casting. There was no turning back if he opened the door and went inside. No, he thought. That was an illusion. He had passed the point of no return long before that moment.

Behind him, a door opened. Peregrine felt a pair of eyes upon his back, but he did not look around. Instead, he grasped the ornate doorknob, pushed forward, and stepped into the monster's inner sanctum, closing the door behind him.

The chambermaid greeted him with bowed head.

"Good evening."

She did not answer. Her coffee-colored face was a blank mask, the same as the other servants in the house. If Peregrine hadn't seen her move, he would have taken her for a wax model of the sort displayed at Madame Tussaud's in London.

Peregrine found himself in a sitting room furnished like the rest of the house with elegant European chairs and tables. A low couch with brocade pillows faced the fireplace. The oil paintings on the walls were landscapes except for a portrait of a noble-looking man from another time over the mantel.

"Have you found my scarf, *chéri?*"

The woman's voice had come through an open door Peregrine hadn't noticed because it was mostly hidden behind a Japanese screen. She spoke with the slight French accent once common to old Creole families in the Delta. Peregrine recognized the voice. He would have known it anywhere.

"No, I thought I had it, but—well, I'm sure *you* understand."

He was glad that his voice was firm and level. He was not worried about sounding frightened or uncertain— although he feared he might sound crazy.

The woman did not answer. Peregrine wondered what she was doing in the adjoining boudoir. He stared hard at the Oriental carpet, trying not to picture her in there with someone like Evangeline or even Mrs. Foster, draining them of their blood and life as he stood next door, waiting his turn to die, but secretly harboring obscure hopes that he would learn some great secret and it would all turn out miraculously different for him.

The servant went to the sideboard and poured a snifter of brandy. She put it on the low table before the couch, curtsied to no one in particular, and went out the hall door, closing it behind herself. Peregrine sat down unbidden, for that obviously was what he was supposed to do, and picked up the glass. The cognac tasted rich and warm, and he felt its effect almost immediately. He took a second swallow, this time bigger, and leaned back to wait.

"My dear general."

The woman seemed to have materialized in front of him.

Peregrine put down the glass as he stood up and bowed. She was smiling up at him when he straightened, more beautiful than ever. She had come out of the bedroom with her long hair undone, so that it tumbled over her bare shoulders. Her skin was as translucent as a cameo held to light. Her lips were shining and full, her profile of such classic shape that she might have been the model for a statue of Aphrodite—and for all Peregrine knew, she might have lived long enough to have been the original goddess. Her sharply drawn eyebrows and lustrous eyelashes served only to accentuate the size and color of her green eyes. She was simply dressed in a plain white gown with raised bodice, the sort of dress a vestal virgin might have worn, golden slippers on her tiny feet. Only two pieces of jewelry adorned her body: a golden bracelet around her wrist in the shape of a serpent chasing its own tail, and a simple golden cross.

"I am delighted to see you again, General Peregrine, but why did you take so long to present yourself to me? Certainly you know that a gentleman never keeps a lady waiting."

10
Seduction

"How do you know my name?" Peregrine asked in a voice that was curious rather than accusatory.

"I know everything about you, Nathaniel. I am Delphine Allard. Secrets are not kept from Madame."

He looked at the hand she had extended, which was as tiny and fragile as a songbird kept in a gilded cage to entertain a drowsy empress.

Madame Allard gazed back at him with a Mona Lisa smile, amused rather than insulted that he had not taken her hand. She seemed to know what he was thinking—that such a hand hardly looked capable of belonging to a monster.

"What are you afraid of, General?"

"Excuse me, madame." He took her hand in his and lightly held it, her skin dry and warm even to the point of feeling feverish.

"You are not really afraid of me, are you, General Peregrine? That is one of the first things I noticed about you."

Peregrine looked back into her eyes and said nothing. There was no point. She already *knew* what was in his mind and heart.

Madame Allard sat down and nodded for him to join her on the couch.

"It is a curious deficiency you suffer, General."

"I beg your pardon?" He had been thinking about how beautiful she was.

"This peculiar condition you suffer, never being afraid, it is because you lack something. Do not look shocked, General. I do not doubt your courage. It is plain that you are a brave man. But your inability to fear is a different matter entirely. A vital part of you simply is not there. Part of your soul is missing. That is the real cause of your indifference to"—she looked around her in a manner that indicated the house on Chestnut Street and its murderous inhabitants—"all of this."

"How is it possible to know such things?"

Madame Allard laughed merrily. "That is what you came here to find out. "You cannot hide your secrets from me, General. No one can."

The rap on the door brought Peregrine's chin sharply up.

"That will be Colette," Madame Allard said. "I have been expecting her. *Entrez.*"

Into the room came the gypsy who had wished to collect a memento mori from Peregrine in the library.

Colette came quietly into the room, her eyes moving from Madame Allard to Peregrine and back.

"I thought you might like more company," Colette said, addressing Madame Allard. "Three can have such a frightfully good time."

"A delicious idea, darling, but I prefer to keep General Peregrine to myself."

There was disappointment but no sign of the temper Colette had shown earlier. She either respected the little Creole girl-woman, or feared her.

"Another time, then."

"Without question," Madame Allard said.

"It was you, wasn't it?" Peregrine said when the monster was gone.

Madame Allard raised one pretty eyebrow.

"When Colette and I were in the library," Peregrine said, "you intervened before she was able to—you know what I'm talking about."

"Colette has a lovely voice and many fine qualities, but she always wants to monopolize the most interesting men. Besides, I have had my eye on you for far too long to let darling Colette have you all to herself."

"You weren't in the library. How did you know what was about to happen? How did you command her to leave me alone? Are you able to project your wishes—even your will—through the walls?"

Madame Allard made a dismissive gesture. "These are trifling matters, General. I can do a great many things that would no doubt astonish you, but they are commonplaces among my kind and hardly worthy of comment."

Peregrine leaned toward her on his arm, his eyes bright and alert. "Your *kind*. That is what fascinated me. Pray tell me what you mean by that, Madame Allard."

She raised her face with pride.

"I am a vampire, General Peregrine."

"And what, pray tell, is a vampire?"

"We can discuss that another time, General."

"Will there be another time?"

She indicated his glass. "Have your drink. It will relax you."

The last thing Peregrine wanted to do was relax, but he picked up the cognac. The vampire nodded as he drank, like a physician happy to see her patient taking his medicine.

"The thing that fascinates me about you is not your fear-lessness, which is remarkable in itself. What makes you unique, General, is your inability to free yourself from your grief. I have known people suffering the horrors of tragedy and loss, but I have never witnessed grief as profound and deep as I see it in you." She closed her eyes. "I can feel it burning in you—your grief, and your anger."

Peregrine locked his jaw and looked away, blinking his eyes rapidly. He wished she would get it over with—sink her teeth into his neck, kill him, and put the whole pathetic tragedy that was his life forever in the past.

"Emotions are like coins, General, with two sides, heads and tails, opposing representations of what is in fact the same whole. Surely you have noticed that the world is made up of dualities: day and night; white and black; inside and out; love and hate; good and evil."

Peregrine was hardly listening. Madame Allard had summoned the ghosts back into the center of his world.

"Every emotion, every power, has its opposite, and that is where it draws its true power. The converse of grief is not joy but vengeance. Grief and anger are waters that well up out of the same dark place in your ruined heart."

Peregrine felt himself fall bodily back into the present moment. He looked back at Madame Allard. The hard light in her eyes reflected nothing but cold calculation and a desire to have her way—whatever she was up to with him. Few men could be as cruel as a beautiful woman, in Peregrine's experience; they grew so accustomed to breaking hearts that they often became hardened to anything but their own desire.

"It is just a question of translation, General. The solution to the pain over your murdered family is not to suffer but to convert the misery into hatred. You have an exquisite untouched capacity for anger. It is a gift, my dear, a talent every bit as rare and precious as what my remarkable friend Liszt is able to do when he sits at my piano downstairs. You have been blessed. The seed that flowers into genius is invariably a wound, and you, my poor dear man, have been wounded to the bottom of your heart. Cradle your lust for vengeance, Nathaniel. Hold it to your breast like a child, like you held your own two poor dead children when they were babies. You can make so many interesting things happen if you devote your mind, your body, and your soul to gorgeous anger. What you want is not oblivion but revenge on the people who killed your wife and children."

Peregrine stared, too stunned to speak, barely able to breathe. He closed his eyes and felt it, the anger, burning hot as a blacksmith's fire in his soul.

"Since there is no love in your life, replace it with hate, Nathaniel. We need something inside, something to give us a reason to continue from day to day. You are a hollow man now, but I can see that changing as I watch you fill your soul with pure and glorious anger."

A bead of perspiration ran down the side of his face, but he did not bother to wipe it away.

"Never have I met a man more marked for doom than you, Nathaniel Peregrine," she said, her voice seeming to come from within him. "Not marked for death, my love," she whispered, her lips now gently brushing his neck, "but doom."

Peregrine started to ask Madame Allard what she meant, but the feeling of her breath against the skin of his neck, so deliciously warm and moist, stopped the words in his mouth.

"The people who murdered your beloved wife and your babies will be made to pay, my darling," she whispered. "Vengeance *will* be yours. That is my promise to you. The cause of the Confederacy is as lost as you are, and what do I care for any of that? My allegiance, such as it is, belongs to France. You will atone for the death of your family a thousand times over, my beloved. You shall drink your fill of revenge. You will find the taste very sweet indeed."

"Revenge," Peregrine said, but that was all he had time to say before Madame Allard's teeth sank deep into his throat.

11

The Killing Field

THE LONELY COUNTRY road crossed the Pennsylvania countryside, rising and falling with the landscape, dividing silent fields of shoulder-high corn, running past farmhouses dark in the first hour after midnight on a July night. The sound of an approaching horseman could be heard from a great distance on the still night, hooves pounding the road, the dirt baked hard by the summer sun. The rider's speed seemed to increase as he drew nearer, a clatter exploding when the horse took the covered bridge at full gallop, the pounding reverberating across the sleeping countryside like a sudden volley of rifle shots.

Nathaniel Peregrine leaned forward in his saddle, his cape streaming behind as if with dark wings partly unfurled. The road passed through a grove of cottonwoods on the far side of the stream, then up an incline, an undulating rise that followed the bend in the watercourse, formed by years of spring floods carrying away earth from the bank. At the top, the rider pulled sharply back on the sweat-flecked beast's reins. The stallion cried in protest and rose up on its hind legs, but the rider remained firmly seated in the saddle.

In the far distance, he saw a flickering line of lights from well-spaced fires. This was the rear guard—the train, the hospital tents, the nether end of the immense

community an army drags behind as it hauls itself ponder-
ously over the earth, depleting the countryside of forage,
leaving in its wake smoldering foundations of houses and
barns, ruined towns, poisoned wells, and the dead. Peregrine had ridden around the flanks of two entire armies to
come up on the rebel force from its rear. The underbelly
that the army dragged with it across the land was its weak-
est spot, especially to a lone rider, approaching the assem-
bled Confederate host from where it least expected attack.

Peregrine tied the horse to a cottonwood sapling and
headed toward the nearest bonfire with preternatural
speed, moving impossibly fast in a low, wolfish crouch,
cutting with fierce purpose through the growing corn rows.

The picket stood leaning against his rifle, eyes closed.
The firelight illuminated his figure so that Peregrine could
see the soldier perfectly. The private's youthfulness was
partly disguised beneath a misshapen slouch hat and an
untrimmed brown beard. He had a smallish nose, thin lips,
his sunburned skin pulled taut over the cheekbones from
forced marches on short rations over great stretches of terrain as the rebel army moved north. The picket's uniform
was homespun cloth, his boots gone beyond hope of repair. The only thing of value the soldier seemed to possess
was his weapon. The picket must have brought his Ken-
tucky squirrel rifle with him when he joined the rebellion.

Peregrine noted all of this from a distance that rapidly
diminished as he approached unseen. The picket sensed
something at the last, but Peregrine was already upon him,
dragging his head back by the long, dirty hair. He sank his
teeth into the soldier's neck with a single, swift, savage
motion. The man's neck tasted of dried sweat and dust
from long months of marching without anything more
than a splash in a creek to serve for bathing. The vileness

made Peregrine want to retch, but instead he bit down harder, ripping muscles and tendons with his razor teeth before the natural sweetness of living blood began to carry him away on its hot tide of delirium.

He had not fed the Hunger in a long while, so he stayed with the man longer than he had intended. He greedily swallowed gulps of blood until he began to feel drunk. Blood did that to a vampire: the first explosion of pleasure deepened into intoxication. The more one drank, the more lost one became to the boundless abandon and sense of power. It was so great that Peregrine sometimes thought he could use the force of his mind to drive the moon backward through the sky.

Footsteps approached. He sensed the other man's alarm. The powerful smell of fear mingling with murderous rage came to Peregrine in the next instant, but still he drank, not releasing the corpse until it had been drained of its last drop of blood, drained like a spider sucks the vital juices from a fly.

Peregrine turned toward the intruder in time to watch the bayonet plunge into his stomach up to the tip of the barrel of the rifle holding it. He felt no pain. The rebel holding the weapon was breathing hard, panting from the run, and the terrible thrill of standing eye to eye with someone he had just stricken with a mortal wound.

"You've killed me," Peregrine said.

"Yankee bastard," the rebel said. There was spittle in the corners of his mouth. He was trembling. Peregrine could tell he had never killed a man up close. Like the rebel Peregrine had just killed, this one was skinny from short rations, his face sunken, with eyes and cheeks hollow, and a ratty goatee.

"You needn't worry," Peregrine said. "You can become accustomed to anything, even killing, given the chance."

Peregrine put his hands around the rifle barrel and held it as he pushed himself backward off the bayonet. His enemy stared at him, too astonished to pull the trigger. A slug in his stomach wouldn't have mattered more than the blade, Peregrine thought, though a gunshot would have brought more rebels running. Once he'd pushed himself off the bayonet, he jerked the rifle from the soldier's hands, then reversed the direction of his swing and smashed the butt into the soldier's jaw. A streak of blood and teeth made a slow parabola in the firelight before splattering on the dusty ground, the sound quickly followed by the muffled crumple of a body collapsing.

Peregrine straddled the prostrate rebel. The man looked up at him and blinked, as if trying to clear his mind enough to comprehend the impossible thing that had just happened. A flicker of horror replaced confusion as Peregrine flipped the gun over in the air, the blade pointing downward.

The soldier's lips moved soundlessly, though the words were obvious enough: "No, please, no . . ."

Peregrine thrust the bayonet completely through the man's body, pinning him to the ground.

Peregrine removed his jacket and hung it over a tree branch. His shirt was torn where the blade had gone in and wet with blood. He unfastened the buttons and ran his hand over the welt where the skin had already closed over the wound. Soon, even that would disappear. Though the shirt was damp with blood, he buttoned it back up, stuffing the tails into his trousers.

He stripped the butternut jacket off the first dead picket, making a face when he smelled how it reeked of sweat, cheap tobacco, and wood smoke. There were blood splatters on the collar, but they were hardly noticeable on the stained and much-patched jacket.

The other man was dead when Peregrine went back to him, bled out through the stab wound. He picked up the man's hat and looked at it before putting it on. The straw planter's hat was in relatively good condition and fit his large head almost perfectly.

He probably didn't need a disguise, but now he had one. He could go wherever he wanted among the sleeping army, unnoticed as he moved toward the front line and the generals making plans for the battle that would be rejoined with first light.

A line of officers' tents was pitched in the yard of a house that had been damaged by artillery fire. The canvas flaps on the tents were folded up to let in the air of the warm summer night. There was a single cot in the tent at the end of the row, and on it a man on his back, asleep.

Peregrine looked about. Except for the watch, the encampment was asleep after another exhausting day of battle.

Peregrine stepped into the last tent and stood looking down on the sleeping man. Beside the cot, before a portable writing desk, the man's jacket was draped over the back of a camp chair, a colonel's insignia on the epaulets. Peregrine made a close study of the man's face, observing his features down to the slightest detail. He had a high, intelligent forehead that met brown hair brushed back straight and neat even in sleep. The nose was slightly rounded at the tip, as was the chin. The faint line of an old scar could be seen on the left upper lip, the mark repeated in a slight gap in the left eyebrow, an old saber wound perhaps.

Peregrine opened his hands and held them over the colonel's face, lowering them until he nearly touched the sleeping man. He closed his own eyes to better *see* the contours of the man's face so that he could re-create the man's image perfectly within his own mind, and then in the minds of others.

Even asleep, the man sensed danger. He stirred and opened his eyes. Peregrine lightly touched his fingertips to the man's temples and the rebel closed his eyes again.

Next, the vampire drank in Colonel John Reeve's memories in great gulps, swallowing them like cool spring-water on a hot day. The recollections of a lifetime poured out of the man and into the vampire.

After only a few minutes, Peregrine knew everything he needed to accomplish his purpose.

"Colonel Reeve, you're up late, sir."

The captain was leaning against a tree, holding a thin silver flask. Peregrine searched his recently acquired memory and was not disappointed. Colonel Jack Wiley, a lawyer from Mobile, Alabama. Mad Jack, they called him, because of his reputation for foolish courage. The men were of two minds about Mad Jack. Half thought he was certain to be the next of Lee's staff officers to be killed. Others—Reeve was in this camp—thought the man led a charmed existence and was sure to go home at the end of the war.

"Jack," Peregrine said, and held out his hand for the flask. The initials engraved in the silver in elegant script— L.R.S.—belonged to a fellow officer. The flask had been Leonard Stacey's, until he made a gift of it to the luckier Mad Jack as Stacey lie dying. The brandy tasted good to Peregrine, though the Change had taken him to a state of being beyond the consolation of liquor or even opium. The only thing that still had the power to intoxicate him now was blood.

"Tomorrow ought to tell the tale, John, though I can't

say I like slugging it out with the Yankees with us both in fixed positions."

"Those people," Peregrine said, and spat, playing his part with perverse enjoyment. "If the Yankees will turn tail and run on an open battlefield, I don't reckon they'll do any different if we attack them in their trenches."

"I suppose not," Mad Jack said gamely, though the hint of a frown made Peregrine wonder if Mad Jack was as mad as his compatriots imagined. He raised his flask to Peregrine in salute. "I trust tomorrow will prove to be an excellent day to see the enemy die."

"I have no doubt of it," Peregrine said, and moved off toward the next encampment. A ring of tents circled a low-burning fire. Just beyond, revealed only when the dying blaze gave off a brief flicker, stood a battery of cannon aimed at the Union lines. Between the lines was nearly a mile of empty ground, the land rising gently as it approached the Union Army. The terrain was a strategic strength for General George Gordon Meade's blue-clad forces sleeping on the opposite side of the broad, open killing field.

There was only one person still sitting out by the fire, a bearded officer formally dressed in boots and jacket, a major general's golden epaulets on the shoulder. The familiar leonine features were instantly recognizable. It was Robert E. Lee, commander of the Army of Northern Virginia. Though outnumbered and outweaponed, Lee had beaten the Union Army time and again, yet this was his boldest move ever, invading the North in an audacious— not to say desperate—bid to force the United States to sue for peace.

Massah Lee, Peregrine thought, studying the Confederate general's profile in the firelight. Lee looked tired but not the soft kind of tired that sleep could remedy. He had been offered command of the United States forces, but chose to side with the South. Three short years had turned him into an old man. The skin around his eyes was deeply lined, and his beard was turning white. There was no way short of a miracle that the South could win the war, but in a way that played to its advantage. Desperate men fight harder. They win because they *have* to win.

Lee glanced up, regarding the campfires burning on the opposite ridge, assessing the enemy's number.

It would have been a simple matter to kill Lee. Peregrine could have done it quickly and silently, without anyone noticing their commanding general's lifeless body until Peregrine was safely gone. But that was not what he had in mind. It hardly would be logical to kill one rebel— even one as important as Lee—when he could just as easily send many thousands of them to hell.

Peregrine closed his eyes and reached out with his mind . . .

The air was filled with voices, the aimless thoughts of sleepless men and their slumbering compatriots, all dreaming of home and the battle to come, a fight that would send many of them down into the earth as food for worms. Peregrine had to focus hard to direct his attention through the gibbering echoes and anxious cries until he found Lee. The interior of the Confederate commander's mind was exactly as Peregrine had expected: clean, clear, well ordered, austere, like a library, like a Greek temple.

Peregrine hid there in the midst of Lee's thoughts for many minutes, choosing not to act until he was familiar with the tone and flow of the commander's thoughts. The thing Peregrine hoped to achieve required great delicacy and subtlety. If he forced the matter, the sober-thinking tactician could become too uncomfortable with the idea to accept it as his own.

The vampire lurked in the trees, watching the methodical logic of Lee's mind as he turned the problem of the coming battle over and over again, like a chess player studying a difficult problem. The solution seemed to present itself spontaneously, as if it had come to Lee as one of those sudden insights, when the answer, so elusive, suddenly makes itself plain.

Lee had doubts about the resolve of the Union soldiers. He questioned the mettle of the Yankee officers. He was contemptuous of Meade, a sentiment Peregrine shared. Lee wondered if the center of the Union line was as strong as it appeared. Maybe if he sent one of his best divisions crashing headlong into the blue-belly center, the line would break, and the resulting split between the army's wings would lead Meade to panic and draw back, opening the way for Lee to drive deeper into Pennsylvania and despoil the countryside until the Northern politicians cried uncle. In his mind's eye, Lee could see General Pickett leading a vast host of the Confederacy across the open plain and smashing the Union line.

Pickett could carry the day. He would do it because he could. He would do it because Lee ordered him to do it, and his men always did what *Massah* Lee asked of them.

That was it, then.

Lee stood up, his legs and back stiff, and nodded his noble, bearded head. The matter was decided. Tomorrow, Pickett would lead a massed charge into the Union lines at Gettysburg that would win the battle for the South and turn the tide of the war decisively in the Confederacy's favor. Lincoln would be suing for peace before the summer ended.

Smiling, Peregrine turned away from Lee and began to return the way he had come.

The vampire knew every inch of the Union lines—the

officers, the troops, their ammunition supplies, their morale, even the quality of their forage, provisions, and drinking water. And more important than all of that, he had walked the ridge himself and examined the tactical position. It was never a good idea to attack an entrenched enemy when you had to run uphill to do it, especially not when the defender's line ran in a way that made it possible to rake the attackers with a withering enfilade of rifle fire and grapeshot fired from close-in artillery.

There wasn't a prayer in heaven that the rebels could carry the Union line, not even with the dashing Pickett leading the way. When the sun came up and the charge was mounted, the soldiers in blue would slaughter rebels by the thousands.

The thought of so much Confederate carnage filled Peregrine with an unfamiliar emotion that he'd almost forgotten existed. For the first time since marauding rebel guerrillas murdered his family more than a year earlier, Nathaniel Peregrine felt happy.

12
Lost

IT WAS AN hour before dawn when Peregrine returned to the hotel in the Pennsylvania town. A thunderstorm was racing in from the west, slashing the night's starless blackness with jagged silver lightning and the diffused glow of bolts trapped within the low, roiling clouds.

No one would be awake at that hour, so Peregrine put up the horse himself. The approaching storm made the animals in the stables nervous. The beasts looked about with frightened eyes with each volley, pawing the ground, afraid to be confined within their stalls with weather coming in. Peregrine spoke to the animals in a soothing voice, and the creatures were quiet.

The first raindrops fell on Peregrine as he crossed to the hotel, each raising a tiny puff of dust from the bone-dry dirt street. The front doors had been left open to let in the cool of the summer night air, a single hurricane lamp burning on the reception desk beside the stairs. The wind was coming up, and it ruffled the pages of a newspaper left on the big square table surrounded by a collection of comfortable chairs in the middle of the room.

Peregrine came into the hotel and stopped, tasting death in the air.

One corner of the newspaper lifted and turned as if by a phantom hand. Outside in the distance, a door banged with the next gust, the wind moving across the night unseen, uncontrolled, uncontrollable. He was like that now. Order and reason were no longer part of his world. A vampire, Peregrine thought, lives in the swirling chaos, a creature outside the law.

The rain started to fall in earnest with a sudden rush of sound. The wind picked up as the thunderstorm arrived and began to howl. There was a brilliant flash of light and the almost simultaneous splintering crack of a tree torn in two before the cannon roar of the thunder. The newspaper blew up from the table as if thrown in the air and flew madly about the room like the fluttering ghosts of those who died afraid and too quickly to ask for their redemption.

Peregrine went up the stairs, narrowing his eyes against the acrid vibration of violence and murder hanging like a poisonous fog in the air. The doors to the rooms on the second floor were open or ajar, several smashed to splinters. Corpses lay in doorways, were flung across beds, or crumpled in corners, as if cowering against an inexorable force of horror.

The wind whooped and moaned around the hotel, rattling windowpanes and shaking shutters, driving sheets of rain against the slat-wood siding. The night reminded Peregrine of the night he'd walked down the second-floor hallway lined with doors in the house on Chestnut Street. Then he had been in jeopardy. Now he *was* the jeopardy, the walking pestilence, the threat that waits in the darkness. The thunder roared, and it seemed to be speaking to him, telling him to take refuge in sudden violence, in whose all-encompassing passion there remained no room for the pain of being a man.

Peregrine had the best room in the hotel, at the front of the building, overlooking the town square. He turned the latch and went in.

"Hello, darling."

Madame Delphine Allard sat on the bed, her arm around the shoulders of the young woman who had served them supper in the hotel's dining room before Peregrine rode off to inspect the Union line and then to go in search of Robert E. Lee. The girl was naked and trembling, her face streaked with tears. Peregrine's nostrils flared as he took in a deep breath, gathering in that single motion the vibrations, scents, and sounds of the hotel, an island surrounded by rain and night. The girl was the only mortal left alive.

"I have been amusing myself while you were away," Madame Allard said. She began to caress the girl with her free hand.

"I noticed," Peregrine said.

The serving girl appeared to be a year or two older than Madame Allard, but that was an illusion. Delphine Allard was nearly two hundred years old. She had lived all over the world, but her base was the house on Chestnut Street, in the city where she'd dropped her mortality and become a vampire.

"So tell me, *chéri,* how does it feel, your revenge? Is it every bit as delicious as I promised?"

"It's a beginning."

"And the remembering? Has it freed you of that?"

Peregrine winced a fraction of a second before the hotel shook with a volley of thunder louder than a battery of nine-pounders firing in unison. From the stables came the scream of a horse crying out in fear. The poor terrified beasts, Peregrine thought.

"I saved her for you, my love," Madame Allard said, and gave him a wicked smile. The girl was looking up at Peregrine, too, her eyes wordlessly begging for mercy. He slowly unbuttoned his cape and let it fall to the floor but made no move.

"If you cannot lose yourself in revenge, my love, then you must lose yourself in pleasure," Madame Allard said.

Peregrine hesitated a moment longer, then moved toward the women on the bed.

PART TWO

HAITI

1914

13

House Calls

Dr. MICHAEL LAVALLE made his diagnosis standing in the doorway of the one-room hut. He pulled up an unfinished wooden chair, the home's only seat, beside the bed, put his medical bag on the dirt floor, and opened it.

The naked child was listless in his mother's arms, almost comatose. The little boy did not move when the cold stethoscope touched him except to roll his enormous eyes away from his mother's face to look up at the physician.

"This lad has dysentery," Lavalle said.

The mother nodded dully. There was hopeless acceptance in her face, as if it was a given that the boy, her one precious possession in the world, would be taken from her so that she could go back to having nothing. She was like most of the women Lavalle had met on that part of the coast: tall and stork thin, with large, clear eyes and skin as black as that of her forebears, who had been kidnapped and brought to the New World in the holds of slave ships. Lavalle was one of a handful of Europeans living on the island's southern coast. The slave revolt a century earlier had killed or driven out most of the Europeans, and in the ensuing years there had been little white mischief to dilute the purebred African racial lines outside the capital.

"Do you know the causes of dysentery, madam?"

The child's mother shook her head. Of course she did not. Since coming to the island Lavalle was reminded daily that a simple discourse in public education would extend the average life span far beyond the pathetic forty or so years that was typical. The government had funds for a luxurious presidential palace and elaborate official rituals—including a staff composer paid a salary to devise dance tunes to entertain the ruling family—but nothing for public health.

"Dysentery is caused by waterborne bacteria," Lavalle said.

The woman gave him a blank look. The doctor sniffed. How sadly typical, he thought. He took out his silk handkerchief and wiped his nose.

"Your boy has been made sick by a germ, a tiny amoeba too small for the human eye to see, that lives in impure drinking water." He held his fingers as close as he could without them touching. Judging from her reaction, Lavalle could tell that he was not educating but frightening the woman. The simple country people cowered in fear of invisible forces. In times of trouble, they appealed to a pantheon of absurd gods and goddesses to protect them from evil spirits. The poor woman could not read a word or write her name; how could she understand amoebic dysentery?

"Never mind," Lavalle said, and smiled to show that he was not unhappy with her. "The little boy is dehydrated. He will be all right, but only if he drinks a lot of water. Do you understand?"

"Oui."

"It is important that you boil water before he drinks it. He is sick from drinking dirty water. Dirty water bad. Understand?"

She nodded.

"You must bring the water to a rolling boil, then let it get nice and cool before letting him drink. Boiling the water will make it safe for the child to drink."

He reached into his bag and came out with a small paper sack filled with a powder he mixed up by the barrel at the hospital.

"Mix a tablespoon of this into each cup."

The woman's expression lightened markedly. Powders and potions were something she understood. She thought he was giving her magic dust, a concoction like one the local witchdoctor would whip up to make someone fall in love or to keep away the evil eye.

"It's a combination of salts his body needs to replenish," Lavalle said uselessly, knowing the woman would prefer to think of it as magic. What did it matter as long as it helped the child? "Boil me a pot of water," Lavalle said. "I will show you."

The doctor stayed until he was sure that the woman understood the simple treatment. He would come back the next day to check on the boy. If he wasn't recovering, he would take him back to Hospital St. Jude in Cap Misère, where he would watch over the child himself. Dysentery was easily treated, but in the backward tropical countryside, it killed many.

The late afternoon clouds where gathering over the Massif de la Hotte Mountains by the time Lavalle got back onto his sturdy horse. Instead of returning to Cap Misère, he decided to allow himself a bit of diversion and headed out for tea at Fairweather House, where Lady Fairweather always made him welcome.

The road followed the curve of the horseshoe-shaped bay. Lavalle looked across the water to the white limestone cliffs rising dramatically to a gabled house. Maison de la Falaise—Cliff House—had been vacant since before Lavalle's arrival, although its owner, a wealthy Belgian, somehow managed to keep the surrounding gardens and park in immaculate condition. Maison de la Falaise and its coca plantation had been on the market at a reasonable price, though life in such a remote and backward corner of the world appealed to few, so the property had remained vacant. Lavalle considered buying it himself once or twice, though he was far too busy running the hospital and helping the poor to properly manage such an operation.

Anchored beneath the house was a sleek black sailing yacht flying an American flag.

Perhaps Maison de la Falaise had finally been sold.

The prospect of a new neighbor—albeit a distant one—pleased Lavalle. Aside from Lady Fairweather, there were no other whites along the coast. Though his practice consumed him, there were times when Lavalle hungered for the company of someone with whom he had something in common. He had never realized how much he liked talking about books and ideas before coming to a country where almost no one could read.

Maybe the American liked to play chess, Lavalle thought. He had not had a game since getting off the ship in Port-au-Prince. The doctor rode on, entertaining himself with thoughts about opening gambits until he turned up the lane to Fairweather House.

A man carrying a machete walked toward him on the side of the sandy road, nodding to Lavalle as he trotted past. It was one of Helen's servants. She had done a marvelous job of managing after Sir Graham's death. The locals were not famous for their devotion to hard labor, but

Lady Fairweather had gotten in her first coca crop as well as her husband ever had.

Something slammed into Lavalle's back with such startling unexpectedness that the doctor's first thought when he found himself looking up at the sky's ragged black belly was that he had been shot. The doctor slowly sat up, looking down at himself, taking stock. Except for a slight concussion, he seemed uninjured. The man with the machete was coming toward him, holding Lavalle's horse by its reins. He must have caught the animal after it bolted. The man no longer held the machete beside his leg at the end of a long, loose arm, but upward, in an attitude of self-defense.

Lavalle got to his feet, wondering what had happened. He wasn't the world's greatest horseman, but it had been a long time since he'd been thrown. His throbbing shoulder helped him remember the blow that had felled him.

"Did you see what hit me?"

The man nodded. Lavalle could see that he was afraid. He took the reins from the peasant and prodded him for more information. The man said "something" had come out of the scrub palms low and fast, flying from the bushes to knock Dr. Lavalle off his horse. Whatever it was, it did not stop but kept going.

"A man?"

"Je ne sais pas ce que c'était," the man said. *"Quelque type d'animal, un tigre peut-être."*

"There are no tigers in Haiti," Lavalle said.

The man was already backing away. Whatever he'd seen, Lavalle would get no more out of him.

He climbed back on the horse and nudged it into a walk, still a little disoriented. A glass of brandy would brace him up. Fortunately, he was almost at Fairweather

House. The lane turned to the right, opening dramatically for the last quarter mile to the white-pillared Palladian mansion.

A woman was lying athwart the road just beyond the curve, her throat torn out.

Even before Lavalle got off his horse, he knew she was dead.

14

The American

IT WAS TWO weeks before Dr. Lavalle's busy schedule afforded him the opportunity to visit the new master of Maison de la Falaise. Jean-Pierre Toussaint, the local prefect of police, had already confirmed the physician's deduction that an American had bought the plantation. Toussaint made it his business to know such things.

As a consciously methodical person, Lavalle was deeply committed to his routines. Every morning he attended to rounds at Hospital St. Jude. At noon, he walked home, ate a light lunch, and took a brief siesta. An early afternoon rest was the custom in Cap Misère, and the doctor found it a sensible one: no one in his right mind would go about his business while the fierce tropical sun was high in the sky. At three every day, Lavalle saw patients at his office in the hospital. Every other day—more often, if there were emergencies—the porter brought Lavalle's stolid gray saddle horse, Napoleon, to the hospital in the late afternoon, and he called on patients in the surrounding countryside.

The rich lowlands around the island's capital supported sugarcane plantations, but along the southern coast there was little arable soil between the mountains and sea. That part of the island was dotted with tiny settlements of a few wretched huts, the malnourished peasantry scratching out enough food from subsistence plots and fishing to maintain a tenuous hold on existence. The mountainsides along the coast were ideal for coffee and coca plantations, but large-scale operations requiring money and managerial skills had abandoned Haiti after the slave revolts a century earlier. Still, there were a few places left where the island's idyllic possibilities were realized, including the Fairweather plantation and Maison de la Falaise.

The gardens at Maison de la Falaise were of a classical French design, formal in their arrangement and perfect proportion. The beds were grouped in interlocking fashion around a stone fountain in the center, in which a Greek goddess gracefully poured water from an upturned pitcher that never emptied. The real focal point to the gardens was not the fountain, the flower beds, the hedges, or the walks covered in white pea gravel rolled smooth, but the *maison* itself. Like a masterful landscape painting, the gardens drew the eye toward the Caribbean-style plantation house backed up near the edge of the cliff. (A bit too near the cliff, for Lavalle's taste. The view near the edge of the precipice made him feel vaguely ill.)

The elegant mansion was the architectural embodiment of all that was good about colonialism, Lavalle thought. It took the sophistication of European culture and interpreted it in a way that was well suited to the local climate and sensibilities. Good architecture was largely a matter of context, in the doctor's opinion. The architect who designed Fairweather House had not understood this as well as the builder of Maison de la Falaise. Fairweather was an almost perfect representation of an English country house, but it was out of place overlooking the azure blue Caribbean. Maison de la Falaise, in contrast, seemed to have grown naturally out of the limestone cliff it sat atop, a perfect expression of how graciousness could flower between the Tropic of Cancer and the equator, when local beauty was tempered with refinement and taste.

A groom met Lavalle at the house and took the reins when he dismounted. Lavalle instructed the man to water Napoleon. It was obvious that the animal needed a drink, but Lavalle had learned to never make assumptions on the island.

The doctor went up the stairs and into the welcome shade of the broad veranda. The shutters along the ground floor were open, making it seem as if the house was a pavilion in some maharaja's garden. Lavalle almost expected to go inside and find a raj reclining on a pile of silken pillows.

Waiting to meet him at the entry was a willow-thin black woman wearing a black cotton skirt that fell to her ankles and a white blouse, a colorful bandanna wound around her head. It was the sandals on her feet that set Marie France apart. Not even Magalie Jeanty, Lavalle's nurse, who had been schooled in a convent, wore shoes.

"*Bonsoir,* Doctor."

Lavalle took off his hat, looking past Marie at the man bounding down the staircase with great energy. It was Maison de la Falaise's new owner, the American.

Nathaniel Peregrine confirmed some of Lavalle's prejudices about Americans but confounded others.

On the one hand, he was tall and lanky, like a cowboy, and with the sort of casual intimacy of disposition that some Europeans found forward rather than friendly. His eyes were, like a bird of prey's, deeply set, dark, and filled with a sharp, active intelligence. Lavalle imagined Peregrine seated on a horse, scouting ahead through a mountain pass for signs of Indians and grizzly bears.

Yet Peregrine was no typical expatriate Yankee. The best evidence of that was the fact that he spoke beautiful French without a hint of accent, something very rare indeed for an American, in Lavalle's experience. He was impeccably dressed, which was hardly typical of the Americans the doctor had known in France, though the deficiency with those other men was more a matter of taste and a lack of acquaintance with good tailors than a lack of funds.

Peregrine's complexion was pale, as if after a long winter. This struck Lavalle as odd, especially after the sea voyage to Haiti. The American said he was devoted to his books and indifferent to the sun and physical rigors. Still, he was a magnificent specimen, Lavalle thought, one of those men born with an abundance of muscle and animal grace, their bodies naturally indifferent to poor diet and insufficient exercise.

Peregrine had a quick wit and was an excellent conversationalist, although he possessed the peculiar American talent of talking easily without revealing significant personal details about himself. The only two important facts Lavalle learned during the time it took to have a glass of wine—which was excellent—was that the American had decided to buy Maison de la Falaise sight unseen after hearing about it from a London broker, and that he had polished his French by an extended residence in Paris.

"Strange that we did not run into each other somewhere in society."

"Perhaps," Peregrine said. "But Paris is large city, not to mention a beautiful one."

"To the City of Light," Lavalle said, and they clinked glasses.

"Besides," Peregrine said, "I tended to spend my time with a small circle of intimates."

"What was her name?" the doctor asked.

"Très bien," Peregrine said, and they clicked their crystal glasses together a second time.

"Cherchez la femme," Lavalle said.

"It does not matter now," the American said. "It was a long time ago."

As for the island, Peregrine was smitten with its beauty.

"I cannot imagine a more perfect setting," he said, waving his hand at the surroundings that seemed to flow in through the mansion's open walls. "I look out my front door, and I see a shimmering explosion of color, the brilliant blossoms against a background of deep greenery. I look in the other direction, and framed by the open windows, the sun is going down in a blaze of red, copper, and platinum over the blue sea flecked with scampering silver scallops where the rays glance off the water. This island and the Garden of Eden have a lot in common."

"Only do not forget that the Garden had its serpent," Lavalle said. "Perhaps this island does, too."

"Oh, without a doubt," Peregrine said. "There is no escaping evil."

"I am a physician and a scientist . . ."

"And you put no stock in religion and superstitious mumbo jumbo," Peregrine said, perceptively recognizing Lavalle's pause as an unwillingness to risk offending Peregrine. "I completely agree."

"The problem of evil, when you reduce it to its essence, Peregrine, is man. This island has natural beauty in abundance. It is people who are the problem."

"I'm not sure I follow you," the American said.

"Whose fault is it that the people live in ignorance and wretched poverty? Infant mortality is unimaginably high. Life expectancy isn't much beyond forty years. The most basic public health program would eradicate diseases like cholera, which sweep through villages here like the Black Plague did in Europe during the Dark Ages, death cutting wide swaths through the countryside. Government could help, but the government here is, as it is most places, perfectly useless. Man is father of his own woes. It is we who are evil."

"We are all a fallen race, sinners from birth."

"Yes," Lavalle said, "but in a practical, not religious, sense."

"But surely a man such as you is evidence of redemption. You have given up your medical practice and blood research in Paris to journey to the end of the earth to serve the poor. A lot of people would call you a saint for making such a sacrifice, Doctor."

"But that is exactly the point. Not that I am a saint or wish to be one," he added, thinking he would be misunderstood. "Haiti is the kind of place where one can turn back the clock and start over. Coming here represents a return to the garden—garden with a lower case *g*—to see if we might do it differently this time."

"A place for humanity to start over."

"Exactly," Lavalle said. "What chance is there to change society in a place like Paris, where decadent habits and wickedness are deeply ingrained after countless centuries of diligent practice? But here, in a place that is remote and primitive, maybe there is a chance to change things for the better."

Peregrine looked Lavalle up and down. "I wouldn't have guessed you were a revolutionary."

"I'm not. Indeed, I am the furthest thing from a revolutionary that there is. That sort of thinking is a big part of what's wrong with the world. Charismatic leaders have never been the answer. I sincerely doubt very much good can come from political movements. The world will be saved, if it can be, one man at a time, starting with a few good men making an earnest effort. That is what I have come to Haiti to do."

"Then you are a humanitarian."

"One does what one can," Lavalle said. "There was no health care for children here before I opened the hospital. I do not mean to sound self-righteous—that is an occupational hazard for people like me—but it is better to light one candle than to curse the darkness, as they say."

"Then I salute you," Peregrine said, raising his glass. "You came here to save humanity. I came to escape it."

"I confess there is a little of that for me here, too, in this place," Lavalle said with a sigh. "I had to get away from the noise and busy-ness of modern life to find myself. I would be lying if I didn't admit that I also came here to save myself."

"You're an honest man, Doctor," Peregrine said. "It is a pleasure to know you. I hope we become good friends."

They finished supper before Peregrine brought the conversation back around.

"When you were talking of evil earlier, I thought you were going to say something about the poor woman who was murdered over by Fairweather House."

Lavalle looked up from his coffee. "How ever did you hear about that?"

"I overheard servants talking."

"Ah."

"They said her throat was torn out, as if an animal had attacked her, but that the wounds mysteriously disappeared. How can that be?"

"These islanders are simple people, Peregrine. Few of

them can read or even write their name. I would not put much stock in their superstitious stories."

"But a woman was murdered."

Lavalle nodded. "It appears so, although she could have died of natural causes."

"Natural causes? What sort of 'natural causes' rips out a woman's jugular?"

"The matter has been turned over to the police," Lavalle said, as if that disposed of the question. "It is in their hands now."

He did not want to tell the American the rest of the story—how he put the body over his saddle and walked the animal to Fairweather House. He had told Helen to stay inside, but Lady Fairweather, a headstrong woman, insisted on bringing a shawl to cover the corpse. Lavalle had remarked to her how curious it was that the tissue damage seemed much less serious than it had been when he first came upon the body. He did not mention the extensive damage to the skin and musculature when the prefect of police arrived a few hours later in a mule cart. By then, the last sign of the fatal injury had repaired itself in the lifeless tissue, which Lavalle knew was patently impossible. Necrotic flesh does not regenerate.

The doctor did not believe in black magic, but he thought it likely that voodoo, as the local witchery was called, had played a role in the death and his subsequent confusion. Possibly Lavalle had fallen victim to the same mass psychosis that led the people to think they were possessed by gods from their primitive pantheon.

The other possibility—and perhaps this was the more likely explanation—was that the concussion Lavalle suffered in the fall from his horse had left his mind in a fugue state, the fantasies of his subconscious mind and reality becoming temporarily intermingled.

Lavalle had not shared any of this with Jean-Pierre Toussaint, the prefect of police. He had no reason to distrust Toussaint, but the policeman was, after all, a native. For all Lavalle knew, Toussaint joined the others in the revels in the hills at night, anointing himself with the blood of sacrificial chickens and goats and dancing around fires, chanting prayers asking to be possessed by ancient gods of the forest.

"Do you suppose voodoo had anything to do with the death?"

Lavalle nearly dropped his coffee cup. It was as if the American had been reading his mind, but that was, of course, impossible.

"The thought had crossed my mind," Lavalle said. "They're all mixed up in it."

"Do you put any stock in it? The servants seem to think its magic is powerful."

Lavalle snorted. "Are you serious? It is difficult for me to imagine even illiterate peasants believing such flummery, much less a worldly fellow like you. This is 1914, man. As Nietzsche pointed out not too long ago, God is dead. There are no ghosts and goblins."

"I don't know that we can be so certain. Maybe supernatural forces exist here more strongly than they do in places like New York and Paris. Science and the electric light have done much to kill man's innate superstitions. What if disbelief is the thing that drives these forces out of the world? Is it possible that here, on the edge of the jungle and savagery, these powers remain very much alive?"

"Only in the minds of ignorant men and women," Lavalle sniffed. "I thought you were a freethinker."

"Perhaps I am more of a freethinker than you."

"Nonsense," Lavalle said, cutting the matter off with a

smile. "The possibility that there is so much as a grain of truth in any religion, much less voodoo, is simply more than I am prepared to accept. Show me the science that proves it and I will believe. Until then, never."

Peregrine leaned forward on his elbows. "My servants?" he asked in a low voice.

"Of course. Your housekeeper, Marie France, is a mambo."

One of Peregrine's eyebrows went up.

"That's what voodoo priestesses are called. I wouldn't take any action on that knowledge if I were you. I don't know that I would hire such a person, but she's already on your staff, and discharging her could lead to complications."

"What kind of complications?"

"Not magical ones, if that's what you mean. Besides, good servants are hard to find. And as I've said, they're all mixed up in it. My nurse, Magalie Jeanty, is the only person beside the Cap Misère priest who doesn't practice black magic, and to tell you the truth, I'm not one hundred percent sure about Father Jacques."

"How did Magalie manage to avoid it?"

"She was brought up in a convent. A Catholic upbringing does, it seems, have some minor benefits. You are not Catholic, I trust?"

"Never touch the stuff."

"Smart fellow."

"I do like a game of chess from time to time," the American said. "Do you play?"

"Not very often, but I do enjoy it." Lavalle did not consider the time he devoted to studying chess problems in the evenings the same thing as playing. "Shall we have a game?"

Peregrine destroyed Lavalle in their first game. The second was a draw. Lavalle won their final game, though Peregrine could have easily beaten him if he hadn't made a critical blunder. It occurred to Lavalle that his host might have lost on purpose. If so, Lavalle thought it damned sporting of him. Perhaps the American was, against all odds, a gentleman. This surprised and pleased Lavalle. It would be good to finally have a dependable friend on the island.

15

Hospital St. Jude

THE MOTHER—ELISABETH Capois was her name—stood beside the bed, patiently watching.

Dr. Lavalle removed the thermometer from the little girl's mouth and looked at it without reaction before reaching over to deposit it in the glass of sanitizing agent. The liquid was flavored with peppermint, which the children liked, one of the innovations Lavalle had made for the small patients he treated. Lavalle looked down the child's mouth and into her ears. He shined a light into each eye to check the response to the light.

Magalie Jeanty stood next to a rolling metal cart, handing Dr. Lavalle the tongue depressor, the swab, whatever he needed next in the examination. She knew his routine perfectly. After listening to the little girl's heart, Lavalle made the appropriate notations in the chart and handed the clipboard back to Magalie, who hung it from its hook at the end of the bed.

"And how do you feel today, my little pumpkin?"

"Bien."

That was how she always replied to the question: *Good*.

Lavalle was going through the motions, noting the decline as it progressed in stages day by day. There was nothing else he could do. Sometimes his work was heartbreaking. Elisabeth followed Lavalle around the portable screen that Magalie moved from bed to bed in the open ward to create a bit of privacy during examinations.

"There is no change," Lavalle said. "I am sorry."

"I will say a prayer."

Lavalle looked at the mother a moment before nodding. It would do no good, but it might give Elisabeth Capois some measure of relief. Who was he to tell her she would be wasting her time by praying to the same remote deity that put her daughter in the hospital through his indifference or malevolence?

Lavalle was pouring himself a small sherry with his back to the door of his office when he sensed Magalie's presence.

"I need a break," he said without turning. "We can continue rounds in a little bit."

Lavalle removed his clinic coat. He had seven, one for each day of the week. His housekeeper boiled, starched, and ironed them serially, the creases in the arms knife sharp. He put the tropical-weight seersucker jacket over his damp shirt. It was too hot to wear a coat, but one had to maintain standards. There was real danger in letting discipline go. Haiti was filled with reminders of how thin the veneer of civilization was over the wildness that lurked just beneath the surface of daily life. The drums in the hills reminded Lavalle nightly. Chaos was out there, just beyond, waiting for its opportunity. And so he wore his jacket, no matter how hot, because even one loose thread could lead to a complete unraveling.

Lavalle was a man of science: meticulous, organized, rational, logical, a paragon of self-discipline. The only thing he really feared was confusion and muddle. And yet he was learned enough to know that in the end, entropy always won. Systems broke down. Energy dissipated. Chaos reigned.

Lavalle had seen the triumph of chaos once before, in Paris. It had been terrible. He made it a special point to never think of it.

Magalie was conferring with Elisabeth when Lavalle left the hospital. The nurse's hand was on the unfortunate mother's shoulder, their heads close together. They were together asking Jesus to heal the child, Lavalle thought. He did not approve of mixing medicine and superstition, but again, what did it hurt in hopeless cases? It was like giving opium to a dying man; if it eased the suffering, what did it matter?

Lavalle put his hat on his head as he stepped outside. He set off briskly, a bamboo walking stick tucked under his arm. The doctor was not at the hospital to see Magalie Jeanty pass Elisabeth Capois a small leather pouch bound with a hank of horsehair. The tidy bundle held a human finger bone, a crow's feather, and a few threads clipped from the inside pocket lining of one of Lavalle's clinic coats. And if he had seen it, would Lavalle have objected? What did it hurt, a little voodoo?

Magalie whispered each line of the prayer in the mother's ear.

Elisabeth stood, the talisman clasped over her heart, and repeated the whispered chant. She called on Ogou Balanjo, the spirit of healing, to return the little girl's *ti bon ange*—little guardian angel—so that the child could live.

Dr. Lavalle's magic had been too weak to help her daughter. It was time to call on the old ones, the way people always did, when there was nowhere else to turn for hope.

Coffee was the one dependable civilized comfort to be had in Cap Misère, Lavalle thought (unless you included the rum, which was either excellent or undrinkable, and also the cigars, which were subject to the same qualitative extremes).

The doctor sat outside in his favorite chair at his favorite table in his favorite café and ordered a cup, black and strong. He was lighting a cigarette when an enormous physical presence, surmounted by what seemed to be an even bigger smile, loomed over him.

"Good morning, Prefect. Would you care to join me for coffee?"

"I'd be delighted, Dr. Lavalle," Toussaint said.

The waiter was nervous at serving the policeman, spilling a little from the chipped china cup into the saucer before hurrying away. Most of the residents seemed uncomfortable around Jean-Pierre Toussaint, Lavalle had noticed. It was a common enough phenomenon among the underclass, which tended to be fearful of authority. It was not as if the prefect was in the habit of oppressing people. If anything, Lavalle thought, Toussaint was too liberal in the way he dealt with the public drunkenness and petty thievery that characterized the balance of crime along their stretch of coastline. There was almost never anyone locked up in the one-cell jail at the district constabulary. Lavalle did not think Toussaint had a policeman's disposition. If he had been born in France, Toussaint would have been a baker or run a candy store. He was related to someone important in the capital, which was the way most people got employment with the island's government. It was simply a matter of chance that Toussaint's employment was with the constabulary.

"Do you have any news on that recent unfortunate matter?" Lavalle asked when the waiter had gone away.

"I am making inquiries," Toussaint said. The opaque comment was the policeman's response to questions about any crime more complicated than a stolen chicken.

Lavalle took it to mean he had exhausted his supply of ideas and was doing nothing.

"It is curious," Lavalle said. "A body with neither blood in its veins nor wounds to suggest where it went."

Toussaint shrugged. "Strange things happen sometimes."

"I should have done more tests."

"Do not let it concern you unduly, Doctor."

"It is my job to be concerned." Lavalle was the unofficial—meaning "unpaid"—coroner in that part of the island.

"And also mine," the prefect of police said. "Unfortunately, Doctor, there is not always an answer. We must trust in the Almighty to sort things out."

"I prefer to rely on hard work and knowledge."

"What does your excellent education inform you about this matter, Doctor?"

"There are facts I cannot immediately explain," he said.

"Do you think witchcraft killed Angelique?"

Lavalle looked up at the prefect.

"I didn't put anything like that in my report," Toussaint said. "It is unwise to mention such things."

"I suppose so."

"Some people find the subject upsetting. Still, it is what I think."

"You think voodoo killed that woman?"

Toussaint nodded his great head.

"You surprise me."

The policeman grinned. That was his response to everything: he grinned. "Maybe I am wrong. I hope I am. But I see sorcery in this."

"I can't believe I'm hearing this," Lavalle said. "You think the cause of death was sorcery?"

"Our ways must be strange to you, Doctor."

"They're strange enough."

The policeman nodded, grinned, and nodded again. "We are fortunate to have an educated man like yourself, an eminent doctor, in Cap Misère. The only white men we see in the south are fugitives and missionaries."

A young woman, very petite and attractive, had come to the door of the café and was looking out at Lavalle, smiling. A prostitute, the doctor thought, new into town from the hill country.

"I assure you I am no missionary," Lavalle said.

Toussaint laughed.

The policeman's good humor was so infectious that Lavalle felt the shadow move away from his spirit.

The conversation went on to lighter, brighter matters. Good coffee, friendly banter, warm sunshine, a beautiful girl to think about meeting in the evening—they were the perfect medicine to cure the doctor's sense that unforeseen forces were combining against him in a way he could not understand.

16

A Woman of Virtue

NAPOLEON'S IRON-SHOD HOOVES galumphed along the sandy road between the ragged mountains and the glittering shore. A full moon was rising in the eastern sky, bathing the twilight in silvery light. In the west, the horizon bled purple from the sunset's afterglow, a slash of scarlet beneath a single thin, crêpe-shaped cloud hovering far out over the water at the rim of the world.

Lavalle looked forward to the diversion of a game of chess with his friend even more than usual. It had been an unusually difficult day.

They took turns at white, and tonight the honor of the first move was Lavalle's. He had already settled upon a Queen's Opening. He was certain Peregrine would use the Dutch Defense, sliding his black king's bishop pawn forward. Lavalle had learned that the American had a fondness for attacking on the king's side. Peregrine would expect him to respond with the Classic Variation, moving the white queen's pawn, clearing the way for Lavalle's queen and bishop to attack. But no! Lavalle intended to throw Peregrine off balance early by instead moving the king's knight pawn forward one square, planning to *fianchetto* the king's bishop and exert white's power over the diagonals, pressuring the powerful center from the wings.

The sound of Napoleon's hooves disguised the drumming when it started, so that it was only by degrees that Lavalle became aware of the low, rhythmic beat, as if he were hearing the collective pulse of the trees on the mountainside.

Lavalle tugged against the reins. Napoleon stopped, agitated and surprised, backing and turning as if to return to Cap Misère. Lavalle glanced over his shoulder, remembering being hit from behind and knocked from the saddle. The road was empty. The moonlight shone almost merrily upon the light chop in the water. If not for the throb of voodoo drums in the hills, the scene would have made a pretty picture.

Lavalle kicked his heels and dragged the horse's head back in their original direction.

"Allez!"

A figure appeared in the shadows ahead. It was a barefoot woman, her blouse knotted under her breasts. Seeing her quick, graceful walk, he imagined for a moment it was Elisabeth Capois. But that had to be wrong, he thought. The mother wouldn't be that far from Cap Misère at night, and certainly not on that night, when she would be sitting up with her dead child, waiting for the funeral in the morning.

Lavalle was almost upon her when she turned and disappeared into the trees beside the road. He didn't see the trail until he was directly across from it, a narrow path wide enough for one person that angled up the steep incline toward a flickering light that seemed to emanate from a clearing halfway to the top. The drumming came from whatever was at the end of the trail. He saw her, already far away, moving fast on her long legs, like a stork silently picking its way through the water toward a fish that remains invisible to human eyes.

Looking around himself, Lavalle confirmed for the

second time that he was alone on the road. He whipped the reins against the horse's shoulder, driving his mount into a gallop, anxious to be gone from that place of black magic.

A glass of good champagne was rare enough on the island. The fact that it was chilled made it even better. Peregrine had brought several cases of Champagne Perrier-Jouet with him on his yacht, and chilled it with a mechanical refrigeration device of his own invention that pumped compressed gas through a radiatorlike collection of copper tubing, the entire affair driven by a small electrical generator powered by a one-cylinder gasoline motor.

"We may be in a very backward place, but that does not require us to forgo the conveniences," Peregrine said as he opened the bottle. He had given Marie France and the rest of the servants the night off so that their game of chess would not be disturbed.

Lavalle returned Peregrine's smile, once again admiring the American's teeth. They were perfectly formed and very white—so white they almost seemed tinted with blue.

"Not that it is easy to forget we are strangers in a strange land," Peregrine said. He inclined his head toward the open window. The sound of insects calling to one another in the night nearly covered the drumming, the distant rhythm rising with the wind.

"I have to confess that at times I am tempted to follow the sound and have a look at what they're up to out there in the forest, from a discreet distance."

"That would be unwise as well as dangerous," Dr. Lavalle said.

"You do not think they would welcome a potential convert?"

"It is not a matter for joking, my friend. These are not Baptists."

"What do you suppose goes on?"

"They dance themselves into hypnotic trances," Lavalle said. "I wouldn't be surprised if drugs are involved. I know rum is."

"Are you the least bit curious?"

"No," Lavalle said. "Joining drunken illiterates dancing with their machetes in a ring around a jungle bonfire is not my idea of an intellectual exercise. Some doors are more easily opened than closed, Peregrine. If there's one thing I know, it's that being educated and sophisticated may not be enough to protect you from savagery. And I don't mean the savagery out there," he said, pointing out the window, "but in here." He put his hand over his heart.

"You are part philosopher, Doctor."

"We all are. Pour me some more champagne, if you don't mind, and let's discuss something a little less unpleasant."

"If you do not want to join me for a little walk tonight to learn a something about voodoo . . ."

Lavalle shook his head.

"Then I suppose we shall have to play chess. But we're going to need another bottle of champagne."

The opening gambit was a success. Lavalle's slashing attack on the center forced Peregrine to capitulate.

"I met Lady Fairweather the other day," Peregrine said as he set up the board for their second game.

"Really."

"I found her charming."

"She has a quick wit," Lavalle said.

"Pity she doesn't play chess."

Lavalle leaned back in his chair and gave Peregrine a

long, appraising look, as if seeing him for the first time. It was funny how learning that you and someone else were interested in the same woman changed things, and not just how Lavalle felt about Peregrine, but how he felt about Helen. Lavalle was, he realized, a lot more serious about Lady Fairweather than he had let on to himself.

"I tried to teach her," Lavalle said. "She has the aptitude but not the interest. Her late husband played rather well, meaning not so well as to be able to beat me except on a lucky night. I don't think Lady Fairweather is the sort of woman who likes to play games."

"She's a good-looking woman," Peregrine said. "An attractive young widow with money to boot. She wouldn't wait long to find a husband back in London. I wonder why she stays here."

"Her husband is buried here, and she still grieves for him. I think she feels closer to him, staying in the house they shared, overseeing the plantation."

"It's a big job for a woman on her own."

"Helen isn't your usual woman."

"Helen?"

Lavalle ignored Peregrine's grin. "Sir Graham was in poor health even before their marriage. He was a good deal older than she, you know. They came to Haiti for the climate. He couldn't take the English winters. I have a feeling Lady Fairweather has helped run the plantation since the day they arrived. She's a perfectly capable manager. I daresay does a better job than many men could."

"Do you like that in a woman—the ability to take charge and get things done?"

"Yes, and I have a feeling you do, too," Lavalle said.

"I am thinking about asking her to teach me to paint. Her watercolors are magnificent."

A vague sense of illness moved through Lavalle. He thought it might be from drinking the chilled champagne until he realized what he was really feeling was jealousy.

"Of course, I don't want to get in your way," Peregrine said.

"I beg your pardon?"

"You saw her first. If you've staked out a claim, I'll stand down. I wouldn't want to lose a friend over a woman. Men on this island who play chess are hard enough to find as it is."

"Don't be absurd, Peregrine." Lavalle laughed uncomfortably. "I have my eye on Lady Fairweather the same as any other man in his right mind, but there are no understandings between us."

Lavalle gave Peregrine a confident smile.

"Yet," he added.

Lavalle was a little drunk when he left Maison de la Falaise. The moonlight was nearly bright enough to read by. He hadn't noticed on the ride in, but in a side garden the branch of a tree that must have split off during a storm earlier in the week rested against the damaged roof of a gazebo. Lavalle would have to remember to speak to Peregrine about keeping after his staff. It wasn't the first sign he'd seen that things were beginning to slip a little at the American's estate. It took a constant exertion of will to keep on an even keel in Haiti. The only thing standing in the way of chaos at Maison de la Falaise was a civilized devotion to order. Peregrine would have to keep after his staff almost relentlessly to prevent them from reverting to their feckless ways.

The drums had stopped on the mountainside, but the silence was almost more unnerving. Lavalle dug his heels into Napoleon's flanks and headed back to Cap Misère at the pace he usually reserved for emergency visits to patients in the hamlets scattered along the coast.

Lavalle usually went over the evening's chess games on his ride home from Maison de la Falaise, but that night all he could think of was Helen Fairweather. The doctor would have to pursue her in earnest, or she would end up in Peregrine's arms.

17
Consolation

LAVALLE WAS IN the lab at the Hospital St. Jude late in the day, checking some samples growing in culture dishes willed with pink agar, when Magalie Jeanty stuck her head in to report that the shipment from Port-au-Prince had finally arrived.

"Just a moment," Lavalle said shortly, not looking up from the lab book where he was annotating results from the latest round of blood research in his neat hand. Lavalle never did more than one thing at a time, if he could avoid it, and he disliked interruptions. It was important for a physician to stay focused and refuse to be hurried. Mistakes resulted from jumping from one thing to another, like a dancer capering to a fiddle tune.

The teamster had pulled his wagon and mule team around to the back of the hospital, where a small, raised loading bay opened into the storage room where Lavalle kept everything under lock and key. The doctor did not think the residents of Cap Misère were dishonest so much as desperate, and any supplies that were not kept out of reach had a way of quickly disappearing.

"Good afternoon," Lavalle said to the driver, and hopped off the dock.

"Bonjour," the man mumbled without meeting Dr. Lavalle's eye. He did not wear a shirt or shoes, his only

clothing a pair of ragged trousers that were too short for such a tall man. He had broad shoulders and massive arms, an excellent physical example. The teamster reminded Lavalle of the Nubian wrestlers he had seen once on a visit to Africa.

The man was probably embarrassed to be a week behind schedule with the delivery, Lavalle thought, although the island citizenry seldom seemed concerned about time, or even aware of its passing. It was fortunate the hospital was not currently in desperate need of any of the medicines and supplies that arrived each month from the Littmann Medical Supply warehouse in New Orleans. There had been several regrettable occasions when his patients had died because of delayed shipments. Once, an entire cargo had been lost in a hurricane, and though a maritime insurer eventually reimbursed Lavalle his out-of-pocket expenses, before the replacement shipment arrived the doctor had been reduced to stitching up people with sewing thread. Life moved slowly on the island, even if disease and death did not.

"Let me have a look at your manifest," Lavalle said.

The much-mended tarpaulin remained over the cargo, tied down with hemp ropes. Lavalle's porter squatted against one wheel with his eyes closed, as if asleep. The teamster had not moved. Lavalle was suddenly impatient.

"I do not have all day. Give me the manifest and get the wagon unloaded."

The teamster kept his sullen eyes on the toes of Lavalle's well-shined boots and began a not very believable story about how expensive fodder had become in the capital. Lavalle cut the man off before he got far into the tale.

"Don't waste your breathing trying to extort money from me," Lavalle said. "I paid your employer in advance for shipping, as I always do. That's the only way I can get him to send a wagon rattling my way, and I assume it's the only way he can depend upon getting the money instead of having the drivers run off with it. You won't get any money out of me."

The man crossed his arms and met Lavalle's eye for the first time. The teamster obviously was a villain. It was a miracle he hadn't disappeared into the mountains with Lavalle's entire cargo. If there had been anyone along the southern coast with money to buy contraband, no doubt he would have stolen it. But this was a game two could play. Lavalle had not gotten where he was in the world by letting people walk over him.

"Not a single *gourde,*" the doctor said, referring to the island currency.

"Then I must return the shipment to Port-au-Prince."

"If you are a gambler you have a lot to learn about bluffing," Lavalle said.

But the man turned away and began to climb up onto the wagon.

"Alexandre!"

The porter, who had roused himself enough to watch the disagreement, stood up when Lavalle called him by name.

"We will unload the wagon with or without the driver's assistance."

The metal leaf springs beneath the driver's seat creaked as the teamster turned around to look back at them. He was sitting forward with his elbows on his knees, but now his right hand dropped down toward the handle of a machete leaning against the seat.

Alexandre looked back at Lavalle, his expression distant and impassive, as if he were somewhere else, thinking about something that did not involve him one way or the other. The porter was at least ten years older and seventy-five pounds lighter than the teamster. Even if the driver didn't have a weapon, Lavalle doubted he and Alexandre together could subdue the stronger man.

"Very well, then," Lavalle said as if suddenly bored. "I will leave it to you to explain to your employer why he lost a lucrative shipping contract to bring supplies to this hospital."

The teamster's only response was to whistle through his teeth and snap the reins against the mules' hindquarters. Lavalle climbed back on the loading dock so that the teamster could see that he was going back inside, that he didn't care, but the driver did not turn around. The wagon continued up the backstreet until it disappeared around the corner.

"Merde!"

The expression of anger shocked Magalie, who had come out to help with the supplies. She and the doctor had been through many difficult times in the past two years, but this was the first time she had ever heard him curse.

Lavalle and Jean-Pierre Toussaint caught up with the wagon five kilometers outside of town. They had been delayed by the need to track down Toussaint's horse, an undistinguished brown mare the police prefect had loaned to the assistant constable to assist with the inquiries started after a body was found two nights earlier near a fishing hamlet up the coast. Lavalle had assisted Toussaint, of course. The cultures he took from the wounds in the dead woman's neck—before the torn tissue mysteriously repaired itself—had not proven to be forensically significant.

The teamster heard their horses coming up from behind

and looked over his shoulder. He stopped without Toussaint having to say a word to him.

Lavalle stayed mounted while the policeman climbed down from his horse and looped the reins under one of the ropes holding the tarp at the rear of the wagon.

"Get down," the prefect told the man. "I want to talk to you."

The teamster set the wagon's brake and did as he was told. Toussaint was as tall as the driver but wider and heavier, though there wasn't anything soft about him, like there was with most men his size. Lavalle assumed it was Toussaint's uniform, not his size, that impressed the teamster. The island people were intimidated by all officials, as were peasants anywhere, weakened by their powerlessness and ignorance.

Smiling as always, Toussaint began to converse with the man, speaking in patois. Lavalle picked out a word here and there. The hospital. The shipment of medicine. Money. The teamster disputed with Toussaint in a desultory way, as if he knew it was useless to argue with a policeman but had to say something.

Toussaint removed his hat. It was a high-peaked cap with a rope of gold braid over the bill, the sort of hat that would have looked right on a general's head. He put the hat on the wagon carefully, as if it were extremely valuable and he wanted to be sure it wouldn't fall off and become soiled. The policeman hit the driver so fast that he did not have time to react before the huge fist doubled him over. Toussaint caught him by the arm and threw him against the wagon. The driver bounced backward, like a ball thrown against a brick wall, hitting the road hard enough to roll over several times. The mules stamped and worried but stayed, held by the wagon's brake.

"That's not necessary, Jean-Pierre," Lavalle said, though too late to have saved the dishonest driver a broken nose and split forehead.

"Thieves must be taught it is wrong to steal," Toussaint said, smiling brightly.

"Now he does."

Toussaint began to kick the man.

"Stop!" Lavalle cried.

But Toussaint did not stop.

Lavalle jumped down from Napoleon with such haste that he turned his ankle painfully in the sandy soil.

"Jean-Pierre, please! I just want the hospital supplies."

"You are a good man, Doctor, but you do not understand how things are done here," Toussaint said, pausing.

"Jail will be punishment enough. You don't have to beat him."

"If I put him in my jail, I will have to feed him," Toussaint said.

The prefect of police turned back to the man and spoke to him in rapid patois. The man somehow managed to get to his feet and staggered down the road, his right arm clasped around his ribs.

"I told the scoundrel he has you to thank that he can crawl away."

"Thank you."

"I will send a report to the capital and have him arrested. Let *them* feed him in their prison." Toussaint laughed, greatly amused by his clever plan to divert the expense to the authorities in Port-au-Prince.

"You needn't bother the authorities further on my account."

"It is my job, Doctor. I assure you, a few months in the dungeons will be the end of his mischief-making."

Lavalle realized it would do no good to protest, so he shut his mouth.

Alexandre was waiting at the hospital to unload. Toussaint took off the tarp and began to help, so Lavalle pitched in, too. In no time the supplies were locked away safe in the storeroom.

"Come into my office and I'll give you a drink for your help."

"I am already late for supper," the smiling policeman said. "If I keep my wife waiting longer, I will be the one getting the beating."

"How will you get the wagon to Port-au-Prince?"

"The wagon is confiscated. It was used in a crime."

"I will never get another shipment delivered here if you keep the wagon. I'll send Alexandre with it in the morning."

Toussaint started to disagree, but apparently he saw the logic in Lavalle's argument.

"As you wish, Doctor. We are fortunate to have you here. Your hospital does much good work. I wouldn't want to do anything to interfere."

Dr. Lavalle lived in a house built by a wealthy merchant in colonial times, one of the few houses in Cap Misère habitable by European standards. He instructed the housekeeper to prepare his supper, and he went into the study. He put his doctor's bag on the table by the door before lighting the lamp. He took off his jacket, hung it in the armoire, and pulled on his comfortable old smoking jacket, patting the pocket where he kept his favorite pipe and a pouch of tobacco.

The liquor chest where the French brandy was kept sat

on a low table. The bookcase behind it held the portion of
his medical library relating to his specialty, rare diseases
of the blood. On a tray beside the liquor chest were two
crystal snifters turned upside down on a white cloth.

Lavalle also lit the lamp on the table, the combined illumination from the two lamps enough to drive most of the
shadows out of the room. Outside, the scratchy insect music softened slightly, as if the creatures were distracted by
the light.

The key to the liquor chest was worn as a fob on
Lavalle's watch chain. He pulled it out now and inserted it
into the lock. There was a soft click as the latch released.

Lavalle lifted the lid and stood there, staring inside.

Balanced on the cork stopping a bottle of cognac was a
crow's foot. Tied to it with a thin strip of black ribbon was
a scrap of white cloth. Lavalle leaned closer for a better
look. It was impossible to know for certain, but the cloth
seemed to be material snipped from one of the clinic jackets he wore at the hospital.

He took a step back and got down on one knee to examine the liquor chest. There were no scratches on the lock
or signs it had been tampered with, though there was only
one key, which was either affixed to his vest or on his
nightstand while he slept.

The housekeeper heard Lavalle's brisk footsteps enter
the kitchen and looked up with surprise. The room was
her province, and the master of the house never trespassed
there.

"Were there any visitors today, Marie?"

"*Non,* Dr. Lavalle," she said, wiping her hands on her
apron.

"Any deliveries?"

She pursed her lips as if in concentration and shook her

head. The woman was guileless, thought Lavalle, who had hired and quickly fired two dishonest servants before finding Marie. The fact that she was slow-witted was at once her best and worst quality. At least she had learned to be a passable cook, under his tutelage.

Lavalle came forward until he was standing closer to the housekeeper than he had ever been. She began to shake a little, sensing that something was wrong.

"I want you to tell me something, Marie, and I want you to be truthful. Were you, or anyone else, in my study today?"

"*Non,* Dr. Lavalle."

"Very well, then," he said, turning away. "Call me when supper is ready."

Lavalle went back to his desk and sat down. He lit the reading lamp, directing its reflector toward the macabre object before him. He took his magnifying glass out of the center drawer. Using the nib of a dry pen, he performed a cursory examination. The severed foot showed no sign of desiccation. His guess was that the bird had been killed recently. He could tell nothing from the ribbon. It appeared to be an ordinary strip of millinery. The cloth might reveal some of its secrets, though, subjected to the proper testing. He would take it to his lab at the hospital, where he could look at it under his microscope and compare it to the material from one of his jackets.

Not that any of that would tell him what the talisman *meant.*

"How foolish of me," Lavalle said out loud.

What it meant? Of course, it meant nothing! It was nothing more than a bit of meaningless superstitious nonsense someone had managed to hide in his liquor chest to frighten him. Well, it wouldn't work. Lavalle was a physician and a scientist. He did not believe in voodoo. Science and logic, not superstition and magic, would find the solution to the odd events of late.

Lavalle poured himself a cognac, noting with dismay his trembling hands. Absent an answer that explained the violent and strange deaths of two people, there was always the consolation of civilization, Lavalle told himself, lifting the glass of amber liquor to his lips.

18

Henri Tortue

"*EXCUSEZ MOI.*"

Lavalle sat up in the dark. "What is it?"

"The prefect of police is here, Doctor," his housekeeper said.

The doctor struck a match and lighted the lamp on the bedside table and picked up the pocket watch. It was midnight.

"*Merde,*" Lavalle muttered, guessing why Toussaint had come.

Jean-Pierre Toussaint was standing in the hall at the bottom of the stairs, holding his grand hat in his hands. For once he was not smiling. A series of unsolved murders could complicate life even for a policeman with connections in the capital.

"It has happened again," Lavalle said, not making it a question.

Toussaint grunted. The door opened and Nathaniel Peregrine came in.

"What the devil brings you out at this hour?" Lavalle asked, shaking his friend's hand. "Don't tell me anything has happened to . . ."

"No, Lady Fairweather is fine, but that's more than I can say for the girl I found in my garden."

"If you would be so good as to get your things, Doctor,"

135

Toussaint said. "We need to accompany him to Maison de la Falaise to investigate."

They brought the body back to the hospital, to its morgue, putting the corpse on an angled tin table with a hole at one end, connected to a hose that emptied into a sump in the floor. Along the back wall was a table containing a scale, and the implements, some surgical in nature, along with saws and hooks and tools that looked as if they belonged in a butcher's shop.

The young woman, somewhere between the ages of sixteen and eighteen, lay on her back, the hands and feet splayed outward, a small white towel draped over her pelvis for the sake of decency. Her mouth hung slackly open in death; the eyelids were parted just enough to reveal two moon-shaped slivers of white. Though in life the woman's skin had been dark black, her complexion had turned an ashen, claylike hue. The gray coloration was exaggerated to a considerable degree by the fact that the body had been almost completely drained of its blood.

"I do not know how a woman can bleed to death without a wound," Peregrine said.

"That is precisely the question," Lavalle agreed, putting on the black rubber apron he wore for autopsies. He had tried to dissuade Peregrine from witnessing the postmortem examination, but the American expressed interest in observing the procedure. His intellectual curiosity and cool detachment from what most people would have been squeamish to see was impressive, Lavalle thought.

"Is it possible that the wound healed itself?"

Lavalle looked at Peregrine across the cadaver. "Have you ever known wounds to heal themselves in the dead body of a person or animal?"

"What other explanation could there be? Perhaps it is an unknown tropical disease that causes the blood to—I don't know what—disappear."

"My suspicion with the first cases leaned in that direction," Lavalle said.

"There have been others?"

"Yes."

"Why didn't you say something?"

"I am sorry, my friend, but it is a police matter," Lavalle said. "You are perceptive to suspect a disorder of the blood is involved. I have not yet ruled it out. There are many such maladies in the tropics that medicine is only beginning to study."

"Blood diseases were your specialty in Paris," Peregrine said.

"That is so," Lavalle said, selecting a scalpel. "It was one of the reasons I decided to open a hospital here. The children of the island suffer from a rare disorder of the blood that deforms their red blood cells into a sickle shape. I have made some progress in my studies of the subject. But this . . ."

Lavalle waved his scalpel over the naked body.

"I am at a loss to explain these deaths. There are disorders that attack the blood, but I know of nothing that would destroy the blood itself. Perhaps some monstrous pathology of the spleen is involved. The spleen filters old and damaged blood cells from the body. Perhaps if the organ became cancerous or infected in some way not yet documented in the medical literature, it might play a role."

"Can you tell from an autopsy?"

"I will certainly remove the spleen and examine it for abnormalities, along with the other organs. I have done so with the other people who exhibited the same symptoms in death. Unfortunately, I have discovered nothing remarkable in the bodies in the previous autopsies. It is tempting to conclude there is no pathological explanation for this phenomenon."

"Meaning?" Peregrine asked.

"That this is a job for the prefect of police."

"You think these people were murdered."

"Most definitely," Lavalle said. "This girl has been almost perfectly exsanguinated. The involvement of an external agency is a virtual certainty."

"What kind of external agency?"

"An animal or a human."

"But who would take this girl's blood?" Peregrine asked. "And why?"

Lavalle shook his head. "I do not know."

"Doctor," the policeman said, "the procedure when the blood is taken from one person and put into another—how do you say?"

"A transfusion," Lavalle said.

"Yes, yes," the policeman said, his smile returned. "You do transfusions here at the hospital."

"Of course. It is the only effective treatment for the tropical anemia I have been studying. But one would not need to take that much blood. Perhaps in a war, with a ward filled with desperately wounded men, but even then there is no doctor I know of who would stoop to such barbarism. Not even the Germans."

As a Frenchman, Lavalle had a special dislike for Germans.

"Blood must be transfused immediately if it is to be of any use. There is no means to refrigerate it on the island."

"That's not exactly true," Peregrine said. "I have a refrigeration unit at my house."

"Is that so?" Toussaint said, his smile growing brighter.

"I use it to refrigerate wine, not blood," Peregrine said. "You're welcome to have a look."

"Maybe I will," Toussaint said.

"Be my guest," he said, turning his attention back to Lavalle. "Doctor, is it possible that there is a person or persons on the island with a rare disease that requires massive transfusions to keep them alive?"

"Anything is possible, but I know of no such condition. This is not the sort of place where people have access to the equipment or the knowledge for such procedures. Something else is afoot, something criminal, I fear."

"Maybe the local juju man needs fresh human blood for his voodoo spells."

Toussaint's smile remained intact, but Lavalle had the distinct impression that the comment made the policeman uncomfortable. The giant policeman stared back at the American long enough without answering for it to start to feel uncomfortable, though Peregrine did not seem to be the least concerned.

"I am going to begin," Lavalle said to relieve the difficult moment. "You gentlemen may wish to take a step back. There shouldn't be much blood when I open her, but you don't want to get body fluids on your clothing."

It was almost dawn by the time Lavalle finished.

Toussaint and Peregrine were in his office, where they'd gone to wait while he closed the body and cleaned his instruments. The atmosphere in the office was dense with cigar smoke. Lavalle's bottle of rum was sitting on the desk, three quarters empty. Peregrine was sitting on the corner of the doctor's desk, swinging one leg.

"Can I buy you a drink?" Peregrine said and poured liquor into a glass.

"Salut," Lavalle said, lifting the drink.

"Another long night for us, Doctor," the grinning policeman said.

"Oui." Lavalle drank the rest of the rum and reached for the bottle.

"Grim work."

"One becomes used to it," Lavalle told Peregrine. He slumped in his chair, and when he looked up saw Peregrine and Toussaint looking back toward the wide-eyed orderly standing in the doorway with a constable.

The body was lying over the constable's mule in front of the hospital. It was a man wearing only ragged trousers, tied facedown on the mule led by a frightened-looking constable. Lavalle knew who it was just by looking at the dead man's heavily muscled arms and back. It was the teamster who had tried to drive off with the hospital's supplies. He told the orderly and constable to get the man down. The men untied the body and lowered it into the dusty street.

"Jean-Pierre," Lavalle said, turning on the prefect of police, his hands clenched, his head throbbing.

"What is it, Doctor?" the smiling policeman said. "Do you recognize this man? He is not from the coast. I do not believe that I have ever seen the fellow before."

Lavalle squeezed the bridge of his nose between thumb and forefinger.

"Get a stretcher and bring him to the morgue," he said, walking away from the others. "Fortunately, I have two autopsy tables."

Lavalle had another drink alone. He didn't know why he would be shocked that the prefect of police tried to cover up his involvement with the man he had savagely beaten the day before. But what was Lavalle to do about it? Toussaint was the law in that part of the country, not the expatriate Frenchman.

Toussaint and Peregrine were both leaning over the body when Lavalle came into the morgue.

"Perhaps you gentlemen would like to conduct the postmortem," Lavalle said, barely controlling his anger.

"You should see this, Doctor."

"Yes, take a look, Lavalle," Peregrine said. "Toussaint told me about your little dustup with this rogue."

"*I* did not put a hand on the man," Lavalle said.

But as Lavalle joined the others, he knew immediately what they were talking about. It had been too dark out on the street to see what there *wasn't* to see: no broken nose, no split lip, not a single sign of the thrashing Toussaint had given the man on the road outside of town. He pushed his way between Peregrine and the policeman and pressed his hands against either side of the man's rib cage. No swelling, no evidence of broken or bruised ribs, not even a contusion to the skin.

"It is impossible," Lavalle said.

Toussaint opened the door and called his constable over. "Go find Henri Tortue."

"Henri Tortue? What are you doing?"

"Who is Henri Tortue?" Peregrine asked.

"The local voodoo priest," Lavalle said, too appalled to exercise discretion.

Toussaint glowered over the doctor. "Are you finished with them both?"

"I must do an autopsy on the teamster."

"There is no reason to waste your time with this fellow."

"I insist."

"No, Doctor, I insist," Toussaint said. "Henri Tortue will know what to do."

"*Mon Dieu!* What can a witch doctor do?"

"Take the bodies to the graveyard, cut off their heads, and bury them in the proper way."

"Why on earth would you cut off their heads?"

"Because, Monsieur Peregrine, it is the only way we can ensure the dead will not rise from their graves to walk the night."

"As vampires?" The American was a little too fascinated with the macabre details to suit Lavalle's taste.

"*Mais non,* monsieur." The grin returned to Toussaint's face. "We may be backward here, but who believes in vampires?"

"Then why cut off the corpses' heads?" Peregrine asked.

"To keep the dead from becoming zombies, of course. Why else?"

19
The Queen

L AVALLE HAD TO move a painting off the couch to have a
place where he could sit down. The sitting room in Peregrine's house was like the residence of a prosperous art
dealer. Paintings were propped against walls and furniture, as if a new consignment were being prepared for a
gallery opening, though there were no art galleries in
Haiti. Over the mantel was the giant image of a purple or-
chid—lush and wet with dew, frankly sensual. Peregrine
had set the watercolor in front of a Matisse he had brought
with him aboard his yacht. The American did have talent,
but Lavalle considered it an act of hubris to cover a Matisse with an amateur effort.

The budding artist had learned much from his teacher,
though other than the subject, there were few similarities
between their styles. Lady Fairweather's paintings were
exactingly detailed representations of reality; she was an
impeccable draftswoman and colorist. In contrast, Peregrine's art was given over to emotion, expression, and an
almost Oriental sort of earthly pleasure. His lighting was
always dramatic and unnatural, flowers depicted as they
might have looked at midnight when illuminated for a
fraction of a second by a burst of lightning. He gave his
pictures strange, mystical titles, like *The Night Watcher,*
The Sentinel, and *The Omen.*

The floor in the room needed sweeping, Dr. Lavalle noted as he toughed a silk handkerchief to his nose. Dr. Lavalle had noted dozens of small signs of deterioration at Maison de la Falaise. He had spoken to Peregrine about letting the gardens and mansion slip into decline, but the American's only interest was painting—and, Lavalle suspected—conquering Helen Fairweather.

There were footsteps in the hall. Marie France walked by, wiping her hands on her apron. She gave the doctor a look. Lavalle did not know what to make of Marie France's smiles. They certainly were not intended to imply warmth or even subservience. She was an enigma. It was the same with all the islanders, including his own servants and even the people whose children's lives Lavalle had saved. Perhaps a white man could never truly be at home on the island or learn to be comfortable with its mysteries.

Lavalle crossed and uncrossed his legs, took out his watch to check the time, put it back into his vest pocket.

Nathaniel Peregrine did not seem to be burdened by the same sense of alienation. Maybe it would come with time, Lavalle thought. Or maybe something about Peregrine— perhaps it was part of being an American—made him comfortable with being an outsider, a solitary, alone.

Except Peregrine would not be alone on his estate if he made a conquest of Lady Fairweather.

"Dr. Lavalle has already arrived," Marie was saying out by the entry. "He is in the salon."

Lavalle looked up, smiling. He was not disappointed.

"This is a surprise!" Lady Fairweather said, and came toward him as he rose to meet her. She kissed him on the cheek, a gesture of friendly intimacy but, alas, nothing more. By God, she was lovely, Lavalle thought, his heartbeat quickening. He could not look on a woman as handsome as Lady Fairweather without feeling desire well up in him. He was, after all, a Frenchman.

"I did not know Nathaniel had invited you to supper, Michael."

"I stopped by to have a look at one of his boys who is a bit under the weather."

"Nothing serious, I hope."

"A minor shoulder injury. Nothing broken." Lavalle put his hands in his trouser pockets and nodded at the painting of the giant flower angled up against the nearest chair, its silky inner chamber glistening suggestively with dew. "Tell me honestly, Helen: What do you make of these odd pictures Peregrine has been painting? They put me in mind of Sigmund Freud's writings, though I don't suppose you've heard of him."

"And thank you, Lord, for the precious gift of friendship. Amen."

"Amen," Peregrine said. He gave Lavalle an arch look, waiting to see if he'd play along for the lady's sake or stand by his convictions—at the risk of offending Lady Fairweather, no doubt to Peregrine's own advantage.

"Amen."

And how could he resist? Helen was so lovely that evening that even Lavalle, an athiest and a scientist, would have gladly worshipped Lady Fairweather as a goddess if she would have allowed it. After a year in mourning black, she had forsaken her widow's weeds for fashionable clothes. She wore a white chiffon dress to the dinner party that emphasized the long, graceful curve of her neck— which was left deliciously bare, except for a simple diamond choker. (How Lavalle yearned to rain kisses up and down the naked declivity betwixt neck and shoulder!) Her long chestnut hair was done up in an elegant way that made

Lavalle remember the women of Paris with a particular kind of longing. Her eyes sparkled with wit, and her complexion was even more radiant than usual.

Sitting there, gazing at her across Peregrine's table, Dr. Lavalle decided the time had come to admit it to himself: He was falling in love. It was not just the medicine in him talking. He despaired for the fact that it had taken him this long to know how he really felt, with his American friend now in the game and clearly at something of an advantage over him in the competition for Lady Fairweather's affections. If Helen knew the truth about the twin daggers of lust and love twisting in Lavalle's gut, she did nothing to let on. Peregrine, on the other hand, had been shooting Lavalle knowing glances throughout supper. Was it possible that he had guessed Lavalle was smitten? It was all an object lesson in why Lavalle disapproved of love, as a matter of principle. Rationality flew out the window when love entered the room. The results of such experiments were impossible to predict, and could be unpleasant, something Lavalle knew only too well from personal experience.

They made small talk while the food was served, Marie France standing at attention by the sideboard, watching her subordinates like hawks. The two serving girls seemed strangely detached, even by island standards. It was almost as if the girls were in a hypnotic trance. Perhaps they were drugged, Lavalle thought; islanders who were too poor to buy rum sometimes smoked hemp. If so, it was but another sorry example of how little control the present master of Maison de la Falaise had over the running of his estate. Lavalle looked at Helen, hoping she noticed the same thing, but she only rewarded him with a smile that made Lavalle feel weak.

"So what do you make of all this awful business?"

Peregrine asked the doctor as soon as the servants were dismissed.

"What business exactly do you mean?" Lavalle said, looking up from his plate and the food he had hardly touched. "You don't mean . . ." He inclined his head toward Lady Fairweather, with a slight shake of the head.

"You needn't worry about protecting my sensibilities," she said. "I know all about the dreadful deaths. People talk, you know."

Lavalle frowned.

"The first of these unfortunate deaths occurred at Fairweather House, Michael," Lady Fairweather said. "I was the one who covered the poor girl, for mercy's sake."

"Yes, of course." Lavalle cleared his throat. "Still, it's hardly an appropriate topic of conversation for the supper table."

"I don't know why not," Peregrine said. "It's a major topic of speculation in our little corner of Haiti."

"It is practically the only thing the servants speak of," Lady Fairweather said. "They are terrified. All the people are."

"And with good reason," Peregrine offered in a sober voice.

"Bah!" Lavalle said with a wave of his fork. "The islanders have always been frightened. Fear and ignorance go hand in hand. A little education would go a long way here."

"What do you think killed those people, Michael?" Lady Fairweather asked.

Lavalle shrugged and speared another bite of pork.

"It's quite a mystery, isn't it, Lavalle: people bleeding to death but without any visible wounds. Although the stranger thing is that there *are* wounds, they just heal themselves. The dead do not heal. Do they, Doctor?"

"Non."

"And yet . . ." Peregrine said, pressing him.

"I do not know. I have insufficient data to render an opinion."

"I don't agree with what the people are saying—that there's something supernatural involved," Lady Fairweather said. "But what explanation could there be? Is there some medical explanation?"

Lavalle put down his fork and knife. His appetite was lost, which was a pity. Despite Peregrine's other deficiencies as a householder, his staff set an excellent table.

"I can think of none."

"Then perhaps the cause *is* voodoo," Peregrine said.

Lavalle looked at his host. He thought he was joking, but he couldn't be sure.

"You're joking."

Nothing changed in Peregrine's face, in his eyes.

"I hope you're joking," Lavalle said.

"Then what, Michael?"

Lady Fairweather was looking to him with such an expression of trust that Lavalle wanted to storm out of the room in shame, because the truth was he didn't have the least idea what scientific explanation could account for the bizarre particulars surrounding the rash of fatalities. Yet there could be opportunity hiding within his medical impotence to stop the strange plague. Lady Fairweather was deeply committed to the welfare of the poor and ordinary, a common affliction of those born to privilege. That fact that he was committed to *her* cause could not hurt *his* cause.

"I have already confessed that I do not know, but the origin of these deaths is something I intend to uncover—and cure—if it takes every ounce of my energy."

She was beaming at him. "I can't think of a more important cause today in our little corner of the world."

"I don't expect it will be easy. I will need help. I might even need your assistance."

"All you have to do is ask, Michael."

"Just say the word, Lavalle."

"That's very generous of you both," Lavalle said, and smiled, trying to look as if the offers moved him emotionally. It was likely that he could find ways to occupy Lady Fairweather. Her time would be better spent assisting him at the hospital than giving Peregrine painting lessons so that he could continue producing lurid portraits of tropical flora. His American friend's help wouldn't be required, unless, of course, Lavalle could think of some delicate laboratory equipment Peregrine would have to travel to New Orleans to collect.

"I have been pondering the question endlessly since the first sad case," Lavalle said, leaning back and adopting the tone he had used as a young professor at the medical college. "Perhaps the root cause is a virus. Or it could be a genetic disposition, like the sickle-blood-cell phenomenon I have been studying. The only thing that seems for certain is that blood is at the root of things. But since one of the remarkable features of this bizarre malady is that there is no blood left in the bodies to study, it is difficult to pursue that angle."

"Like the case of the dog that didn't bark in the Conan Doyle story."

"I beg your pardon, Peregrine?"

"The popular series about Sherlock Holmes, the detective. The solution for Mr. Holmes in one of the stories turns on him realizing that a dog that normally would have barked at a stranger the night of a murder didn't. Ergo, the killer was someone with whom the dog was familiar."

"If only medical mysteries were as easily solved," Lavalle said.

"You will think of something and find the answer," Helen said, putting her hand over his. "As it says in Matthew, 'Fear them not therefore: for there is nothing covered, that shall not be revealed; and hid, that shall not be known.'"

Lavalle looked away from her, at a loss to think of a reply except to remind her that quoting Scripture was a ready resort of the naive, the poorly educated, and the superstitious. Peregrine was staring at him, evidently relishing Lavalle's discomfiture.

"'And fear not them which kill the body,'" the American said, still smiling at Lavalle with a certain hit of victory, "'but are not able to kill the soul: but rather fear him which is able to destroy both soul and body in hell.'"

"Peregrine, you surprise me," Lavalle said with disapproval.

"Yes," Lady Fairweather said with considerably more enthusiasm than Lavalle. "You *do* know the Bible!"

"I plan to start a hematological survey of the local population," Lavalle said, desperately improvising, for he couldn't think of a single passage of Scripture with which to redeem himself.

"You would study people's blood?" Peregrine asked.

"Not everybody's blood. I doubt everybody would agree, and besides, I haven't the resources. But I would examine a statistical cross section. It could prove revealing."

He looked at Lady Fairweather, thinking of the opportunity such a survey would give him to make up lost ground with her.

"In Paris, my area of specialization was disorders of the blood. It is one of the reasons I chose to come to Haiti—to study the anemia found here among a segment of the population."

"Let me be the first to volunteer," Peregrine said.

"And you must test me, too," Helen said.

"I'm sure what we're looking for will be found, if it exists to be found, in the blood supply of the indigenous population. The solution lies in the peasantry."

"You never know," Peregrine said. "The broader the sampling is, the more statistically representative it will be."

"That is true enough."

"You can draw a sample of my blood, too. It will set an example for others to follow. We must show that we support Michael's important research."

"And you never know," Peregrine said, "maybe you'll discover I've caught this dread disease and be able to figure out a way to cure me."

"It would be my sacred duty to try," Lavalle said, his eyes on Lady Fairweather's. "I am a physician. I am here for the people in their time of need. Indeed, that is why I came to this island to open a hospital for the children."

"You are a saint, Michael," Lady Fairweather said, her awe of Peregrine's Bible knowledge forgotten.

Lavalle shot a glance at his rival, as if to boast the reversal of fortunes: *Advantage Lavelle*. His eyes quickly returned to the ravishing Lady Fairweather. She was a feast for the eyes! Peregrine set a fine table, but the lovely Helen was by far the dish he most wanted to taste. If the American hadn't been sitting at the table with them, Lavalle would have taken Lady Fairweather up in his arms and pressed his lips against hers. He was perhaps a move or two behind in the game, but the chess match was far from over. A chance remained for him to capture this queen.

20
Nemesis

THE ANSWER HAD something to do with blood. That much seemed obvious to Dr. Lavalle, even if nothing else did.

He sat slumped forward in the saddle, content to let Napoleon plod along at a walk, while he brooded over the game before him, a match he was compelled to begin without all his materials and the obstacles already arranged in a way to make defeat seem likely.

Lavalle wished he were back in Paris, sitting in a hansom cab instead of riding his horse back to town on a dark and deserted road. At home in the city, he would be able to get up in the morning, post letters to distinguished experts, and spend the afternoon at the university, poring over books in the library, searching for something that might point him toward a solution.

In Haiti, he had no resources, no allies except the woman he loved, a friend who was his rival for the woman, and a policeman he did not trust.

On the island there were no certainties, no givens, no colleagues to help him identify the single thread of epidemiological cause and effect that explained the series of deaths. The only research facilities at Lavalle's disposal were what he had brought with him boxed up in wooden shipping crates. The Haitian public health system was nonexistent. The government was corrupt. The police were undependable. The people were illiterate. The fact that voodoo ruled the islanders' lives said everything about the hurdles Lavalle would have to clear to apply science to the issue.

But if Lavalle could end up with Helen Fairweather in bed, perhaps it did not matter if the answer eluded him.

Napoleon tossed his head as if in dispute.

"You are right," Lavalle said, and patted the animal's neck. The deaths would continue, and since he had told Lady Fairweather he was joining the game, he ultimately would have no peace until the matter came to some resolution.

The doctor turned his head to the right, standing up in the stirrups as he peered into the darkness. Napoleon paid no mind to the disturbance in the bushes. It was nothing but the wind moving the leafy shadows, making them shake as if concealing someone hiding beside the road.

Vampires . . .

Lavalle nudged Napoleon into a slow trot.

It had been Peregrine who brought up the absurd idea of vampires the night after the autopsy, when Toussaint admitted he was having the victims' heads cut off to keep them from turning into zombies. That was an equally preposterous notion—the existence of "zombies," the favorite folk terror on the island. But perhaps there was something worth thinking about in Peregrine's comment about vampires.

Lavalle had read an account of a variety of bat plaguing cattle in the tropics. The parasite was called the "vampire bat," which was appropriate enough, since the creature fed on livestock blood. If he remembered correctly, the treatise hypothesized that the bats' saliva contained an anticoagulant, which served to keep the blood flowing once the creatures nicked the host's skin with their razor-sharp teeth.

It did not seem likely vampire bats were responsible for the island deaths. Bats were small creatures, too tiny to take down a man. Unless, perhaps, they hunted in packs.

A thin wisp of cloud moved slantwise across the moon, drawing a veil across its face. The doctor squeezed his eyes shut for a moment, forcing from his mind the image of a cloud of bloodthirsty bats descending on him from the sky. When he got home he would look up vampire bats in the encyclopedia of natural history in his study. There might be a clue there, a germ of an idea, something to shape his inquiries.

The cloud moved away from the moon, blown by the trade winds. The face seemed to leer down at Lavalle, mocking the doctor with the knowledge of what had transpired on those lonely jungle paths. To what countless horrors had the moon borne silent witness? And not just there, on the rim of the world, on the far shore of a wild island, but everywhere. Even civilized men were capable of monstrous behavior. Lavalle knew *that* well enough.

A clump of palmetto shook beside the road, the movement too vigorous to be the wind. There was something there, a feral cat or even a wild hog. Whatever it was, Lavalle's horse sensed it. Napoleon tipped his head and blew out a rough breath through flaring nostrils. Dr. Lavalle kicked his heels against the horse's flanks and brought the animal to a canter.

It was so deceptive: the brilliant sun, the turquoise water, the greens, reds, blues, yellows, and purples of the landscape. The more subtle reality was that Haiti was a place of secrets, and perhaps no one was as innocent as he seemed. Lavalle was not. It was likely Peregrine was not. The American had never explained to the doctor's satisfaction why he had forsaken civilization for exile in a seeming paradise of black magic and fugitives. No doubt Peregrine harbored his own secrets.

Helen would be home already. It was unfortunate that Fairweather House and Cap Misère lay in opposite directions from Maison de la Falaise, for Lavalle would have preferred it was he, not Peregrine, who escorted her home. Lavalle reached backward and rested on the saddlebag containing the vials of blood he had drawn from Lady Fairweather and Peregrine. He disliked thinking of the vials touching each other, two cork-stopped glass tubes filled with blood that had so recently run through their hearts.

"Mais non," Lavalle said to himself, shaking off the anger rising from within. It required special effort to keep jealousy from souring his friendship with Peregrine. Jealousy was an explosive emotion, dangerous anywhere, but especially on a remote tropical island with no real rule of law.

A limb cracked in the bush along the right side of the road, the dry snap of a dead branch breaking loud enough to hear over Napoleon's hoofbeats.

Lavalle squinted into the darkness. There *was* something there. He could see that from the way the foliage moved, shaken by the violent passage of whatever was keeping pace with the doctor's horse.

"Yah!" Lavalle cried, and gave the horse two hard kicks.

Napoleon broke into a full gallop, neck thrust out, ears back. The doctor leaned forward on the animal's neck, the reins in both hands, his knees gripping the saddle. Whoever it was, whatever it was, kept pace with rider and mount. It had to be someone on a horse, though Lavalle had the sense that his nemesis was much smaller and more nimble than a man on a horse. Could it be a man running on foot? That was impossible. No man could run as fast as a horse, much less running through the jungle scrub at midnight, dodging trees, branches, and other obstacles with only the light of the hide-and-seek moon to find the way. What manner of man or beast was this, flying through the night, chasing along for who knew what dark purpose?

Lavalle switched both reins to his left hand and pulled the revolver from his pocket. He held the weapon as far from his face as he could. He did not aim. He was not so foolish as to think he could hit his enemy while riding at a full gallop. His intention was to frighten the thing. Man or beast, either would respect the sharp report of a pistol shot. And with luck, he might even hit something.

The doctor pulled the trigger, startling Napoleon into a frantic gallop on the dirt road, animal and its clinging rider stretching out faster and faster.

Holding his breath, he chanced a quick look.

It was still there, running beside them.

Lavalle held out the gun again and squeezed the trigger. Whatever it was veered closer, angling toward the road to intercept the doctor and his mount. Ahead in the distance was the outline of Cap Misère, angular shadows against the starry sky. The huts and modest houses were dark, but a lantern would be lit outside the police station and in front of the Hospital St. Jude. The bordello would be well lit, the lamps there not being extinguished until shortly before dawn.

If he could only make it to town, Lavalle knew, he would be safe.

The thing was actually pulling ahead of him, which seemed patently impossible, since Napoleon was a very good horse indeed and had the advantage of carrying his rider over an open road. The other continued to angle toward the road, moving to cut him off before he could get to safety.

"Please help me, God," Lavalle whispered, too frightened to be confounded by his sudden conversion to faith.

The doctor pointed the revolver toward the scattering bushes and pulled the trigger again and again until there were no explosions but only the impotent metallic clicks of the hammer falling on spent brass casings. He must have hit or frightened the thing, for it held up just short of the road as Lavalle flew by on his horse. The doctor did not dare look back as something reached out for him. Something clutched at the trouser of his right leg, but horse and rider were too fast. In another few seconds, Lavalle was flying past the first dark house on the edge of town.

He did not rein in Napoleon until they approached the fountain in the town square.

Whatever had been following him was not there when he looked back.

A door opened. One of the whores looked up at him hopefully, not seeing the revolver as he put it back into his jacket pocket with a shaking hand.

Lavalle walked the sweat-flecked animal home, waking up the manservant who had fallen asleep in front of the stable, waiting for the doctor's return.

Carrying the saddlebags that contained his traveling medical kit and the vials of blood, Lavalle dragged himself up to the house feeling utterly drained, and let himself in through the back door with his latchkey, locking the door behind himself. He had never been so glad to be home. He went into his study and put the gun into a desk drawer. He could wait until morning to clean and reload the weapon. He didn't even put his coat into the wardrobe but threw it over the back of a chair and went to pour himself a brandy.

Lavalle should have gotten Toussaint out of bed to assemble a posse and search the bush outside town, but that could wait until morning. If there was someone dead along the road outside of town, the body would still be there in the morning. How fortunate he would be if he could boast to Lady Fairweather that he had killed the enemy of the people! It would take more than a glass of brandy to make him think he had managed to kill the beast.

A floorboard in the hallway creaked.

Lavalle looked up. The house was locked.

The board complained again.

"Annette?"

There was no answer.

Locked doors did not mean his house was secure, Lavalle thought. Locks had not stopped whoever put the voodoo talisman in his study. A shadow flickered across the doorway, the hint of a man's outline in the weak light of the single lamp. There was no time to get the revolver and reload it. Lavalle snatched a scalpel from the open case of surgical tools on the side table.

"I give you fair warning that I am armed," he called out.

Again, no reply. He was surprised his housekeeper hadn't been awakened by his voice, or the mere sound of him coming into the house. He often wanted a cup of hot cocoa before bed. She was a light sleeper and accustomed to his demands. Unless she was—Lavalle refused to let the thought take form in his mind.

"You would be well advised to turn around this minute and leave the way you came in. Spending time in Jean-Pierre's jail will be the best thing that will happen to you if you do not leave this house."

There was a small sound, like someone shifting his weight from one foot to the other, but it seemed to come from *behind* Lavalle. The hair stood up on the back of the doctor's neck, but he did not turn. He did not want to take his eyes off the door, and he knew it would have been impossible for the shadow man to have moved into the room and gotten behind him, moving too quickly to be seen.

Nearly a minute passed. Lavalle had frightened off the intruder, he told himself.

There was a puff of air on his neck, warm air—someone's breath, Lavalle realized, but by then it was already too late. The lamp went out at the same instant something struck his hand, sending the scalpel flying away. Lavalle was falling, knocked forward to the ground. His assailant was on his back, a viselike grip on his shoulder. Before he could cry out, something sharp tore into the skin of his neck, piercing his jugular vein.

The doctor did not cry out to God this time, for he knew that not even God could help him now: he was going to die.

21

The Public Welfare

Dr. Lavalle stabbed the hypodermic into his vein with a quick, expert movement. He depressed the injector, sending the drug into his bloodstream. Through the hollow steel needle came the sharp, rising joy mingled with a sensation of raw animal power. The cocaine raced through his body, leaving no room in him for anxiety, fear, and helplessness. The formless torment that had possessed him since the housekeeper found him unconscious on the study floor that morning was ended.

Lavalle's *medicine*. What would he do without it? Cocaine was the only thing that made life bearable among the godforsaken heathens dwelling, as he did, at the very end of the earth.

Lavalle slumped in his chair, eyes closed, smiling a crooked smile. The hypodermic was forgotten in his hand, the bubble of blood trembling over the wound on the inside of his left forearm unnoticed.

Where did the runner run when his sanctuary was betrayed? There was always somewhere else to go, as long as his money held out—and he had plenty of money, as the last surviving member of an ancient and wealthy French family. If not for Helen Fairweather, he would be already gone, but he could not bear to think of her with Peregrine.

And what was it about Peregrine? Lavalle could not remember. There was something that happened after the encounter with the person who had tried to attack him along the road. Lavalle reached for the memory, but it remained just beyond his grasp. He had gone home, badly shaken by the experience on the road, then something about Peregrine, before Lavalle fainted from nervous exhaustion and spent the night on his study floor. It didn't matter, the doctor thought finally, and abandoned himself to rising bliss.

His heart was beating fast, and the breaths he drew deep into his lungs seemed to glow with energy. Lavalle's skin tingled from the acuity of his hyperreceptive nerve endings. The drug had penetrated the tiniest capillaries, flooding him with well-being and strength.

It had been a long time since he had invited his old friend, cocaine, into his body for a visit. He had forsworn the drug after the terrible ordeal of his wife's death, and yet Lavalle had known all along that once an addict, always an addict. He always kept some of the drug in his apothecary as a topical numbing agent for minor surgeries. Sometimes he would take a vial out of the locked cabinet and look at it, testing his resolve. What false exhibitions of strength! Once he was over the physical craving, it was easy enough for a disciplined mind to resist the needle, at least as long as life went along on a steady, predictable course, everything under the careful control of Monsieur le Docteur. Yet Lavalle knew, in the secret innermost chamber of his heart, that it was only a matter of time before something would come along to shake him out of his complacent stability; and when the stress became too great, the doctor knew he would return to the drug. It had never been more than a question of time. Once the soul is surrendered in weakness, it is never completely reclaimed.

Outside the window of his hospital office, a bird began to sing. It was not a pretty sound, like the songbirds in the parks back in Paris, but a harsh and wild complaint, the creature crying out perhaps in fear at the sight of a snake lurking among the mangoes, waiting for its chance to strike.

If Lavalle went away from Cap Misère, Magalie Jeanty could care for the sick children until chaos overwhelmed what little progress he had made there. That would happen whether he stayed or went. Things ran down. They fell apart. Entropy always triumphed in the end. It was a law of physics. And it was only worse in the tropics. Mold, rot, and decay constantly did their quiet work where the sun was hot and it rained almost every afternoon. In France, a man could build something and sit back to admire the progress he had wrought. There was no such respite in the islands. The fight against creeping corruption could never pause, and if it did, the forces of decomposition easily won. Man might have been nature's master, but on the bit of rock where Lavalle had come to hide from the past, nature refused to be subjugated for long.

But he could not go away without Lady Fairweather.

And Peregrine—there was something about Nathaniel Peregrine that Dr. Lavalle could not quite make himself remember.

Someone knocked on the door.

Lavalle sat straight up, his eyes bulging.

"Just a moment."

He threw the needle into his center desk drawer and slapped at his right sleeve, clawing at the cotton fabric rolled to above his elbow.

"*Excusez-moi,* Doctor." It was Magalie Jeanty. She gave Lavalle a curious look. It was because he was sitting in his shirtsleeves, he guessed. "The prefect of police has returned."

Lavalle stood as the smiling Toussaint came in past the nurse, but was overcome by the rush of blood to his head. He leaned forward, supporting himself against the desk, and extended his hand.

"You are looking pale, Doctor," Toussaint said, lowering his great bulk into one of the two chairs in front of the desk. "I hope you are not feeling ill."

"I didn't get much sleep. What did you find along the road?" Lavalle asked.

"I made a thorough search. We found nothing, Doctor. No blood, no body."

"I didn't think there would be a body." Lavalle noticed he had been tapping his right foot and compelled himself to stop. "I thought I may have wounded him."

"You should do some target shooting, Doctor."

"Ensuring the local safety is your parish, not mine."

Toussaint leaned back in the chair until its groans could be heard over his booming laugh. "Is there something you are not telling me, Doctor?"

"Of course not." Lavalle noticed the red stain on the inside of his right elbow. He crossed his arms to hide it from the policeman.

"Your housekeeper said she found you on the floor of your study this morning. She said you were weak and feverish and disoriented."

"I have a touch of malaria that bothers me from time to time," Lavalle said. "It's been giving me a bit of a go lately, I'm afraid. To be perfectly frank, I collapsed from nervous exhaustion in my study. The stress of running the hospital, these murders, the incident on the road, the malaria—I fainted dead away."

The policeman was listening carefully to him, his smile taking nothing away from the expression of cold appraisal in his cunning eyes.

"Then you were not attacked in your study?"

"What?"

"You are jumpy today, Doctor."

"My nerves are frayed." Lavalle noticed he was tapping his foot again. "Why would you think I was attacked in my study?"

"Your housekeeper heard you cry out about an intruder, but she was too frightened to come out of her room while it was dark."

"That is absurd." Lavalle frantically searched his mind. Had he been attacked? He knew he most certainly *hadn't,* yet there was a germ of uncertainty about it. He couldn't remember anything between pouring himself a brandy and being woken up on the floor.

Toussaint was watching him, waiting.

"The only possible explanation is that I cried out in my sleep."

"People do not always want to tell the police everything," Toussaint said. "That is perfectly understandable."

"I'm telling you everything."

"*Non,* Doctor. You have not been honest with me."

The cocaine saved Lavalle from the sinking feeling those words should have brought. "Oh?" he said finally.

"You were not honest with me about the reason you left Paris."

Lavalle had hoped this moment would never come, but now that it had, it was almost a relief.

"No one comes to Cap Misère without a very good reason, Doctor, and I knew you had to have yours."

"It is beautiful country," Lavalle said. "Eternal summer, the sea, the flowers. The only things the island lacks are culture and money."

"One thing we do not lack, Doctor, is fugitives," Toussaint said.

"There are no other fugitives like me on the island."

"No, indeed not, Doctor. You are in a class by yourself: white, wealthy, an eminent physician. You are the most distinguished murderer we have as a guest."

Lavalle felt as if he were crashing inward on himself. The drug was wearing off. It wasn't just that, of course, but the discovery—and the guilt.

"I am curious," the policeman said. "You are a highly intelligent man, Dr. Lavalle. Why did you choose to use your real name? You could have made it more difficult for me to discover your crime."

Lavalle shrugged.

"I think I can guess," Toussaint said. "You thought Cap Misère was too far away for anyone to know. And you were nearly right. Unfortunately for you, it was necessary for me to file a report on you to the capital after the incident with the teamster. The man was dead, of course, but the formalities must be observed. Reports are a matter of great importance to the government, though I doubt anyone ever reads them. It seems a circular printed on your behalf had belatedly arrived at La Sûreté headquarters. Sooner or later these inquiries even get to places like Haiti."

"I refuse to pretend to be someone I am not simply because of . . ." Lavalle had to search for the words. "Simply because of an unfortunate entanglement. Leaving France was merely expedient, but pretending to be someone I am not would be dishonorable."

"You are a proud man, Doctor. And you know what we are told about pride."

Lavalle's chin came up. "Of course I am proud. I am a doctor and a scientist. I have an obligation to use my training to benefit society. This is all the more so because of what happened during that unfortunate incident. What good could I do society in prison?"

The smiling policeman held up his hands.

"Easy, Doctor. I quite understand. We are fortunate to have a man like you in Cap Misère to alleviate the suffering of the little ones. What does it matter to me if some unpleasantness occurred on the other side of the sea? I have never been to Paris, of course, but I imagine it is much like Port-au-Prince. Even the biggest scandals become passé after a few months. Who cares what happened two or three years ago? What purpose would it serve to send you to a prison cell in France, or even to the guillotine? And when would we ever get another physician to come to Cap Misère? I am a realistic man, Doctor. Your secret is safe with me."

"I want nothing more than to devote myself to the public welfare," Lavalle said with all the humility he could muster.

"Concerning these strange attacks that have the people frightened, Doctor: I believe you narrowly escaped whatever is responsible for these killings last night."

Lavalle nodded, perfectly happy to move on to a different subject.

"I need to add additional patrols. The public safety is at stake."

"I agree."

Toussaint's smile grew brighter. "Expanding patrols to keep the town safe will require hiring more constables. Unfortunately, I do not have the funds at my disposal to defer such an expense. Therefore, I have decided to assess you a special police protection tax."

Lavalle and Toussaint looked at each other a long moment, the doctor's expression thoughtful, the policeman continuing to grin.

"I see your point perfectly," Lavalle said equably. "I am

glad to help in this time of public emergency. How much do you need?"

Lavalle cringed inwardly at the figure, enough to hire a platoon of policemen. He opened the center drawer to his desk, pushed aside the syringe, and took out a book of checks.

"You are a wealthy man, Doctor."

Lavalle did not reply except to tear out the check and offer it to the smiling policeman.

22
Blood Work

LAVALLE PREPARED THE first slide for study, extracting blood from the vial, adding dye to make the cell structure easier to see under the microscope.

A second injection of cocaine had filled the doctor with compulsive energy, and it was far better to lose himself in productive work than to obsess over Toussaint's blackmail, Helen and Peregrine, and the faceless killer.

Lavalle had very little hope that a study of the province's blood supply would provide insight into the recent murders, but the crimes might serve a greater purpose. The superstitious peasants would never agree to cooperate in a study that required them to provide blood samples, but now Lavalle had an excuse to enlist Toussaint to ensure cooperation for the general collection. The policeman was in his employ—which was one way to look at the situation—so Lavalle might as well put him to good use. The data would advance his research into the sickle-cell syndrome. Comprehensive data might even lead to an epidemiological breakthrough.

The doctor's hands were a little shaky from the cocaine injections, so he got the bottle of rum out of his drawer and filled a teacup with liquor. He never drank while he was working, but what did it matter anymore? It was impossible to maintain civilized standards in the jungle. He had been foolish to try.

Lavalle opened the louvers, squinting against the blinding tropical sunlight flooding into the laboratory. He clipped on the first slide and angled the microscope toward the light, adjusting the mirror to reflect light up through the bottom of the slide and illuminate the blood study. He bent over the instrument with one eye closed, using his thumb and forefinger to adjust the focus.

He saw the bad news immediately.

The doctor turned away from the microscope, shaking his head. He carried the teacup of rum over to the window and looked out through the slats. Across the street, two men were butchering a hog hung by its hind legs from a front porch. A pack of wild dogs watched from the dusty street, waiting for a chance make off with a bit of offal.

Medical research was a paradox, Lavalle thought. (His mind was not usually given to such musings, but the cocaine sent ideas tumbling through him, like a landslide of boulders falling down the hill, each one knocking others free as it fell.) Research could turn up things that would save a person's life, he thought. He took a sip of rum. But research could also condemn a man to death.

Lavalle went back and took another look through the microscope. He made a notation in his lab book, his handwriting more hurried and crabbed than usual, this also from the drug. He had more than a little familiarity with acute myeloid leukemia. Indeed, it was one of his special areas of expertise. He had been Paris's greatest expert in the disease. The rich, the noble, the famous—they all sought him out when they were diagnosed with the disease. Not that there had been much Lavalle could do for them, of course, but people always wanted the finest physician money could buy when the case seemed hopeless.

Poor Peregrine. He had acute myeloid leukemia, his time left to live measured in months, maybe weeks.

And when he was dead, and Dr. Lavelle had won back Lady Fairweather's heart—she had become unaccountably smitten with the American—they would leave Haiti together, the two of them, and go somewhere new. Lavalle would have to be more careful the next time, if for no other reason than to keep Helen from discovering he was a fugitive.

Lavalle eyed the hypodermic needle but elected to pour himself another rum instead. That was the way it was with him and cocaine. Once he dipped into it, he always wanted more.

The vial containing Lady Fairweather's blood was unopened on the lab table, neatly corked, marked with the tag he had attached to it the night before.

"Sweet Helen," the doctor said. He picked up the tube and began to bring it to his lips. He turned the vial toward him as he was about to deliver his kiss. It was then that he realized the mistake. In his cocaine-addled state of mind, he had mishandled the two vials in preparing the first slide. The vial he held in his hand was not filled with Helen's blood but Peregrine's.

It was not Peregrine who was dying, but the beloved Helen.

23

Les Invalides

"I WILL SAY a prayer for you, Lady Fairweather."

Lavalle winced inwardly at his nurse. Magalie Jeanty's convent upbringing had permanently warped her sensibilities.

"I'll give you some privacy," Lavalle said, snapping shut his doctor's bag. He left Helen's maid to help her pull the dress back over the modest chemise she'd worn during the examination.

Lavalle went out onto the porch, dropped the bag on a table, and let his bones fall back into a rattan chair. He felt bad for Helen, and he felt bad for himself, since everything had gone completely wrong for him over the past few days. But mainly Lavalle felt bad because he had been up all night, indulging in his vice. A servant brought a cool glass of mint tea. Lavalle took a packet from his vest pocket and with shaking hands sprinkled cocaine into the glass. The mint in the bitter drink cut through the dry, pasty taste in his mouth, which instantly went numb.

"Just what the doctor ordered," Lavalle said out loud, suddenly rejuvenated.

The gardens at Fairweather House were as magnificent as ever. It was late afternoon, and the landscape was filled with slanting golden light. It was impossible to imagine how Lady Fairweather managed it. Helen was notoriously easy on her staff. She'd never had a servant flogged, and Lavalle had never so much as heard her raise her voice with the help. Workers in Haiti typically performed only up to the standard their masters enforced. One needed to look no farther than Peregrine's property to see the lack of work ethic on the island. That plantation had been kept in good condition only through the famously brutal energies of the previous owners and their hirelings. Unfortunately, the American had proven unequal to the task of keeping his people in line. Peregrine's lands and house grew visibly more decrepit and wild each time the doctor visited.

Lavalle looked up at the sound of footsteps. Helen was so lovely that for a moment he actually forgot. The faint shimmer of perspiration at the edge of her hair brought the truth crashing back down on him with a force that not even the cocaine could relieve. He thought of the night at Peregrine's, when he had marveled at her glow, not recognizing death in its disguise.

"I am going to die."

Lavalle could not bring himself to say it, so she had said it for him.

"I think I've known for several weeks," she said, sitting across from him. "I don't have any strength, and I bruise easily. I wondered what you would find when you looked at my blood in your microscope."

"My dear Helen, I cannot begin to tell you how sorry I am."

She gave him a crisp nod. "What is it, then?"

"Excuse me," the doctor said, blinking rapidly. "This is difficult for me."

"I know how you feel, Michael. About me—about us."

Lavalle nodded, unable to speak.

"It is all right, darling. I am at peace. This is the Lord's will."

"How can you say such a thing?"

"Because I know it in my heart and soul."

"I wish I had your faith."

"You sound so bitter when you say that."

"I *am* bitter. I love you, Helen. And now that I've said it, I have nothing to look forward to but losing you."

"You must not despair, Michael. Maybe part of this is about helping you find your faith."

"Helen, please."

"If you can do nothing else for me, Michael, at least wish you had faith. All you need to do is wish for faith. If you can do that much, God will take care of the rest."

"God wouldn't want me. I've done things. The other night you said I was a saint, but I'm a deeply flawed man."

"As are all men and women. That's all the more reason for you to learn that God loves you and forgives you for your sins."

Lavalle considered it. Did he even have it in him somewhere to wish for such a thing, to let the trials and inevitable tragedies of life weaken him to the point that he surrendered the scientific rationality that was the basis for his entire life?

"I will try," he said in soft voice. Lavalle didn't know whether she could tell he was lying, but she leaned over and kissed his forehead, so perhaps he was convincing enough.

"As to my illness . . ."

Lavalle told Lady Fairweather about the leukemia and the prognosis, which was hopeless. She listened calmly and asked several excellent questions, nodding at the answers, her good mind able to easily grasp the medical concepts Lavalle outlined.

In the course of his professional career, Lavalle had told many people they were dying, but none had heard the news with such calm and peaceful acceptance. Lady Fairweather's inner strength was nothing short of amazing. If her fortitude flowed from faith, then even he would have to admit religion served a purpose.

"So there is no known treatment, no hope of recovery."

"Nothing short of a miracle, I'm afraid," Lavalle said, instantly regretting the words.

"Then I shall pray for a miracle but remain obedient to God's will. Have you told Nathaniel?"

"What?" The question caught Lavalle completely off balance. "No, of course not. I would never discuss your case with him without your permission."

"What would you say if I told you Nathaniel guessed that I was sick? We talked about it the other night after you left."

Lavalle felt a stab of jealousy. "He's a perceptive man, but I don't know how he could have guessed."

"He suffers from a similar condition himself."

"He said that? How could he know?"

"He did not explain that to me."

"How very odd." Maybe Peregrine had been afflicted by his own peculiar blood condition for longer than Lavalle had guessed. Judging from the composition of the American's blood, Lavalle was amazed that Peregrine had been able to sail his yacht to Haiti, let alone carry on the appearances of a normal life, considering that he most certainly had a fatal blood disease, though one heretofore unclassified in any of the medical books.

"Since he told you of it himself, there can be no harm in my confirming as much."

"Nathaniel has leukemia?"

The concern in her voice was particularly galling, especially so soon after Lavalle's confession of love.

"I do not know exactly *what* Peregrine has. It's nothing

I've encountered in the literature, and with all modesty, I've studied every monograph on the subject of blood pathology worth reading. His blood has a tremendous excess of red blood cells, which carry the oxygen to the body. But his red cells are unstable. There is an unnaturally high degree of premature cellular necropsy—cell death."

"Is he dying?"

"I am afraid so. I don't know how anybody could live with such abnormal blood."

"I feel sorry for you, Michael. You have two close friends on the island, and both are invalids."

"Save your pity, my dear. I will find a way to get by." He thought of the syringe waiting back at his house. "I always do."

"Nathaniel says he has learned to live with his condition."

"That is highly unlikely, from a medical standpoint."

"He says he can help me overcome my own illness."

"My dear Helen," Lavalle said in a long sigh. "There is nothing I would rather do than give you hope, but there can be none. No doubt Peregrine means well, but it was cruel of him to lead you on."

"Promise me you'll try to help Nathaniel, even if you can't help me."

"I will do what I can, of course. I am a physician."

"But the two of you are also rivals of a sort."

Lavalle almost asked Lady Fairweather whom she preferred—him or Peregrine—but he lacked the nerve. It would only make him feel worse to know it was Peregrine she loved.

"That hardly matters now. Not for any of us."

"Please try to help him. I care for you both very much. Promise me, Michael. Do it for my sake."

"I promise."

Lady Fairweather smiled, at last satisfied. Peregrine's health notwithstanding, Lavalle planned to flee the island as soon as Helen died. What did it matter if he lied? She would never know.

"Have you ever noticed that there is something peculiar about Nathaniel?"

Lavalle snorted. "He is an American. They're all peculiar."

"It is nice of you to try to lighten my spirits."

Lavalle shrugged. More cocaine would lighten his own.

"I think there is something different about Nathaniel, though I can't quite put my finger on it," Lady Fairweather said. "I think there are secrets in his past."

"There are secrets in all of our pasts."

"Not mine, Michael."

"No, I suppose not," Lavalle said, and smiled sadly. "You are too good for this world. Perhaps you should have been a bit more like me."

"You're a good man, Michael."

That was not true, of course, but not even Lavalle was a big enough cad to contradict the dying woman.

24

Basic Research

LAVALLE GASPED WITH frustration and rolled off the prostitute.

The doctor lay on his back in the dark, panting, feeling his sweat soak into the sheets. At least the linens were clean. He always insisted on that when he visited the brothel.

The whore sat up in bed. He could see her profile in silhouette against the open window. She wasn't the youngest or the prettiest, but her body came closest to matching Lady Fairweather's elegant frame. The smell of the perfume he'd given the prostitute to wear was still strong in the air. It was Helen's perfume. Lavalle had stolen a little of it that afternoon while Lady Fairweather got ready for her examination, in order to make this little charade more realistic.

Seeing Helen nearly naked, touching the softness of her breast with his stethoscope, had filled Lavalle with a crude desire that she was far too ill to satisfy without risking hemorrhage. He had had his chance, between her husband's death and Peregrine's arrival, but he had let it pass by. One always thought there would be an opportunity for these things, but there was never any way to know how much time was left. The future was an illusion and the end usually never very far away.

"Are you finished, Monsieur le Docteur?"

Lavalle struck a match and brought it to his cigarette. He filled his lungs with smoke and answered with the exhalation.

"Oui."

No doubt she was finished with him, too. He had pounded away for nearly an hour without attaining release. That was the way it was when he was on the cocaine. The desire was powerful but usually not the ability to finish, no matter how raw or exhausted he and his paid lovers became.

The woman got up, pulling the sheet around her. The door opened and closed. It was Lavalle's preference to be left alone when it was finished. He made it a habit only to come to the brothel when the lust was more than he could bear, but once he was done, he did not want the whore's company. As exotic and forbidden as it was to make love to an island woman, afterward he felt disgusted with himself in a way that he never had with a Parisian prostitute.

Poor Helen. He had seen her in his mind's eye the entire time he had been ravaging the black woman, even as he had smelled her stolen perfume on the whore's skin. The charade had worked far too well. As much as he wanted to fantasize about fucking Lady Fairweather, he could not for a moment forget the awful fact that she was doomed to waste away before his eyes over the coming weeks, her face turning cadaverous, her lusterless skin hanging off of bones that would weigh very little when the time came to lift her into a coffin.

Feeling very low indeed, Lavalle lit a candle. From his jacket he took out the little black leather case that held the silver syringe he reserved for his personal use and a vial of white powder.

*   *   *

There was another horse tied to the hitch outside beside Napoleon, a black stallion that looked familiar to Lavalle.

"Just the man I was looking for."

Lavalle spun around to see that Peregrine had come up behind him without his notice. He must have come out of the brothel, but the doctor hadn't heard footsteps. Peregrine had a way of creeping up on Lavalle that the doctor found particularly disconcerting, an attribute, no doubt, of the American's lack of the deeper European sense of culture and deportment.

"Should you be out this time of night?" Lavalle looked the other man up and down. He showed no outward sign of illness. Just the reverse, in fact. Peregrine projected his usual air of vigor. He was dressed all in black, with leather English hunting boots that came up to his knees. The stallion was Peregrine's. "How do you feel?"

"Quite fine, thank you."

"That's difficult to imagine, having had a look at your blood under the microscope."

"Which is exactly what I came to talk to you about."

Lavalle unfastened Napoleon's reins from the hitch. "If you want to come along to the house, I'll give you a brandy and we can discuss your case. I don't suppose a brandy will do you much harm."

"It hasn't so far," Peregrine said, and grinned in the darkness.

The American's ill health notwithstanding, Lavalle wished he had Peregrine's fine white teeth.

"I rode over to Helen's earlier," Peregrine said, swinging his leg over the saddle. "She told me the bad news."

Lavalle felt like brooding, but the cocaine made him talkative. Still, he managed to keep silent for a few

moments as they rode side by side along the darkened
street. Lamps and even candles were a luxury for most of
the people in Cap Misère, who went to bed with the sun.

"She said you knew she was sick."

"I sensed it."

"How?"

"I don't know. Like I said, I sensed it. I know things
sometimes. I pick them up. It is difficult to explain."

"Like a gypsy fortune-teller?"

Peregrine laughed softly. "Something like that, but
without tarot cards or crystal balls."

"Sometimes you say the damnedest things, Peregrine."

"You haven't heard the half of it."

Lavalle's stable boy took their horses, and the men
went into the house. The doctor lit the lamps in his study
and poured them both snifters of his finest cognac. Peregrine deserved as much, given how little time he had to
live.

"Is there anything you can do for Helen?"

"There is nothing anyone can do for the poor woman."
Lavalle looked at Peregrine past lowered eyebrows. "You
shouldn't fill her head with false hopes."

"I don't know what you're talking about."

"Don't be evasive, Peregrine. You told Lady Fairweather you could help her."

"I can," Lavalle said with what seemed to be perfect
earnestness.

"Stop it! She's dying and we both know it. There is no
treatment for acute myeloid leukemia and certainly no
cure."

"That may be true, but with my help she can live as long
as she likes."

Lavalle stared with slack-jawed disbelief, but his mind,
quick even without the cocaine to drive his thoughts ever

faster, soon generated the hypothesis that Peregrine wasn't merely trying to provoke him.

"How long have you been sick?" Lavalle asked, sounding more like a kindly physician than a drug-addicted, lovesick man.

"For many years."

"I find that difficult to imagine. Your blood cells are severely damaged."

"I know."

"How aware are you that the condition is influencing your thinking? Are you subject to bizarre fantasies? Do you sometimes find it difficult to distinguish between reality and something you have dreamed?"

"The problem is not with my mind, Lavalle."

The doctor did not contradict the American, but looked at him with a self-satisfied smile.

"You think I'm mad."

"You have been saying things that are not rational. That you *know* things. That you can somehow save Lady Fairweather from a quick and tragic death. Frankly, I am surprised I have not seen evidence of this incipient psychosis before, my poor friend. It must be linked somehow to your blood condition. We have spent many an evening playing chess and talking. I should have noticed."

"Do you think you can help me?"

"With your condition?" Lavalle sat up straight. "I will have to do more tests. I would be lying if I told you to be optimistic. The damage is too severe."

"I came to Haiti because you are one of the world's preeminent specialists in disorders of the blood."

"It is kind of you to say so, but even if it is true, how do you know about my work?"

"Because I sought out the best doctors in Europe looking for a cure."

Lavalle took a mouthful of cognac but held it in his mouth, his mind racing.

"Do you know . . ."

"Of course. In a way, the fact that you're a fugitive made it more convenient for me. And the fact that you had gone away to live in a remote place also suited my purposes. I am an extremely private person, Lavalle. I do not want anyone to know about my illness."

But the doctor was hardly listening.

"I have done a very evil thing," he said into his glass.

"Yes, but your crime is of no consequence to me. You have an unhappy love affair and a crime in your past. I have an unhappy love affair with a Creole woman and many crimes in my past, and before that a sorrow I still cannot bear to think about. The only thing I care about, Doctor, is that you help me. I will give you money, if you need it. I have more wealth than I could ever spend."

Lavalle waved his hand dismissively.

"If you change your mind, my resources are at your disposal," Peregrine said. "If Toussaint bleeds you dry with his blackmail, you can come to me for help."

Lavalle nearly choked. "How do you know about Toussaint?"

Now it was Peregrine's turn to look satisfied. "You were wrong about the islanders not welcoming a white man to their voodoo ceremonies." He burst into laughter. "If you could see your face, Doctor!"

"I cannot believe you would be so foolish as to involve yourself in peasant witchery, Peregrine."

"It's harmless. Well, mostly." The American winked. "You'd be amazed at the things you would learn if you could bring yourself to deal with the peasants on their own level. I tried to talk Toussaint out of blackmailing you, but you know how it is with the police in a place like this. The government assumes they'll make most of their salary through their own initiative. And they always do."

"Then the prefect should live very well for the next few years, thanks to me."

Peregrine slid his chair closer and leaned forward, forearms on his knees. "I'll tell you my plan. I'll help Helen. You don't have to worry about her. She will not die. What you do need to do is devote your talents to finding a way to treat us both. Helen will be trading one disease for another, her leukemia for what I have."

"Peregrine, please! You're talking nonsense."

"No. You don't know what you're dealing with, but when you do, it all will become plain. I have not been entirely honest with you, though in fairness I must point out that you have not been overly honest with me, either. I am a rare creature, a member of a small and secretive race."

"Of course you are."

"You do not need to indulge me. I am no lunatic. Do you remember being followed the other night, coming home from my plantation house?"

Lavalle felt the blood drain from his face.

"And then you were attacked in your house—in this room, in fact."

Lavalle ran his hand again and again through his hair, searching his mind.

"You can't quite remember, can you? The memory was repressed, but this will help you remember."

The American reached over and touched Lavelle lightly on the forearm. The doctor threw his hands up in horror as the experience fell back down on him with enough immediacy to leave him shaking—the shadowy form coming up fast from behind, an irresistible force that swarmed over him, driving him to the ground, helpless against the strange sensation that someone was forcing his way into Lavalle's mind. But even worse was the sense of menace, the sensation of being at the mercy of a lethal malice that was utterly devoid of mercy. And yet, he had survived.

"I knew that you were considering fleeing Cap Misère," Peregrine said as Lavalle looked out from between his lowering arms. "I needed to assess the chance that you would stay, that you would agree to help me—and Helen. What I saw in your mind convinced me, so I did not bother you in any other ways. It would have been such a waste to have killed you when you could be such a valuable tool."

The American smiled so that Lavalle could see two wicked supernumerary fangs extending from the upper jaw. Peregrine moved the muscles of his cheeks in a grimace and the teeth disappeared under his lip.

"Your supposition is entirely correct, Doctor. My blood teeth retract into the upper jaw when I do not need them. You see, my friend, I am a vampire. I am also, I almost regret to say, responsible for the recent deaths that have been such a concern to you. I require meals of fresh human blood. I suppose it has something to do with the sorry state of my own blood. I will leave that up to you to determine. You're the physician and scientist, not I."

Lavalle felt a peculiar tingling sensation in his head, as if something was gently moving within his brain. Maybe he was having a stroke. His blood pressure spiked after each cocaine injection, putting him at risk. The lack of sleep, the overindulgence: Could this all be an elaborate paranoid hallucination?

"A vampire possesses many powers that would seem strange to you, Lavalle. That is how I know that at this moment you are wondering if the cocaine binge you have been on has filled your mind with fearful fantasies. What is that word you use to describe it? *Paranoid*. You have been reading Dr. Freud lately, haven't you? He has strange ideas. Do you think he is right about sex being the root of most people's unhappiness? It is an interesting idea. I shall have to read him for myself to see if I agree."

"You *can* read my mind."

"But of course, and I can be far more subtle about it than I just was, but I wanted you to feel me inside your mind. Probing your thoughts is how I was able to verify that despite your many virtues, my good doctor, you are at heart a coward. You will do what you can to help Helen and me because you realize there is nowhere you can go to escape me if you don't."

It was suddenly very close in the room. Lavalle took out his handkerchief and patted the perspiration from his forehead.

"Whatever you need I will supply it. Money. Equipment for your laboratory. Cocaine. I had Toussaint send a man to Port-au-Prince to fetch you some. I realized you were worried about running low the other night when I was rummaging around inside your mind. You won't have to be concerned about the shipment from New Orleans being late again. You can have as much cocaine as you want, as long as it doesn't get in the way of your work."

Lavalle began to shake his head slowly. What the American was telling him defied his every certainty. It was madness.

"Not madness," Peregrine said.

The doctor pressed his fingers against his head. "I can't accept this. I *can't*."

"Think of it this way, my friend," Peregrine said, his voice reassuring. "You have just made an unprecedented medical discovery, one of those unsuspected leaps that turn the world on its head and redefine all understanding.

Someday your name will be mentioned in the same breath as Copernicus, Galileo, and Newton. You will be the first scientist to investigate the heretofore undocumented condition that transforms ordinary men into beings with superhuman powers, along with one monstrous need. You find the cure for me and others of my tortured race, who are compelled to prey on people like cattle. Your research may even extend the life span and intellect of the entire human race. The knowledge you gain will bring an end to a race of demons. In the process, you will transform men into gods. And you, Doctor, will be remembered throughout history not as a murderer, but as the visionary father of the New Man."

Peregrine waited for Lavalle's reaction, but the doctor was too stunned to speak. His awe at the secrets glimpsed that night was too far-reaching to take in all at once. He sat leaning forward in his chair, his face near the vampire's, his breathing quick and shallow. This must be how it felt for a bold explorer who, happening upon an unsuspected and wondrous new continent, is overcome with the rich enormity of possibilities.

"I will dedicate myself to this research as if my life depended on it," Lavalle said finally, his voice shaking with emotion.

"And that's the very thing you need to understand," Peregrine said, and smiled. "Your life *does* depend upon it."

25

The Agony

LAVALLE CUT THE girl open quickly, relying on instinct and adrenaline—and, of course, his *medicine*.

"The light, Dr. Duplessy."

But the young physician was already adjusting the lamp over the incision in the child's abdomen as Magalie Jeanty attended to the anesthetic. Lavalle had expected his new assistant to be incompetent, but to his profound surprise, Duplessy proved quite capable.

Like many Haitian men, Dr. René Duplessy was tall and thin. He kept his black head shaved, a carryover from his brief career as an army doctor. He was the graduate of a medical school in Havana that Lavalle had never heard of, but the Cubans must have known what they were doing to turn out someone as solid as this young doctor. Duplessy was Peregrine's find. After locating the promising physician, Peregrine had spread enough bribe money around Port-au-Prince to secure his release from the army.

Thanks to Dr. Duplessy, Lavalle would no longer have to divide his time between research and the hospital. As an inducement to Lavalle to work all the harder at unlocking the mystery of vampirism, Peregrine had promised to pay Duplessy to remain at the hospital even if Lavalle left the island. Peregrine had intervened after the second time

Toussaint blackmailed Lavalle, but they both knew it was only a matter of time before someone would betray the French doctor to the authorities in the capital.

Lavalle reached into the girl's abdomen and found the diseased appendix. The organ was swollen fat with poisonous infection and ready to burst, which would lead to peritonitis and the girl's death. After another cut Lavalle threw the rancid organ into a kidney-shaped bowl.

"The child's parents nearly killed her waiting for the witch doctor's potion to work. When will these people learn?"

"I do not know, Dr. Lavalle," Duplessy said. He did not yet know his superior well enough to know when Lavalle's questions were merely rhetorical.

"Would you like to close up, Dr. Duplessy? Magalie, you assist. I have a house call to make."

"As you wish, sir."

Lavalle turned, smiling, to wash the blood from his hands. *As you wish, sir.* Good army protocol was a wonderful thing, especially when one was on the receiving end.

Napoleon was saddled and waiting in front of the hospital. Lavalle had been on his way to Fairweather House when they brought the girl in, writhing in pain. He climbed back on his horse and headed out of town at a gallop. The darkening sky did not concern him. The murders continued every week or two, but Lavalle had nothing to fear. It was a different story for the others. The people along the coast barricaded themselves inside their hovels at sunset and did not come out again until dawn. Of the establishments in Cap Misère, only the brothel remained open after dark, the appeal of sex and liquor too powerful to be resisted. Most customers stayed overnight. The risk of shame did not outweigh the fear of having your throat torn out but the monster that was, by a peculiar twist of fate, the mentor to Dr. Lavalle's research.

Lavalle followed a servant upstairs to Helen's bedroom. She was on her back beneath a down comforter, though it was a hot, humid night. She reminded him of the child back at the hospital after she had been chloroformed: small, still, feverish, the weak spark of life barely flickering on the edge of eternal darkness.

"I apologize," Lady Fairweather said weakly just as Lavalle decided she was unconscious. "I was too weak to get out of bed today."

"There is no need."

Lavalle sat down on the bed and took her hand. She had lost perhaps a kilogram of weight that week, all the more alarming in one who had not carried any excess weight even when she was healthy. Lady Fairweather was already beginning to look skeletal, as Lavalle had imagined she would when they put her into a casket.

"Have Colette bring you a glass of wine."

He shook his head. "I have work to do when I get back to the laboratory."

"Ah, yes, your research. Tell me, Michael, how is it going? Are you making much progress?"

Lavalle looked at her closely and saw nothing but her usual English detachment. Most people in her position would have been desperate for some thread of hope to cling to, though his solution of the problem of Peregrine's condition would do nothing directly to help her.

"A little, my dear. I would be lying if I told you I expected a quick breakthrough. It is one thing to identify a disease of the blood, but quite another to cure one. The leukemia you suffer from is a perfect example. It was described in the medical literature long ago, but treatment remains elusive. Perhaps someday there will be an answer, when we unlock the secrets of the cell and come to understand what causes these malignancies. If we could only understand what factors lead a disease to be switched on in the body, so to speak, perhaps we could find treatments to turn the same switch off."

"Tell me what have you learned so far," she said, and closed her eyes. Lavalle doubted she had much interest, but conversation gave her something to think about besides her misery.

"An excess of red blood cells, for one thing. It is quite remarkable. The red cells carry oxygen to the body. Peregrine has them in abundance beyond anything I've ever witnessed in mammalian blood. No wonder he has such unusual physical strength. His body is supercharged, like a mighty engine that is able to generate extraordinary power. My guess is this is the reason his health has not completely collapsed. His system keeps him one step ahead of this disease, indeed of all diseases—but only just barely."

"Do you think you will ever find a cure?" There was a faraway quality to Helen's voice. Perhaps she was becoming delirious. The end wasn't very far away for her, unless she changed her mind.

"Perhaps someday. It would help to relocate the research somewhere near a major teaching hospital, perhaps in the United States, where the facilities are up-to-date and there are colleagues whose assistance I could enlist. Money is not an issue for Peregrine. You can buy a lot of expertise with unlimited funds."

"Then will you both go to Boston or Philadelphia when I am gone?"

"I don't know. There would be complications."

"You mean because of the problems you left behind in France."

Her eyes were open again and she was looking at him, not blinking.

"Did he tell you?" Lavalle said, feeling his anger rise.

"Who—Nathaniel? No. Before he died, my poor husband told me you had to leave Paris and would go to jail if you ever went back."

"That's all?"

She nodded, barely moving her head.

"Do you want to know what happened?"

"Only if you want to tell me, Michael." She summoned the strength to smile. "You know that confession can be good for the soul."

"It was over a woman," he said, unable to meet her eyes.

"I thought perhaps it was."

How best to frame the story? Lavalle thought. It was a good thing he'd been frightened into laying off the cocaine and had regained some perspective.

"I fought a duel over a woman. I know that must sound hopelessly romantic. But I am, after all, French."

Helen smiled. The poor, misguided Christian soul: fortunately for Lavalle, Lady Fairweather didn't have it in her to condemn him.

"The man was killed, unfortunately. And so I came to Haiti to open the children's hospital, which had always been one of my dreams." He took a deep breath before going on, knowing the boldest lies are often the easiest to believe. "And, frankly, to atone for my sins."

He almost expected her to burst into laughter, but she continued to look at him with the same compassionate smile.

"You're a good man, Michael. No matter what happened in the past, in your heart you are a good man."

Lavalle enjoyed the adulation for the few moments he was able to keep himself from acknowledging that none of it was true.

"Now, as for you, my darling Helen."

Lady Fairweather's head came up a little from the pillow.

"I do not mean to be melodramatic," Lavalle said, "but you realize your time is growing short."

She nodded.

"I understand your hesitancy to take our friend up on his unusual offer. I cannot recommend it to you as a physician. There are too many unknowns. The first law of medicine is 'Do no harm.' There is no telling how long it will take to find a way to reverse the process. To be perfectly honest, a cure for vampirism may never be found. But . . ."

Helen Fairweather's eyebrows rose. She had known there was going to be a *but,* and she was waiting for it, knowing Lavalle would eventually come around to employing it.

". . . as your friend—as someone who loves you, Helen—please let Peregrine help you. It is your only hope."

"That's not true, Michael. I have the only kind of hope that matters. My hope, and my faith, are in the Lord. I am going to a better place."

"No one wants to die," Lavalle said hotly, like a prosecutor objecting to an absurd claim in court.

"I do not mind dying, if it is God's will."

"I thought you loved me." Lavalle felt a stab of uncertainty, which was immediately replaced by jealousy, the twisting of the dagger in his entrails. "Or it is Peregrine you love?"

"I care very much for both of you, Michael."

Dr. Lavalle threw up his hands. "Then how can you leave us? How can you lie there and let life slip away from you when there is an alternative?"

"Don't think that it is easy," Lady Fairweather said as a single tear began to trace its way down her feverish cheek.

"This has caused me more agony than you could imagine. I would have this cup taken away from me the same as you, and yet I am determined to let God's will be done."

"But why, for the sake of all you hold holy?" Lavalle slid off the bed onto his knees. "I'm begging you to reconsider. I am *begging*," he said, his hands clasped together in supplication.

"I can't become like him." She was shaking a little. "I refuse to become like him."

"A vampire, you mean."

She shook a little as she nodded, as if nearly bereft of strength. "To be forced to prey on the innocent—I would rather die a thousand deaths than hurt even one person, Michael."

"But Peregrine says you don't *have* to kill to get the blood you need."

"As if he doesn't? You are too intelligent for such a disingenuous argument, Michael. If Nathaniel can't control his appetite for blood, how could I expect to be any stronger?"

"Because you *are* strong. I've never known a woman who possessed half as much will as you, Helen. You've proven that with the way you've run your plantation. Look at it in comparison with Peregrine's place. And besides that, you are *good*. You could never let your desires lead you to stoop to killing. You don't have that in you."

"If only I could believe that were true. Nathaniel was good once, too. He's confided in me a little about his past life. He was once a husband, a father, and judge. Then his family was murdered, and he met the beautiful creature who transformed him into a—I can't even say the word. It is too monstrous. I can never become one of them. I could never prey on the living for their blood to prolong my own life. Blood is like a strong drink to a drunkard or drugs to an addict: it exerts a power over these pathetic creatures they cannot control."

Lavalle stood up and walked to the window. Did her remark about drugs mean she knew of his dalliance with cocaine? Was she hinting that she knew? Perhaps her husband had known more, and had told her more, than Helen let on.

"Who knows what tax such a change could levy against my eternal soul?" Lady Fairweather said to his back. "Have you read Bram Stoker's novel *Dracula*? They have all lost their souls, these undead beings."

"I do not have time for novels," Lavalle said briskly. "Does Peregrine strike you as 'undead'? He seems very much alive to me."

"You will not be able to persuade me to ignore the moral dimension to this, Michael. I know Nathaniel far too well to believe he is evil, but we can never forget that he has done many, many evil things."

"He has changed. There have been no more deaths."

"Is that true?"

"Yes," Lavalle lied. "Not a one."

Lady Fairweather relaxed back into her pillow. "Then I have done at least that much for him. You must do the rest, after I am gone."

"Do you really think he'll let you die?" Lavalle said, exasperated and afraid at the same time. Peregrine expected him to convince Lady Fairweather to change her mind. "He is in love with you, you know. No, that isn't putting it strongly enough: he is obsessed with you. He will not rest unless he can possess you."

"He said as much when he was here last night. Do you know what I told him?"

Lavalle did, but he waited for her to say it herself.

"I told him he could kill me, if he wanted to, for I was

already in great pain and death would come as a relief. I also acknowledged he could turn me into a vampire against my will, if he wanted. In this remote corner of the world, Nathaniel clearly has the power to do whatever he wishes. But if he did force me to become like him, I told him I would hate him forever. Far better for me to go to the peace of my grave loving him—and loving you—than to be turned into a monster doomed to hate him with every fiber of my being during an eternity spent dragging myself from one vile, bloody crime to the next."

Her hand slid across the comforter and took his, her grasp for one brief moment as firm and strong as it had once been.

"You must both be as brave as I am, Michael, and face death without bitterness or remorse," she said, her voice trembling with emotion. "My death and your death, when it comes. We must be obedient to God's will."

26

The Fallen

NATURE IS AN indomitable power in the tropics, the heat, rain, and sun creating paradoxically twin drives for growth and decay that can be resisted but never overcome. The coastal jungle quickly reclaims gardens, farm plots, and plantations that are not constantly maintained.

The plantation surrounding Maison de la Falaise had the look of abandonment about it, as if disease or war had carried away the inhabitants, leaving the vines, ferns, and monstrous orchids to reclaim their humid kingdom. The gravel of fine white shells paving the lane from the road to the great house had almost completely disappeared beneath Bahama grass and overgrown oleander bushes that slapped Dr. Lavalle's legs as he rode, leaving the trousers above his riding boots wet with dew.

But the workers had not run away—or been murdered. They had merely abandoned their former duties. Their presence was plain enough in the drumming and firelight flickering against the trees from a clearing beyond the cottages where the field hands lived. Peregrine allowed voodoo to be practiced openly on the plantation. And why not? The American had abandoned all pretense of civilization, even to the extent that he participated in whatever dark rituals were carried out around the huge bonfires that sent sparks mingled with pagan incantations into the starry Caribbean night sky.

Lavalle did not turn Napoleon toward the ceremony but continued to the house. If Peregrine was off with the witches, dancing around the fire, he would wait until the American returned to the house to deliver the news.

Maison de la Falaise was lighted but in a haphazard way—a lamp here, a candle there, more dark than not. The house was disintegrating at an amazing rate. One corner of the porch was sagging—termites had gotten into a pillar—but Peregrine apparently had no interest in having his people repair it. One of the shutters had come loose during the last thunderstorm and hung against the house at a crazy angle. It was madness to let the property go, especially when Peregrine had the employees and money to maintain the plantation as it deserved to be kept. But then there was a madness to the American that Lavalle was only beginning to appreciate. Peregrine had given up on Maison de la Falaise as he had given up on almost everything and seemed content to wallow in misery as his world disintegrated around him.

There was no way of knowing how Peregrine would react to the sad news of Lady Fairweather's death. Lavalle would have preferred to flee the island than to be the one to tell him, but he knew there was no way to escape the vampire, and even if he tried, Peregrine would hunt him down.

Science was the doctor's only hope now, which was fitting enough, for he had lived his entire adult life as if the laws of science, as postulated and proven by research, were the only laws that applied to him. If he could make Peregrine understand he was beginning to make progress with the research, the monster would not kill him. It ought to be easy enough to convince him, with Lady Fairweather dead, that the best course for them was to leave their green hell for somewhere civilized, where Lavalle could avail himself of the laboratory facilities required for the breakthrough that would lead to a treatment for Peregrine's bizarre condition.

A woman was sitting on the top porch stair of Maison de la Falaise, her figure silhouetted against the light shining through the open entryway. She sat with head slumped forward, knees far apart, like one of the bawds at the whorehouse in Cap Misère. The doctor didn't see the second woman until he got closer; she was lying on her back at the bottom of the steps, arms and legs splayed out, as if she had been shot at the top of the stairs and fallen backward, dead.

Napoleon sensed death, the way animals do, and began to shy. The reins snapped against the horse's neck as Lavalle pulled them sharply back just short of his destination.

The woman's head rose enough for her to look up at him through the long tangle of hair falling around her face. Lavalle was caught completely off guard. It was a *white* woman. Where had she come from? Lady Fairweather was the only other white woman on the coast, and she was dead.

Lavalle jerked the reins again when Napoleon began to back away. There was no avoiding the scene, repugnant as it was. Lavalle swung himself out of the saddle, grunting as his boots hit the ground. He looped the reins around the branch of a tree felled in the last storm. He could feel the woman's eyes on him, but something made the ever-charming Parisian doctor wary.

Lavalle knelt next to the prostrate woman long enough to assure himself of what he already knew. Marie France's corpse was still warm to the touch. The savage wound in her neck was the cause of death. He was surprised he hadn't seen the shoe on her right foot and recognized her sooner, for Marie was the only black woman Lavalle knew on the island besides his nurse, Magalie Jeanty, who wore shoes. The left shoe was missing. Perhaps it had come off when her lifeless body was pitched down the stairs. Or maybe she lost it while trying to run away from Peregrine, the coldhearted killer. The American's interest in sorcery hadn't prevented him from killing the voodoo priestess. The larger question, though, was would he kill Lavalle?

The doctor looked up at the white woman, who was watching him with what appeared to be a drugged fascination. Lavalle had her to worry about now, too, not that he would put a stranger's welfare ahead of his own, even one so lovely. She was young, scarcely past childhood, and far too innocent looking to be anywhere near a creature like Nathaniel Peregrine. Her face had the same refined, idealized preciousness seen in the face of a little girl's doll. Her skin was the most amazingly perfect shade of white, as if she were made from porcelain. Lavalle guessed she was sixteen, maybe eighteen at the most. Despite his fear, and his determination to look after his own best interests, he could not help but feel a twinge of yearning for the delicious young thing.

"Hello, my dear," Lavalle said.

She did not answer but got to her feet and turned to go into the house. Lavalle went up the stairs after her.

"Excuse me, young lady, but I am not sure it is a good idea for you to go inside."

When she did not stop, Lavalle stepped quickly forward and put his hand gently on her shoulder. She turned, her lips the shimmering red hue of wet cherries. The impulse to take her in his arms and kiss her took command of Dr. Lavalle with such force that he was barely able to keep himself from behaving poorly. There was a dreamy, far-away quality to her eyes. Peregrine must have drugged her, Lavalle thought, perhaps with a draft of opium.

"It is not I who am on drugs," she said. She spoke in French, but her accent reminded Lavalle of the Creoles he knew in Port-au-Prince. "I see you have gone back on the cocaine, Dr. Lavalle," the girl said. "I can smell it in your blood."

She pulled a lady's handkerchief from a sleeve and daintily patted her lips. Some of the red from her mouth transferred to the lace. Her lips were wet with blood, Lavalle realized, his eyes growing wide. She, not Peregine, had killed Marie France. That could only mean she was . . .

"A vampire," she said, and smiled sweetly, finishing his sentence with the same tender expression and tone she would have used to help a beau too shy to ask for the next dance. "But of course I am a vampire, Monsieur le Docteur. Surely you do not think anyone as perfect as I could be mortal?"

Lavalle turned to run but his body inexplicably froze in midstride. He could not make his legs move by exertion of muscle or will. It was as if he had become completely, instantaneously paralyzed. But unlike in nightmares where Lavalle found himself unable to command his legs to work, now he could not even drag himself away from the thing he feared. He stood there, an awkwardly posed living statue, sweat trickling down his neck and the hollow of his spine. There was nothing to do but wait to see what she was going to do to him—and if Peregrine would intervene on his behalf before it was too late.

"Won't you please have a seat in the parlor, Doctor?"

Lavalle felt an invisible force jerk him back around toward the main salon, his movement a series of jerks and spasms, as if he were a marionette controlled by strings in the puppet master's hands. There was a fire burning in the fireplace. Lavalle could not turn his neck, but he saw that much from the corner of his eyes. Someone was moving back and forth, throwing things into the growing conflagration. Lavalle's body was tugged around and abruptly dropped into a chair.

The other figure was Peregrine. He ignored Lavalle, busy burning his paintings one at a time. The flames mingled the watercolors' reds and golds with the rich, sometimes lurid colors of the tropical flowers the American had learned to paint from Lady Fairweather.

Lavalle had no love left for Peregrine, yet it was excruciating to see him destroy the art he had spent so much time creating. The doctor disapproved of the American's style, but watching Peregrine burn his art was like being forced to witness Saturn devour his children. There was something almost inhumanly hateful about the act. When an artist destroys his own creations, it is akin to infanticide.

The woman moved into Lavalle's field of view. She was holding a lamp in both hands like a votive offering, the glass hurricane chimney a few inches from her face. Lavalle did not know what she intended to do with the lamp, but it made him nervous.

"Sometimes I think you are entirely driven by self-pity, Nathaniel," she said. "There is nothing easier to get than a new lover."

Peregrine did not answer or look up from his grim work. He fed another painting into the flames, squinting against the firelight as it flared brighter.

"Love is not meant for creatures like us, my darling."

The American turned toward the dwindling stack of his paintings, walking in a benumbed shuffle.

"Did you love your English wench more than your wife?"

Peregrine stopped and stood up straight, his back still to them both.

"I didn't love her more than my wife, but I did love her."

The female vampire shrieked with laughter.

"Helen and my poor wife were more alike than a monster like you could ever imagine, Delphine. They shared the same simple goodness of soul."

"Oh, do please stop! You were just like this when I found you in the French Quarter after the Confederate raiders butchered your family. Do you remember what a simpering fool you were? You were killing yourself by degrees with opium, afraid to put a gun against your head and get it over with. It is unfortunate the Change has put you beyond the influence of narcotics. You and the decadent doctor could go on quite a spree together to forget your beloved Helen."

Lavalle held his breath as Peregrine stood there, but instead of the great explosion of wrath the doctor expected, the American started again for the stack of artwork he was progressively destroying.

"If you're going to burn the pictures you painted with Lady Fairweather, get it over with!" she cried, and threw the lamp. It smashed against the wall above the fireplace, spraying burning oil and fire across the room.

Peregrine seemed undisturbed that his house was on fire until the paintings propped on the mantel burned through to reveal the oil painting behind them.

"My Matisse!" he cried, but it was already too late, the oil painting burning brilliantly as the reclining nude disappeared behind a curtain of golden flame.

The woman's response at seeing what she'd done was to burst into mad laughter.

"What fun is it to destroy if you don't destroy things that are valuable, Nathaniel? You can buy more paintings when you come back with me to Paris. I am tired of New Orleans. And besides, we have worn out our welcome there for another generation or two after our latest visit."

With growing panic Lavalle watched the flames climbing the walls, licking toward the center of the ceiling. The draperies behind Peregrine caught fire. Lavalle could feel the heat on his face from across the room.

"Why did you kill her?"

Lavalle felt a glimmer of hope. If the American regretted that Marie France had been killed by the other vampire, maybe he would protect Lavalle from the lunatic, and from the flames.

"He doesn't care about Marie, you fool," the woman mocked Lavalle. "He is talking about Lady Fairweather."

Lavalle's eyes grew wide.

"Oh, yes, you are correct: I killed Lady Fairweather, not that she was anything but as good as dead," the woman said, returning her attention to Peregrine. "I merely ended her suffering. You should thank me. If I really wanted to be cruel, I could have left her to endure the torment of having you and Dr. Lavalle moon over her in her final weeks."

"You are a horror, Delphine," Peregrine said.

"Yes," she said as if receiving a compliment. She nodded toward Lavalle. "Do you want the pleasure of killing this parasite or is he mine?"

"Let him go. There's been enough killing."

Lavalle would have thrown his arms around the American and hugged him, had he been able to move a muscle.

"You must be joking, *chéri.*"

"It is finished for me here. I have no further need of him."

Peregrine turned his hawk's face toward the doctor. He

blinked his eyes with a deliberation that reminded Lavalle of a bird of prey looking down on the world. Lavalle wondered why he had never seen the remote coldness in Peregrine's eyes before. It was like looking into the eyes of a raptor; the only thing he saw in the American's dark eyes was a sharp, predatory intelligence devoid of mercy.

"I am not taking you with me, Doctor."

"But what of your dreams of Lavalle finding a so-called cure?" Delphine Allard asked. "As if any of us would ever choose to give up power and immortality to go back to being a weak, pathetic human."

"I would have, if I could have shared mortality with Helen. I know, Lavalle, that you think unlocking the secret of what made me what I am is beyond the power of science, at least today. You thought you were using me, but it was just the reverse. My thinking was that if Helen believed you might one day find a cure, she would agree to the Change so that we could be together forever."

"She saw through your strategy," Madame Allard jeered. "She was a better chess player than either of you two men."

The fire broke through the ceiling over the fireplace. Pieces of flaming joists crashed down in a shower of sparks, the heat so fierce that Peregrine had to move away.

"The science . . ." The sound of Lavalle's own voice startled him. He could speak again! He tried to stand up, but that was still impossible. "The science," he began again, "isn't there yet. But perhaps in twenty years. Maybe fifty. If I were immortal, I could work on the problem until the solution is found for us all."

Madame Allard came closer and began to stroke the back of her fingers against the stubble of Lavalle's unshaven face.

"What do you think, Nathaniel? Should we make him a

changeling so that he can continue your insipid quest to regain your exalted status being human worm food?"

Peregrine shook his head. "Lavalle is precisely the wrong sort of person to be given a vampire's power."

"Why? Because he is so much like me—vicious, cowardly, and caring only for his own pleasure?"

The American said nothing.

"Did you know that he told Lady Fairweather the reason he had to leave France was because he'd killed a man in a duel over a woman?" She put her face directly in front of Lavalle's, so close he could feel her breath as she spoke. "Why didn't you tell her the truth? Why didn't you tell her you went on a monthlong cocaine binge and murdered your pregnant wife and your best friend after becoming so delusional you were convinced they were having an affair and planning to murder you if you didn't kill them first?"

"Please don't speak of that," Lavalle begged. The tears only added to his humiliation, but he could not bear to think about the horrible thing he'd done in Paris.

"I think Dr. Lavalle would make a *perfect* vampire, Nathaniel. Have you told him what it feels like to become drunk on the blood of human cattle?" Her eyes burned with the fire of a madness as intense as the one that was about to consume them along with the great house. "The feeling you get when you inject cocaine into your veins is *nothing* compared to the delirious bliss a vampire knows drinking blood. Shall I show you? My victims share my pleasure, at least they do until their hearts stop beating."

"Let him go, Delphine, and I will go with you to Paris or wherever you wish to go. Enough killing."

"You will?" Madame Allard sounded as excited as a child promised a treat.

Lavalle hardly noticed when his hands began to slip back from their awkward grip on the chair's arms. An almost electric shock shot through him when he realized he could move again.

The doctor was on his feet, running, even before his mind could form the intention to flee the fire and the pair of supernatural killers. The archway to the front hall was in flames. He threw his arms over his head to keep his hair from catching on fire, and soon was flinging himself down the front steps.

Napoleon! He looked frantically around, but there was no sign of his horse. Either someone had stolen him, or the beast had become frightened enough of the conflagration engulfing the house to slip his reins and run away.

Lavalle began to run down the lane.

The drumming—why did the drumming continue while Maison de la Falaise went up in flames? Did the people at the voodoo ceremony know Peregrine planned to destroy the great house and leave? Maybe they didn't care. Maybe they were *glad* the mansion was burning. If not for the infernal drumming, Lavalle would have thought them all dead.

Unless they *were* dead. Unless they were zombies.

Something gave way in Dr. Lavalle's mind and he began to shriek in animal terror as he ran through the darkness. It was not that he believed in zombies—he could barely believe in vampires, and he knew they were real—but that the science, mathematics, and physics he had used to shore up his life were falling in on themselves, the foundation of his sanity eaten away by the chaos, by the unexplained, and the unexplainable . . .

Lavalle ran screaming through the night, knowing that if vampires existed, then perhaps zombies did, too. And

even if there were no zombies, he had been proven insuf-
ferably narrow-minded and myopic to have circum-
scribed the world into small, orderly circles whose
boundaries were defined by scientific inquiry. There was
more to the world than Lavalle had dreamed of in his
mind, which lacked only for imagination.

But worst of all for Dr. Lavalle was knowing that, taking the argument to its logical conclusion (as he felt compelled, as always, to do), the existence of categories of
beings beyond the understanding of mortals meant that in
all likelihood there really was a God, somewhere out there
far, far away, at the end of all things, at the beginning of
all things. And since God existed, then it was entirely reasonable to postulate that Dr. Michael Lavalle—murderer,
drug addict, lecher, liar, fugitive, racist —was going to die
and go straight to hell.

Lavalle nearly ran into Madame Allard on the road. She
had evidently run ahead of him through the jungle with
impossible vampire speed, as Peregrine had once done,
and was now waiting, not even panting, for him.

"You didn't really think I was going to let you get
away," she said. "Nathaniel is such a weakling. He would
let you go, but I, however, am quite strict about not leaving loose ends when I finish enjoying myself and move on
to new diversions."

Lavalle pulled away when she reached for him and ran
back toward the house, his legs moving so fast that he kept
stumbling and falling forward, though he somehow managed to stay on his feet and keep moving from the horror
behind. He could hear her back there, laughing. She could
catch him whenever she wanted, but it amused her to toy
with him, like a cat playing with a mouse, prolonging the
act of killing for sheer perverse enjoyment.

The flaming great house appeared out of the trees, first as a brilliant light above the leafy canopy, then in its entire horrible blazing glory. The structure was fully wrapped in flames that danced and jumped into the overarching darkness. There was no escape for Lavalle there.

Peregrine sat on the bottom step of the porch, oblivious to the inferno behind him, head in hands, eyes downcast, ignoring the smoke coming off the back of his smoldering jacket.

"Help me!" Lavalle shouted, but the American did not even look up.

She was close behind him now, so the doctor had no choice but to keep running. The fire illuminated the rim of the cliff ahead, beyond it a yawning abyss that concealed the long drop to the rocks and water below. Lavalle had a fleeting, desperate idea to stop at the last possible moment and see the monster hurtle past him, but he was running too fast. Madame Allard's fevered fingers reached out to lightly brush his neck over his jugular as Lavalle felt himself hurtle over the edge.

There was the sickening sensation of falling, and the vomit rising, when something smashed into Lavalle from behind.

He instinctively knew, in that split second, that Delphine had thrown herself after him, unafraid of the fall, knowing that not even the screaming drop to the rocks below could end her demonic existence.

In his last moment of life, as the rocks loomed boldly into his vision, blotting out everything else—dark, jagged, unforgiving—Dr. Lavalle felt the vampire's teeth tear savagely into his neck. There was a short, sharp eruption of bliss seemingly as powerful as a star exploding into nova, and after that . . .

Nothing.

PART THREE

SAN FRANCISCO

The Present

27

The Cage Club

IT WAS A rainy night on a dirty, litter-strewn street of San Francisco. The closed factories and shuttered warehouses had been slated for gentrification a few years earlier, before the Internet bubble burst. The pricey apartment lofts and hip advertising agencies decorated in industrial chic were still only blueprints tucked away in a filing cabinet in the office of a real-estate developer one step ahead of bankruptcy. The buildings on McKennit Street remained empty, the broken windows boarded up, steel accordion gates padlocked across entries to keep out transients. But the homeless and lawless looking for something to steal or smash had learned to stay away from McKennit Street. The neighborhood belonged to the Ravening Brood, and they had a reputation for dealing harshly with trespassers.

A young woman walked boldly down the deserted street, oblivious to the grim atmosphere. She was tall, nearly six feet in her bare feet, with the lithe, willowy body of a ballerina. She wore her long hair down; the color appeared to be black, but when she passed beneath the streetlamp, the light reflecting up off the wet pavement revealed the deep purple highlights. Her face was narrow and intelligent, with classic high cheekbones and a noble forehead above her large, luminous eyes. Her skin was pale, as if the only natural light that ever touched it came from the moon and stars.

The girl's manner of dress was eccentric, as if part of her wardrobe was from the closet of a Victorian lady, the rest from a gypsy's caravan. Her black ankle-length skirt nearly concealed the high-heeled boots, which served only to accentuate her height and angularity. The long-sleeved blouse, also black, was held closed at the throat by an antique cameo. Her fringed silk shawl was decorated in reds, purples, and blues, an elaborate Oriental pattern. As cold rain began to fall again from the night sky, she clasped the wrap more tightly around her, the finger tendons standing out more sharply against the soft flesh on the back of her hand. She wore silver rings on all her fingers and both thumbs, and her nails were painted with black lacquer. The ankh pendant around her neck was silver, as were the half-dozen smaller Celtic and traditional crosses. The dozens of bangles and bracelets on her wrists were silver, too. She wore only silver jewelry. Black, silver, and bloodred—those were Ophelia's colors.

The girl stopped to open her umbrella as the rain began to pelt harder. A rat stuck its head out of a hole gnawed in a corner of disintegrating plywood over a doorway. The rodent squeaked at her. That made her smile, because it reminded her of the line of poetry about dead men who lost their bones in the rats' alley.

The black rain came down hard enough to wash some of the trash from the street and sidewalks, the runoff flowing filthy in the gutters. Ophelia stepped over a foul rivulet and entered a narrow alley that dead-ended in a brick wall. Halfway to the end, just past a reeking Dumpster overflowing with beer cans, wine bottles, and fast-food garbage, was a steel door that slid open sideways along an overhead track. The handwritten sign on the door

decorated with a skull and crossbones warned trespassers
that survivors would be prosecuted.

The door opened with a shriek of rusty metal.

Ophelia stepped inside.

The door slammed closed behind her.

The only light inside came from a ten-watt bulb on the
other side of a grate, making the light splay out in bars
across the floor. A deep pulse came up through the con-
crete floor, like a leviathan's heartbeat or the sound of a
sinister machine at work deep in the bowels of the earth.
Ophelia felt it through the soles of her boots as she went
to the freight elevator and bent for the greasy rope to raise
the gate of vertical wooden slats.

She was going down. She stabbed the button marked
basement. The elevator, its ancient electric motor long in
need of service, shuddered to life with a loud hum and the
smell of ozone, and began its descent.

The cavernous cellar stretched out into a vast darkness
interrupted by bits of red glow shining through the holes
in the brick walls near the ceiling where the water pipes
and heating and electrical conduits ran. The building had
once been the warehouse for a downtown department
store that had gone out of business when Eisenhower was
president. Beyond the first few rooms, which were filled
with boxes and bales of crumbling business documents,
the cellar expanded into a large room that had been divided into a series of cages where merchandise was once
organized. Some were filled with old store display cases
or broken office furniture, others with battered man-
nequins posed in ways that were intended to represent
various sex acts.

The music became progressively louder as the elevator
carried Ophelia to the lower level. It was the metallic

sound of synthesizers programmed to suggest music
made by machines untouched by human emotion, except
perhaps for angst and rage—industrial Goth music.

Ophelia exited the elevator and strode through the dark
passageways, knowing the way as well as any. Some of
the cages she passed were strewn with garbage, others
outfitted for ritual purposes. There was the Initiation
Cage, the Transformation Cage, the Judgment Cage.
Some of the cages were purely for fun and games and
equipped with chains, shackles, cables, transformers, and
wires for electrical sex play, restraints, whips, clips, ropes,
and nooses. Some of the cages had mattresses on the floor
where the fledglings—but usually only the females—had
to submit to the pleasure of master vampires. Ophelia had
put an end to that, once she took over the Brood. The mattresses still got their share of use, especially on weekend
nights when there was X in the Cage Club and dancing
sometimes degenerated into spontaneous orgies. Ophelia
remained aloof from such activities. She didn't care for
drugs and was mostly indifferent to sex. But mainly, being
Brood Mistress required her to maintain a certain distance
from the other vampires.

The Brood was gathered in the Great Hall, an open area
at the back of the basement from which the cages had
been ripped out. The room was bathed in red and green
light. A powerful strobe light was trained on the platform
along the rear wall that held the speakers and music gear.
Zeke was running sound, a spectral form in a floor-length
black trench coat looking even more sinister than usual in
the flickering light. Next to the sound platform, pressed
into the corner was the boiler, a hulking contraption
sprouting ductwork that made it look like a giant spider
lurking in the shadows.

The way the other vampires whispered to one another

when Ophelia strode into the middle of the room made her immediately suspicious. She was always on the lookout for treachery. If there was one thing you could always count on in a Ravening Brood, it was that somebody ambitious and evil was always ready to overthrow the Brood Master or Mistress and seize power. Broods were governed according to a strict hierarchy, like the Jesuit brotherhood on which they were patterned with a consciously perverse irony. Though others held authority commensurate with their rank, with the fledgling vampires at the very bottom of the pecking order, ultimately the individual Brood members were scarcely more than slaves relegated to serving the Master's or Mistress's desires.

Ophelia looked at Zeke through narrowing eyes, which was the only thing she needed to do to get him to turn down the music so that she could hear herself think. Her own taste in music ran toward classical, but she would never have expected the Ravening crowd, by and large a rough, crude group, to appreciate true beauty.

Her eyes went from one vampire to the next as she joined them in the middle of the room. Conspiracy was definitely afoot. She could smell it on them. In mortal life, she had been born with Chiron conjunct with Pluto, which made her unusually psychic. Ophelia slipped her hand into her antique beaded purse, reaching for the death talisman. Whoever was planning to depose her would pay dearly for the mistake.

"Surprise!"

Ophelia had to stare at the grinning idiots for a few moments before seeing the cake on the table. It was shaped like the ankh Ophelia always wore around her neck, the black icing decorated with bloodred candles.

"Happy birthday, Mistress!"

A fledgling named Letitia, who imagined herself a

favorite of the Mistress, put her arms around Ophelia. Ophelia stood there stiff, barely tolerating the expression of affection.

"I told you she wouldn't like it."

Blade was grinning at her, enjoying her discomfiture. He knew her better than the others. They had once been lovers, when he was Brood Master, before Ophelia deposed him. He was lucky she hadn't made the Brood shun him—or worse—she thought, not for the first time regretting the mercy she'd shown him.

"There is nothing happy about me," Ophelia said. "Not today. Not ever."

"I told them vampires don't celebrate birthdays," said Damien, a fledgling who obviously regretted that he had been pulled into this embarrassing charade by Letitia and her lover, Pendragon.

"The undead have no need for sentimental gestures," Ophelia said.

Letitia and Pendragon edged back away from her, unable to look at the others after their blunder. But Damien was the one Ophelia wanted to eviscerate most. He had been part of their silly plot to ingratiate themselves with the Mistress, but now he thought he could turn on his fellow conspirators and escape her wrath. Ophelia would make the others pay in time, but Damien would pay the dearest price. He would never gain admission into the Brood when his apprenticeship in vampirey was over.

"Come on, Ophelia, lighten up," Blade said in a condescending voice. "It's your eighteenth birthday. You're *legal* now."

Ophelia's hand clenched around the death talisman, but something told her to let the insult go. She would deal with Blade, too, but in her own time. She didn't like to use her power in showy, indiscriminate ways. That led to resentment, and resentment led to cabals and combinations and plots. Ophelia could never forget that Blade's high-handedness with the Brood had led to his own downfall—as well as to her own elevation to Mistress of the Ravening Brood.

"I appreciate the gesture." She smiled at Letitia. "The black icing is lovely."

"It's chocolate heavily dosed with food coloring," Pendragon said.

"But nothing else," Letitia said.

"Thank you, Letitia and Pendragon," Ophelia said, pointedly ignoring Damien. She could feel the third fledgling's psychic withdrawal from her presence. He *knew* he was dead meat to her. If there was anything Ophelia despised more than treachery aimed against her rule over the Brood, it was someone who thought he could get away with manipulating her.

"It would be a shame to let the cake go to waste," Ophelia said with carefully contrived good humor. "It will go well with a nice glass of blood."

28

Dr. Glass

THE AIR IN the ECT room smelled of disinfectant and alcohol. The room was unusually chilly even for the hospital, which tended to be over-air-conditioned in summer and overheated in winter.

There were three people in the room. Standing and looking over a clipboard with a Montblanc pen was Dr. Lucian Glass. A Filipino nurse named Emerlinda Vicenceo stood beside the ECT machine. She was there to assist Dr. Glass, if need be, though the psychiatrist generally preferred to do things for himself. The last member of the trio was the twenty-two-year-old woman strapped to the treatment table. Candy Priddle wore only a hospital smock. There were goose bumps on her bare legs and arms, and Dr. Glass wondered if they were from cold, from fear, or a combination of the two.

"We're going to give you an IV that will make you more comfortable. You're not afraid of needles are you?"

The young woman shook her head. She was skinny and had an overbite. Dr. Glass had first seen the tattoo above her breast when she put on the smock in the emergency room, where she'd been brought in for swallowing a bottle of aspirin. Then she was wearing a dirty "wife-beater" T-shirt and cutoff jeans that rode so high on her legs that her underwear was all that kept her decent as she lolled on the examination table. Dr. Glass had taken one look at the way she was dressed, and her limp, dishwater-blond hair, and guessed that the girl was pure trailer trash. Candy's manner of speaking—she could barely get a sentence out without using a double negative or committing some other grammatical travesty—proved the case. The psychiatrist thought he had an uncanny ability in a quick glance to judge a patient's socioeconomic niche. He was a real-life Henry Higgins, he was.

"We're going to start off with something to make you relaxed," Dr. Glass said, speaking in his smooth, sonorous voice while he introduced the liquid Valium into the IV drip. "You're going to like this, Candy. You're going to say, 'I want some more of this, Dr. Glass.' If you're a good girl, we'll see what we can do."

The tranquilizing effect was instantaneous. The frightened-rabbit look went out of Candy's eyes, replaced with the stupefied expression of compliance. If Nurse Emerlinda hadn't been present, Dr. Glass could have done whatever he wanted to the girl, even if she wasn't strapped securely to a rubber-wheeled body cart. Candy Priddle had been hospitalized for the suicide attempt, but Dr. Glass's larger diagnosis was that she suffered from bipolar disorder. After nearly six months of treating the young woman, he knew that in her manic phases she was prone to aggressive nymphomania. She had undergone more abortions than any patient Dr. Glass had ever treated. He had had her tested several times for AIDS, but to his amazement she had avoided it, though she'd fallen prey to several other sexually transmitted diseases in the time she'd been his patient.

"Some doctors would give you a general anesthetic for this procedure, Candy, but I find the treatments are much more effective if you are in what we call twilight sleep.

You're awake but you're not awake. Do you understand?"

The girl on the gurney tried to smile.

The door opened and in came a brisk-looking middle-aged woman wearing a crisp navy blue suit.

"Ah, Margeaux."

"I just want to put you on formal notice, Dr. Glass. I am opposed to this course of treatment for Candy."

Candy's head—he hadn't put on the head restraint yet—fell drunkly to the side so that she could grin up at Margeaux Lloyd.

"I am well aware of your feelings, Margeaux," Dr. Glass went on in his unctuous voice. He was not in the least threatened by Candy Priddle's caseworker. "With all due respect, I am the one with an M.D. after my name. As much as I hate to pull rank, I am the psychiatrist, you are the psychiatric social worker."

"We should discuss this in the hall."

"She won't remember a thing, Margeaux. Trust me."

"My point exactly."

"Such hostility. It's not really your style, is it?"

"No." He noted his antagonist's inner collapse with secret triumph. He could have her job for this kind of effrontery. He even had a witness: Emerlinda Vicenceo.

It was easy to be magnanimous. Dr. Glass held all the cards, the physician's authority sacrosanct. "The management of Candy's case is my responsibility. Once I get her stabilized, you can go back to trying to keep her on a steady keel with weekly counseling sessions."

"The FDA classifies an ECT as a Type-Three device—the highest-risk category."

"Electroconvulsive therapy is safe and effective," Dr. Glass said. "I have been administering these treatments for years."

"The Benedict and Saks study found that ninety percent

of the patients getting ETC received inappropriate treatments," Margeaux said. "Death, brain damage, seizures, epilepsy, and memory loss are all possible side effects."

Emerlinda Vicenceo's wary eyes went back and forth between them both. She didn't want to be a part of this. As much as Dr. Glass wanted to put the mere M.S.W. in her place, he knew the better strategy was to remain aloof. Perhaps it had been her intention all along to provoke him into losing his temper in front of the nurse, hoping to use it against him.

"If the surgeon general certifies the treatment as safe and effective, that's good enough for me," he said with the same patience. "Now unless you intend to interfere with Miss Priddle's physician of record—which I don't have to tell you would be a very serious disciplinary matter for the licensing board to consider—I suggest you disengage. You're quite welcome to stay if you want. If you observed a few of these procedures, you'd see how harmless they really are."

But Margeaux was already on her way out of the room.

"I'm going to give you a little succinylcholine chloride," Dr. Glass said, turning his attention back to his patient. "It will relax your muscles. Back in the days before we learned to give muscle-paralyzing drugs, ECT patients sometimes convulsed so violently that they broke their bones. Some even broke their backs."

Dr. Glass looked up to see the nurse frowning at him.

"I'm always completely frank with my patients," he said. "I treat them like adults. Not that Candy has any idea what I'm talking about. How are you doing, my dear? Are you doing okay?"

The young woman blinked, but she probably wasn't paying any attention to what he was saying.

"I'm going to put a strap over your forehead to keep you

from hurting your neck." Dr. Glass slipped the heavy leather strap through the buckle and cinched it snug. "You can put the salve on now, Nurse."

Emerlinda applied the conductive graphite compound to both temples of the girl's head.

"Some doctors only use one electrode, but I prefer the bilateral approach. That way we treat both hemispheres of the brain equally."

"How many volts, Dr. Glass?"

"Let's start Candy out with three hundred volts for two-point-five seconds."

The nurse repeated the formulary as she set the dials, and Dr. Glass nodded confirmation.

"Bite down on this rubber, my dear. It will keep you from swallowing your tongue." Dr. Glass worked the bit into Candy's mouth. She resisted a little but was conscious enough to know that she had no choice but to do what he commanded.

Dr. Glass went over to the control and put his finger over the button. "We're going to give you three treatments today, Candy. There will be about five minutes between treatments, but after the first one, you probably won't be aware of what's happening. Are you ready?"

Dr. Glass activated the electrical current without waiting for a sign of readiness from the woman. It was only a rhetorical question, after all. Whether or not she was ready to have a jolt of electricity sent through her brain was of no consequence whatsoever to the psychiatrist. Candy Priddle's body lurched violently upward against the restraints, her eyes bulging from the fire consuming her brain from within until it seemed they would pop out of their orbits. The shock lasted only a brief moment—far too brief to suit Dr. Glass's personal tastes. She fell back, limp, unconscious, a heavy sweat soaking her face and making the cotton hospital smock cling to the erect nipples on her breasts. She wouldn't move again until he turned the electricity back on.

The gown had pushed up over her pelvis during the first treatment, revealing the patch of dirty-blond hair between her thighs. Dr. Glass had a vision of Candy nailed to a cross, which he quickly shook off. The psychiatrist made sure the white doctor's jacket was arranged to hide his reaction before turning to the nurse.

"Do you have anything fun planned for the weekend, Emerlinda?" he asked. "Some gardening perhaps? The weather has been lovely."

"My mother is coming over, and we're going to plan the reception," she replied. Candy Priddle was forgotten as soon as she began to update Dr. Glass on her wedding plans.

Dr. Glass returned to his office with plenty of time to fix a nice cup of tea before his one o'clock appointment. He was a punctual man and demanded the same of others, including his patients, as a simple matter of courtesy and respect. The exact moment the numbers on his digital clock clicked over at the top of the hour, his receptionist phoned to say his next patient was ready; the clocks in his office were synchronized with the one in the waiting room.

"It is good to meet you, Miss Warring," the psychiatrist said, standing up to meet the girl. "I am Dr. Glass."

The young woman nodded briskly but did not extend her hand. Dr. Glass never made the first move with his patients. Not in the beginning, anyway.

"Please make yourself comfortable."

The oddly dressed young woman did a quick survey of the office, which was decorated with the same spare modern elegance as a psychiatrist's office in Copenhagen that Dr. Glass had seen pictures of in *Architectural Digest*.

"Should I sit on the chair or the couch?"

"Whichever makes you feel more comfortable, Miss Warring."

"Ah." Her eyes flicked in his direction, the gesture made more dramatic by the almost theatrical use of eye shadow applied in the manner of a princess from ancient Egypt. "The first test."

Dr. Glass smiled back at her. "The second, actually." There was no point denying it. The school counselor said she was an exceptionally intelligent young lady.

"And what was the first? Something about the way I walked into the room, or was it that I didn't offer to shake hands."

"Very good, Miss Warring. But please do be seated."

She went to the couch, which was shaped like a lazy *S* perched on four narrow chrome posts. Though she didn't look in his direction, Dr. Glass was aware that she was monitoring how he was watching her as she lay back and draped her legs—hidden in a long black skirt and spike-heel boots—upon the couch. The many silver bracelets on her wrists clinked softly as she made herself comfortable.

"Do you mind if I call you Mary Beth?"

Dr. Glass heard her suck in the breath between her teeth. "Yes, I would mind. I would mind it very much. My name is Ophelia."

Dr. Glass nodded pleasantly and leaned back. The chair he was in was larger and more authoritarian looking than the one the patients used, if they were too insecure to indulge in the soft, Freudian comfort of the couch. Dr. Glass adjusted his half-moon reading glasses and read the tab on folder. His receptionist had dutifully labeled it *Warring, Mary Beth*. Which was as it should be. Mary

Beth *was* Ophelia's birth name, and her legal name, as far as that went. But what was a name if not a label that could be changed whenever it suited you? The thought that he could get up one day and simply decide to be someone else had a certain appeal to Dr. Glass. He opened the folder and scanned the school psychologist's evaluation. The report, which was laughably facile, was also sadly typical.

"Are you waiting for me to explain about my name?"

"Hmm?" Dr. Glass looked up from his reading. The girl was lying there with her eyes closed, her body language telling him that she was perfectly at ease, which was certainly not what he usually encountered with new patients. "No, not particularly."

"Good. I find it boring to talk about. Most people don't ask me about it anymore, though it was of obvious interest to the school shrink. I suppose that's all in the paperwork you've been reading."

Dr. Glass smiled, closed the folder. He leaned back and crossed his legs. A minute went by in silence. Then two. Then three.

"Are you awake, Ophelia?"

"Yes."

"I was just checking. I thought that maybe you'd drifted off."

"I'm perfectly content to lie here quietly until my half hour is up, Dr. Glass."

"My time is rather expensive for that, but if that's what pleases you."

A smile flickered over her lips, which were painted in lipstick of such a deep purple that they seemed almost black.

"Why did you decide to call yourself Ophelia?"

The girl sighed.

"You're a fan of Shakespeare, I suspect, though I doubt you would have been any more happy with Hamlet than the Ophelia in the play."

"Very good, Dr. Glass. One point for you."

"Ultimately we all invent ourselves, though most people aren't as cognizant of the fact as you. Or as bold about the persona they create to inhabit."

"There is no need to be condescending, Doctor."

"I meant it. Your manner of dress—it's very striking, if I may say so."

"Thank you."

"What do the others your age at the high school think of it?"

"Who gives a fuck?"

Dr. Glass nodded.

"How long have you been a Goth?"

The question displeased her.

"And I would guess that your name, Ophelia, has as much to do with the vampire role-playing game you're involved in as it does with your interest in Shakespeare and poetry in general."

That got her attention, Dr. Glass noted with satisfaction, seeing her posture stiffen.

"It's not a game."

The psychiatrist gave her anger a full minute to subside.

"What is it about vampires that fascinates you most, Ophelia?"

"The darkness. They're all about darkness. Darkness and blood."

"Most people are repelled by blood."

"Not me." She smiled, her eyes still closed. "Blood is power."

"Did you start dressing like a Goth and become interested in vampires about the time your mother died last year?"

The girl laughed, but without joy, and looked across at him. "That is such a pathetically obvious question, Dr. Glass. But I have a question for you: Why were you staring at my breasts?"

"I wasn't," Dr. Glass replied smoothly. "I was, however, admiring the collection of crosses you have around your neck. The ankh is the ancient Egyptian symbol for eternal life, but then I'm sure you know that. But the crosses—I thought vampires had an aversion to crosses."

"That's an old wives' tale, like the idea vampires can't go out in the sunlight and have to sleep in coffins. Vampires don't sleep in coffins because they have to, Dr. Glass. They sleep in coffins because they like it."

"You don't look as if you get a lot of sun, Ophelia."

"I'm a night person."

She was actually rather attractive, despite the bizarre getup, Dr. Glass noted. Her body was better suited to the ballet, or even modeling, than to slouching around with a bunch of punked-out losers. But there was something about the whole package—her looks, her clothing, her intelligence, her defiance. She seemed plugged into something primal—dark, but primal.

"Have you ever heard of the Shadow, Ophelia?"

"I'm not stupid, Dr. Glass. I know about Jung. Not a lot, but some."

"Of course."

She looked over at him again, interested in spite of herself. "Do you believe in the collective unconscious, the animus, the Shadow, and all of that?"

"Jung certainly has an interesting way of looking at the human psyche. I don't know if myth has as much power over our lives as he argues, but it's certainly possible. What do you think about it?"

"I think that I have decided to become my own Shadow."

Dr. Glass leaned forward slightly. "Really?"

"There's no point denying our darkness. The only way to be truly free is to cross to the Shadowside and take responsibility for the pain, the decay, the death. Others deny these ultimate realities. We celebrate them."

The Shadowside, Dr. Glass thought, smiling to himself. The term was from the vampire game Ophelia was wrapped up in, reality and illusion blurred in her depressed late-adolescent mind. The young woman would benefit from medication, perhaps even from a course of electroconvulsive therapy.

But still, Dr. Glass thought, there was a certain primitive aspect—even archetypal, on a Jungian level—to what she said. He was interested in learning more about the Ravening, this decadent children's supernatural playacting game. But most of all, Dr. Glass was interested in learning more about Ophelia, queen of the local undead.

29
Hauntings

OPHELIA WAS THE fifth generation of her family to live in the big Victorian house on Mulberry Street. Her great-grandfather Jonas Warring bought the house in 1919. He had been a lawyer whose expertise was water rights. Jonas Warring made a fortune arguing on behalf of railroad interests and against ranchers and small towns in the West, where everything depended upon water access.

The rambling three-story manse was perched at a seemingly precarious angle on a steep hill, like the houses built along the street rising sharply up from the waterfront. The house had a view of the San Francisco Bay, Alcatraz Island, and Oakland at the other end of the Bay Bridge, when fog didn't obscure the view. Ophelia's grandfather had been born in the house on Mulberry Street, though Ophelia's father had come into the world the modern way, in a hospital delivery room. In one of those reversals of convention that seem odd in some places but not in California, Ophelia was born at home, with the help of a midwife. Ophelia's mother had always disliked hospitals, perhaps because she psychically intuited the horrible end she would suffer, hooked up to all those hoses and machines during her last tortured weeks of life.

The Warring residence had fallen into disrepair. Old homes require constant attention, and it had been several

229

years since Stephen Warring, Ophelia's father, had stopped caring about that sort of thing. The windows were streaked with grime, and paint was starting to peel on the eaves. The decorative planters along the front of the house, where Ophelia's mother had planted colorful annuals each spring while she was still alive, were a tangle of dead vegetation and scraps of windblown trash.

Like flies to spilled soda pop, houses showing distress in fashionable San Francisco neighborhoods attract a steady stream of realtors, developers, speculators, and young professionals searching for a bargain. Ophelia had learned to spot them from her bedroom window as they stood on the porch, looking earnest and hopeful; she no longer bothered to answer the door when they rang the bell. The business cards and notes they left stuck in the doorjamb contributed to the litter that collected around the foundation.

The problem wasn't financial. Though Stephen Warring no longer kept office hours at the law firm his grandfather founded, he still had plenty of money. The explanation was that he had stopped caring. The condition of the house was the outward sign of a collapse not of the financial kind, but rather one of the will—a withdrawal from the world of appearances and everyday concerns. The disease Stephen Warring suffered from was not one of the body, like the cancer that had claimed the life of his wife and knocked him from his position as one of the town's prominent citizens, but rather a sickness of the soul.

Ophelia suffered from the same affliction, although the symptoms were entirely different from her father's.

Dusk was gathering as Ophelia turned up the sidewalk to her house. She was dressed in her usual Goth attire. She had attracted a lot of stares—and derisive comments—

when she changed her name and became a child of the night, but the people in her neighborhood and at the exclusive private school she attended had grown used to it and now barely gave her a sidelong glance.

There was a Prada backpack slung over her shoulder, an accoutrement from her previous life that she sometimes still used because of its functionality. Inside the pack was her digital camera and a black leather book of unlined paper she used to write poetry and random observations about life. *The Book of Lies,* she called it.

Directly across Mulberry Street from the Warrings' was a house that truly was abandoned, though it wouldn't have attracted more than a glance by a realtor cruising by in a BMW, looking for fixer-uppers. The house at 1666 Mulberry Street had sat empty for all eighteen years of Ophelia's lives—her life as Ophelia, and before that, her other life, the ordinary one, which had been filled with fear, helplessness, and despair. The Haunted House, as Ophelia had always known it, was empty of inhabitants but not of furniture. She had peeked through the windows on many occasions at the elegant old-fashioned furniture, the oil paintings on the walls—nineteenth-century landscapes, she guessed—and plants. One of the city's more aggressive security firms maintained the burglar alarm and patrolled the property at night, a side benefit for the neighborhood, which remained remarkably free of the usual urban mischief. A cleaning crew came by every two weeks to dust, and a plant maintenance van stopped by slightly more often to take care of the ferns, rubber plants, and big jade plant that sat in the front hall and must have been more than a hundred years old, judging by its carefully manicured size.

The house was never visited by its owner.

Ophelia's mother had told her a trust maintained the

property. Its owners were apparently too wealthy and busy to visit the home. Or maybe, Ophelia thought, they were all dead, and there was nothing left but the trust, using the proceeds of some careful investment to maintain a simulacrum of life in the house long after its owners had surrendered to death and decay.

The house across from Ophelia's was haunted. Everybody said so. Even her mother. The house's ghost was a sea captain who had grown rich on voyages to the Far East back in the days when ships were powered by sails. The captain was a sad figure, a man whose family had been killed during the Civil War. Ophelia had seen evidence of the haunting on several occasions over the years. There were lights in the upper rooms—not electric lights, but more like candles, as if the ghost made his visits by the light of an earlier century, when people relied on whale-oil lamps and tallow candles to see after dark.

Growing up across the street from the Haunted House had shaped Ophelia's imagination as a child. She began to consciously collect San Francisco ghost stories when she was thirteen. She knew all about the Bleeding Staircase and the Knocking Crypt, as well as many more obscure occurrences known mainly to the local cognoscenti of the supernatural. Ophelia sometimes took her friends on walking tours of the city's haunted places. For the past year, she had maintained a Web site devoted to local hauntings. The site grew week by week, with new stories and photos, the collection of which had taken Ophelia abroad on her present mission. A tour company had offered her a job leading after-dark tours, but she had no need of money, and no interest in interacting with tourists and other ordinary mortals.

*   *   *

The house was dark when Ophelia unlocked the door and went inside.

The foyer had a musty smell, the floor littered with un-opened mail and newspapers still wrapped in plastic de-livery bags. The *Chronicles* and *Wall Street Journals* were all at least six months old, the unread newsprint turn-ing brittle and brown. Ophelia had canceled the subscrip-tions. There was no point having newspapers clutter up the hall if her father was just going to drop them on the floor when he came and went on his infrequent trips away from the house. Ophelia sometimes thought about bag-ging them up as garbage, along with the rest of it, but she let it be. It was her father's business, not hers.

Stephen Warring was sprawled forward across the kitchen table, an empty vodka bottle and a tumbler near his hand. He did not move when Ophelia turned on the light. She stood in the doorway long enough to assure herself that he was still breathing before filling the teakettle on the big Viking chef's stove to make herself a cup of herbal tea. Ophelia straightened up a bit while waiting for the wa-ter to boil. A dirty kitchen was the one thing she could not abide. Her mother had loved to cook, and the room had al-ways been spotless when she was alive. The kettle began to whistle. Her father did not stir. She could have set the house on fire and he wouldn't have budged. If she did set the place on fire, she might be doing them both a favor.

Ophelia turned off the fire, finished loading the dish-washer, put in some soap, and started it. She got down a saucer and china cup—her mother had insisted on drink-ing tea and coffee from china cups—put a bag of Red Zinger into the cup, and added water. She gathered up her pack and tea and paused long enough to put her hand gen-tly on her father's shoulder. He did not stir. He was too drunk to go to his bed, and even if Ophelia could get him to wake up, he was too big for her to help him up the stairs.

Ophelia kissed him on the back of the head, turned out the kitchen light, and went upstairs in the dark.

While her tea cooled, Ophelia transferred the digital photos from the camera into her computer.

The only evidence of Gothic preoccupation in the young woman's bedroom was Ophelia herself and the Victorian mourning clothes she affected. The room remained exactly as it had been when her mother died during Ophelia's sophomore year of high school. She and her mother had decorated it together; they picked out the wallpaper and drapes, went shopping for the desk and matching bookcases, now loaded down with books, all of which Ophelia had read, some of them many times. It was not a feminine room in the exaggerated way some parents do up their daughters' bedrooms. Ophelia had never been that kind of girl. Even as a child, she had sensible, mature tastes. Her room, as she and her mother had decorated it, looked more like the home of a studious college-age woman with aspirations of becoming a poet—which had been Ophelia's intention since she started to write couplet verses in first grade.

Ophelia had changed, but her room had not. She kept it as it was as a sort of monument to her past life. Being in the room was like being in her own tomb, but it was oddly reassuring. No doubt it had something to do with the reason spirits of the departed remained behind in the place where they had once been alive and happy.

The only purely girlish icon in the room was the princess doll her mother had given her one year for Christmas. It was gorgeous and had cost a small fortune. The doll was kept in a place of honor on the dresser, a glass case protecting its elaborate white satin gown from dust. Beneath the expansive full-length skirt and ruffled petticoats was a full bottle of Demerol. Ophelia had taken the bottle from her mother's room after they took her to the hospital to die. Sometime, when she could stand the pain no longer, Ophelia would swallow the bottle's contents and become a ghost herself.

Earlier that day, after school and her visit to Dr. Glass, she'd taken a taxi to a private Episcopal school where the chapel was haunted. There were nuns buried in the chapel basement, and according to rumor, baby bones were buried there, too. In a rare stroke of luck, Ophelia had managed to take a dozen interior photos of the chapel before a teacher discovered her and asked her to leave. That was a coup, even if she was disappointed that she hadn't been able to find the door leading down to the crypt.

The images flew into the Mac G3, and she processed the best pictures in PhotoShop and had them up on the Web in no time. Computers were Ophelia's one material vice. She had to have the newest and fastest.

When she was finished, she took out her journal and her favorite antique fountain pen and got ready to write some poetry in her *Book of Lies*. She was tempted to start out, *Dr. Glass, the fatuous ass . . .* —but that was far too obvious. She closed her eyes and waited for the muse to come to her. There was strange energy in the air that night. The house on Mulberry Street was even sadder than usual.

She leaned over the *Book of Lies* and wrote:

> *All houses are haunted,*
> *And in every past there is a ghost.*

A light went on across the street.

Ophelia looked up, her Egyptian-mascara eyes wide as

she pushed away from her desk and went to the window, the black onyx pen still in her hand. Across the street, a light had been switched on in an upstairs bedroom at 1666 Mulberry Street.

A ghost, Ophelia thought, but then she saw the silhouette of a man move past the window, a shape far too well defined, she thought, to be a specter.

Someone was in the Haunted House, someone alive and breathing.

Perhaps its owner had at long last returned home.

30
The Graveyard

JANET WARRING SLEPT beneath a tombstone carved from
Paradise Black Marble, the trade name for calcitic marble quarried in Canada. Her daughter had picked the
monument from a catalog at the St. Regis & Eberhart
Mortuary. Ophelia's father had been too deranged with
grief to look after the arrangements, so it was up to their
only child, then a sophomore in high school, to meet with
the mortician and plan Janet Warring's funeral.

Ophelia chose what the catalog called a "companion
marker," a double-wide headstone with ample room for
her parents' names, birth, and death dates. The funeral director, a sympathetic young gay woman in a navy blue
wool pant suit, had approved of Ophelia's choice of black
marble, which she termed "tasteful." She did not try to
talk Ophelia out of buying the largest tombstone available
without special order, a monument that was five feet wide,
three feet six inches high, and eight inches thick. The
price, $6,088, included engraving the stone with the fam-
ily name, the given names for her mother and father, the
dates bracketing their time in the world of the living, and
a twenty-five-word "endearment phrase" for each parent.
The funeral director had suggested *Beloved Wife and
Mother* on Janet Warring's half of the marker, but Ophelia had something different in mind. She had already

decided on a quotation from "Adonais," Shelley's ode to the dead poet Keats. The words carved into the rock over her mother's bones were these: *Awaken'd from the Dream of Life.* Ophelia and her father were still trapped in life's nightmare, but her mother had "awaken'd."

The headstone sat on a rectangular marble base in a pleasant, shaded part of the cemetery. When she arrived for her Sunday afternoon visit, Ophelia put a single rose on top of the tombstone before spreading a light blanket on the grass over the grave. She arranged a row of votive candles along the stone base. As she crouched on her knees, the grass felt thick and rich beneath her. When she was at the cemetery, sitting on her mother's grave, she had nearly the same sense of security that she remembered from when she was a little girl, sitting on her mother's lap.

Ophelia took out *The Book of Lies* and put it on the blanket in front of her. She liked to read the poetry she was working on to her mother, the same as she had done when Janet Warring was still alive. Tucked inside the journal was a letter with the return address of the admissions office at Smith College printed on it. She took it out and propped it up against the headstone behind the candles. Ophelia's mother had graduated from Smith. The women's college had the reputation for being one of the best places for a young poet to spread her wings. Sylvia Plath had gone to Smith, and her journals and handwritten drafts of poetry were part of the school's collection.

Plath was one of Ophelia's icons. They had more than a few things in common. Like Plath, Ophelia earned an early reputation for brilliance, had a passion for poetry, and experienced periods of soaring aspirations for the highest levels of success that alternated with bleak episodes of the darkest despair.

And, of course, Plath had committed suicide. Ophelia intended to do the same, when the time was ripe.

She sat cross-legged on her mother's grave for ten minutes, communing with her mother's memory, summoning—she hoped—her mother's spirit from out of the earth or down from the sky or wherever it was your energy went when it was finally freed from being shackled to a dying animal.

"I know you wanted this even more than I, so I waited to share it with you," Ophelia finally said, indicating the letter from Smith.

"My test scores were good, as you know. And I've kept my grades up. I promised you I would. To tell you the truth, it wasn't all that difficult. Everything is so dumbed down. I haven't kept up with the extracurricular activities—student senate, the debate team, the volunteering, and the rest of the things I used to do. I haven't been able to make myself do it. That might make a difference. It's not enough to be smart; you have to be socially engaged in the politically correct fashion. But maybe I can rest on my laurels. I used to do a lot. But I just couldn't put up with the hypocrisy anymore. And the futility. What difference does it make if everything you care about can be destroyed, lost, taken away?"

The flames on the votive candles danced as the breeze came up, the only answer Ophelia would get from the beyond.

"I might as well get it over with."

Ophelia held the letter up to the light so she could see the outline of the paper inside the envelope. Smith was the only school she had even bothered to apply to. Her counselor told her she needed some other options, that she was walking a tightrope without a net. She hadn't listened, though, which was part of the reason the private prep school she attended had insisted she talk to Dr. Glass. If it hadn't been for the pain it would have caused her mother's ghost, Ophelia would have just as soon dropped out.

She tore the envelope open along its narrow end, careful not to damage the letter inside. She pulled the letter out, unfolded it, and began to read out loud.

" 'Dear Ms. Warring . . . ' "

Ophelia folded the letter back up, slipped it back into the envelope, and put the envelope back into *The Book of Lies*.

Someone was moving obliquely across her field of view, walking in great, long strides. She looked up with irritation. She liked to have the cemetery to herself, which is why she came late in the day on Sundays, when there were no funerals and only rarely other visitors. The man was dressed all in black, like her. He appeared to be in his thirties, but wore his long hair black in a ponytail. He was not too far away for Ophelia to see the sharply drawn features. He had a serious, almost fierce look on his face. The flash of silver on his wrist was not a bracelet, as she first thought, but one of those stainless-steel "sport" watches men with too much money and testosterone wear. If the interloper saw her watching him, he gave no sign, so Ophelia did not bother to look into the basket to make sure the small .22-caliber pistol was close at hand, since a cemetery was a good place to get mugged and raped.

The gun was her father's. Ophelia had stolen it to keep him from using it on himself, though she doubted he realized the weapon was even missing. Ophelia always brought the gun to the graveyard. She sometimes carried it with her when she went out on the town, though not always. Ophelia knew how to look out for herself, and she didn't want to become too comfortable with the gun. If her father could use it to put himself out of his earthly misery, she could certainly do the same. If it ever came to that, Ophelia planned to shoot herself in the heart. The thought of putting the barrel in her mouth and then pulling the trigger was too overtly sexual.

The man kept going, up the hill into the older section of the graveyard, a necropolis of mausoleums from the nineteenth century. Ophelia stared at him, hoping to think him out of sight, but he stopped in front of a mausoleum at the top of the hill. He stood there a long moment, looking up at the name carved above the bronze doors, then sat on the marble bench in front of the portico.

Ophelia read from *The Book of Lies* for a little while, but she soon felt herself becoming tired. It was a warm afternoon, and she had been feeling particularly exhausted. Ophelia was having a lot of trouble sleeping. She hardly ever got to sleep until around two, and then she always woke up at three-thirty. She usually had trouble getting back to sleep, and then she would wake up again about the time it started to get light. She lay down on the blanket and closed her eyes and instantly fell into a dreamless slumber. Some weeks the only real rest she got came from these naps on her mother's grave.

It was getting dark when Ophelia awoke.

She sat up, feeling confused and disoriented, the way she usually did after being asleep. After a few moments she began to blow out the votives and pack them away in the tea tin she used to carry them. She folded up the blanket and put it in the basket, with her journal.

Curiosity made her leave by an indirect route, up the hill past where the man had been sitting earlier. There was no sign of him now. Ophelia decided he must have left while she was asleep.

The mausoleum he'd been sitting outside was a stately

Greek Revival structure that might have been patterned after the temple of Athena Nike on the Acropolis. Ophelia's aura began to tingle as she approached it, the way it did when she sensed she needed to be aware of something beyond what the eyes could see. She slowed as the feeling grew stronger until the ominous sensation brought her to a dead stop.

What was it?

The unsettling sensation, like a slight electrical shock, trilled up and down the back of her neck as she strained to reach out with her psychic powers and identify the source of her peculiar sense of danger.

Her eyes found the first solid sign. The doors on the mausoleum, two heavy cast bronze portals that looked like something from the entry of a palazzo in Venice, did not join where they would have met, had they been closed. The right door stood just far enough out from its partner for Ophelia to see a thin vertical line of darkness, a glimpse of the chamber within. The mausoleum had been opened.

The rustling sound of a breeze moving through the trees disguised and almost swallowed the faint sound floating out the tomb door and down the hill to where Ophelia stood in her long black dress, leaning forward with an expression of strained attention on her face, as if she suspected a tiger was hiding just ahead, ready to pounce. At first she thought her imagination was playing tricks on her, but then she knew she was really hearing it.

From within the mausoleum came the unmistakable sound of a man softly crying.

Before Ophelia began to back away, her eyes rose to the name carved in the white stone above the bronze doors, the family name of people who built the crypt a hundred or more years ago: *Peregrine*.

31

The Hunter

OPHELIA REALIZED AT once that she'd been drugged. At first all she could do was lie there, dazed, unable to move or even open her eyes. After a few moments, her eyes opened and she found herself in perfect darkness. Control trickled back into her limbs as the potion used to poison her wore off. She pushed up into a sitting position and took stock. She had too much power to be killed easily, though it might have appeared otherwise to the monsters and perverts who stalked the city in the night. She put her right hand around her ankh to draw extra strength from it. It might have looked like costume jewelry, but Ophelia had used a ritual to fill it with the immortal energy of the ancient Egyptian rulers who had discovered the secret, now mostly lost to time, of transcending death.

She lifted herself up off the floor and—one hand before her, the other around the ankh—began to explore the darkness. She sensed she was alone, but she knew that was only true in a limited sense. The one who had drugged her might not have been in the room, but he was out there somewhere, waiting.

Her hand found the wall. She followed it to the corner, paused, then turned ninety degrees, knowing that eventually there would be a door, although whether it would be unlocked was a question she would address when the time came. The toe of her boot bumped against something solid but without substance. She knew what it was even before she knelt down to lightly touch the body with her fingertips. She hadn't sensed it because it was dead. Corpses did not register a psychic signature with her, though the ghost that went with the body would have been another matter.

Judging the distance around the body, Ophelia stepped around it, careful where she walked in the dark room. For all she knew, there could have been a gaping pit inches from her feet, but she did not think so. The person who had done this to her had something different in mind, and she had a pretty good idea what it was.

The door was just on the other side of the body. Her hands found the knob. It turned freely, the lock clicked, and the door came open toward her. A dull light shined through the dirty window at the end of the hall. Ophelia guessed she was in a hotel. It might have been a dormitory or hospital, but somehow she knew it was a hotel. She began to move slowly down the hall, listening for a sound, a tingle of intuition, anything that would alert her to the presence of the one stalking her. The doors were off most of the rooms. Some of the windows were broken out. The place was abandoned, probably slated for demolition, which would make it easier to dispose of the bodies. She smiled to herself in the darkness. He was a clever one.

When she got to the end of the hall, she was able to look out the window. She was up a dozen stories. She didn't recognize any of the buildings. It could have been any city in the Western world—San Francisco, London, Prague. There were trucks and bulldozers below, the equipment vaguely foreign looking. There was no traffic on the street in front of the building. Except for the rats scuttling in the walls and the one who brought her there, Ophelia was completely alone.

Water dripped somewhere in the distance, a hollow echoing sound, like condensation dripping in a cave. She heard the scrape of shoe leather at precisely the same moment her psychic alarm shrieked *danger*.

Ophelia glanced at the elevator. There was no point in even trying it. The power to the building had been shut off long ago. She dashed into the stairwell and began to run up the stairs two at a time, holding her long skirt in her hands. It was a classic error—running *up* the stairs in a building, where there would be no hope of escape except out a window or off the roof. But it was too late to change her mind because she could hear him coming after her.

It was just plain too late, Ophelia thought, feeling suddenly weary.

He was gaining on her, close enough for her to hear his heavy breathing. Instead of continuing the futile race, she slammed through the fire door at the next landing and ran down the hallway as fast as her feet could carry her, hoping there were no obstructions to trip her. She flung herself into the first room and stopped, listening.

Though it made her lungs burn, Ophelia held her breath at first so her panting wouldn't give her away. She could hear him coming down the hall, looking into the rooms one at a time as he went.

Enough light filtered through the boarded-up window for her to see that the wall where the bathroom was had been torn out, leaving splintered plaster, laths, and exposed pipes. The only place to hide was the closet, which didn't have a door but stood at a right angle to the door and at least afforded concealment. If he was careless, there was a chance he wouldn't see her.

Ophelia pressed her back against the closet and tried to be perfectly still.

He was at the doorway. She could hear his breathing and feel his presence. She could even *smell* him, for her nose was very sensitive.

He stepped into the room. He *knew* she was there. He was taking his time, enjoying it, probably hoping she'd whimper, maybe even beg him for mercy.

With the sound of a quick shuffle he filled up the closet doorway, blocking her only escape. He was tall and muscular, with a goatee. She knew the type well enough. The ones who chose that form were all sadists at heart. He intended to kill her, but not until he made her suffer. The crude tools of an apprentice were in his hands: a butcher knife in his left hand (he was left-handed, Ophelia thought), and an old milk jug in his right. He would torture her, kill her, and carry her blood back to his vampire master in the jug to curry favor. If he served his sponsor well enough, he would one day be made a vampire, too, as his reward.

"There is no use struggling, though I will be disappointed if you don't."

"You're right. There is no use struggling."

Her hand shot out and grabbed him by his ponytail. Ophelia could sense his surprise give way to horror as she sank her teeth into his neck and tore out a huge chunk of flesh. She drank his steaming blood in great gulps and then hurled his dying body to the floor.

"You fool!" she jeered. "You thought you were stalking a mere sorcerer's apprentice. You will have to learn to recognize a master vampire when you see one if you ever hope to become one!"

Ophelia moved the mouse up to the program menu and selected *Quit,* disconnecting herself from the Internet.

"What an idiot," she said to no one in particular, pushing herself back from the desk in her bedroom where her computer sat. Her opponent clearly had some experience at the Ravening, but not nearly enough to even think about taking on Ophelia. It would be a long time before her newly killed adversary amassed the power and skill required to become a vampire.

Ophelia got the tarot cards out of the box on her dresser where she kept them. She shuffled them on her way back to the desk and dealt the first one, faceup, as she sat down again. It was the Fool.

"Ah," Ophelia said to herself.

Strange to turn over the Fool first, for the Fool was the first card in the tarot deck. She recognized herself in his figure. The Fool in his motley was slightly ridiculous in his dress. He carried all his meager possessions tied up on his back, set out for his journey through the world. The Fool could be a hopeful figure. The possibilities were wide open for the Fool, if he would only decide to unpack his things and make a go of it. But the nearby cliff indicated the possibility of disaster should he take a misstep. Ophelia was never sure whether to regard the small dog barking at the Fool's heels as being there to warn him of danger or harry him into plunging to his death.

She reached for the next card, using the edge of her black-lacquered fingernail to separate it from the deck.

The High Priestess.

Two power cards in a row—extraordinary. There was energy in the room. Ophelia could feel it. It made her aura tingle. She lit a pair of black candles on the desk and turned out the lights before coming back to ponder her future.

The High Priestess was an enigmatic figure. She came

shrouded in darkness but filled with secret, occult knowledge. She was one who could see behind the curtain, who could reveal what was hidden, illuminating the future.

Ophelia sat back in her chair and closed her eyes to meditate on the matter. She would have liked to believe that *she* was the High Priestess, but she knew it was only too obvious that she was the Fool. It came up again and again, no matter how she read the cards. So who was the High Priestess? It had to be someone who had recently come into her life, or was about to enter it. Otherwise, Ophelia couldn't think of a single person who could help her unlock the possibilities for a future she had all but decided to forgo by swallowing the bottle of pills hidden under the doll her mother had given her.

Dr. Glass?

Ophelia started to smile, but the left side of her mouth went up higher than its opposite to form a smirk. She was too intelligent to put any faith in psychiatry. Besides, she had seen him staring at her tits. He sat there all the time she was on his couch, fantasizing about fucking her. Ophelia didn't have to be psychic to know *that*.

Putting the question aside for the moment, she turned over the next card. The picture showed a half god, half goat at the foot of a black mountain, surrounded by chained people indulging in their earthly desires, slaves to their obsessions. The Devil card, powerful and dangerous. The card was for someone powerful and wanton, someone who could be impossible to resist, not because he was too charming but because he refused to take no for an answer.

The card was a warning.

Ophelia reached for the next card, but looked up when a light came on outside her window. She rose from her chair and moved to the window in a crouch, as if not wanting to be seen by anybody who might be looking up at her window in the dead of night.

A light had come on downstairs in the house across the street, illuminating the ferns and heavy antique furniture. Looking in through the open draperies, she saw an over-size Chinese vase beside the marble fireplace, over it some kind of landscape painting. It was odd to see the lights on like that, for the house was always dark at night. Even when the security patrol was checking on things, Ophelia could never remember them turning on more than a light in the hall. Tonight, the downstairs was ablaze, as if the house was wired so that a single switch turned on every light on the first floor.

She could see someone moving in the parlor, not enough of a body to see if it was a man or a woman, just a bit of motion masked by the furniture and by the angle of vision from Ophelia's bedroom. She was thinking about going downstairs for a better view when a man walked to the bay window at the front of the parlor.

Ophelia crouched down lower, but it would have been almost impossible to see her there. The candles on her desk threw off only enough light to see a dull golden glow and shadows from across the street.

It was a man, and he stood holding his arms behind his back, looking down at the street.

Ophelia's eyes grew wide.

It was the man from the cemetery.

He shifted his weight and looked up the hill, glowering, as if he saw something that displeased him greatly, though Ophelia was sure the displeasure on his face was the sort that came from somewhere within.

He looked up at her.

Ophelia threw herself down in the window seat, pressing her face into the silk pillows. She knew he couldn't have seen her there, but she had an uncanny sense that he had anyway. She stayed hidden for half a minute before daring another look.

The man was no longer standing in the window.

Ophelia let out a long sigh of relief.

A masculine silhouette appeared in the door across the street. It opened and he came out, shutting the door behind him but not locking it, moving down the stairs with so much deliberation that Ophelia was sure he was going to come across the street and pound on her door, demanding to know why she had been watching him. But at the sidewalk he turned and began walking down the hill, toward the bay.

Ophelia grabbed her cloak off the bed and flew out of her room.

He was still in plain sight when she moved outside, keeping in the shadows. She went down to the street and, staying opposite him, followed at a distance of several blocks, certainly enough to be discreet.

In a Jaguar sedan parked up the street, a man sat with his face bathed in the blue light reflected from his iBook computer, which was hooked into the Internet via a wireless network card. He had about given up hope of luring Ophelia back into the game, but now that she had come out of the safety of her house onto the street, it would be even more fun.

Dr. Glass closed the notebook computer and put it on the passenger seat. He opened the door, closing it quietly, pushing the remote lock as he set off down the hill after Ophelia.

32
Investigation

OPHELIA WAS WORKING on the Web site when the doorbell rang. She looked up, scowled, then went back to work on the new photos she was placing on the Hauntings home page.

The doorbell rang again.

It wasn't as if her father would answer the door, even if he had been home, instead of away on one of his ill-defined errands. He rarely left the house, but when he did, Ophelia had no idea where he went. Certainly not to the grocery store. Marketing had become her responsibility by default, not that either of them ever cooked. He didn't have to leave to buy liquor; they delivered it once or twice a week in boxes brought to the back door. It would have been a relief of sorts to think he was seeing someone, but Ophelia knew that wasn't where he went when he disappeared. It was a mystery. She was just glad he went *somewhere*.

Whoever was downstairs began to pound on the front door.

"If it's another Realtor I'll rip his lungs out," Ophelia said. She shoved herself away from her desk and went to the window. Parked on the hill in front of the house was a midnight blue four-door Ford Crown Victoria sedan with too many antennas and the sort of absurdly cheap-looking mini-hubcaps you see only on government vehicles.

Ophelia's immediate thought was that something had happened to her father. He had given up driving, so at least he could not be arrested again for driving while intoxicated. (The BMW was parked in the garage, not drivable after his accident.) But his color had been exceptionally bad lately, and Ophelia was worried about his heart. She went down the stairs two at a time and opened the door as the policeman was about to knock again. There were two of them: a man and a woman, each unsmiling.

"Can I help you?"

"Miss Warring?" the woman asked.

"Yes."

The policewoman showed her badge. She was the one in charge.

"I'm Lieutenant Minelli. This is Sergeant Packer. Could we come in?"

Ophelia's anxiety made her more agreeable than she would have been otherwise. She opened the door and stood out of the way. The two cops looked around the foyer at the piles of newspapers and mail and exchanged a look.

"Is it my father?"

Lieutenant Minelli and Sergeant Packer glanced at each other again.

"No, Miss Warring. Is your father home?"

She shook her head.

"We'd like to ask you about last night."

"What about it?"

"Where were you?"

"I was home until after ten."

"Alone?"

"I suppose my father was home, but I didn't see him. I was playing a computer game."

"And after ten?"

"I went for a walk."

She didn't tell them that she'd followed the man from across the street, the man she'd seen earlier at the cemetery, crying outside the Peregrine mausoleum. She'd lost track of him down by the wharf. Ophelia half suspected he had known she was following him, but it was only a hunch. After that, she'd gone on to the Cage Club, where there were a few people hanging out, but she didn't want to mention that to the police. The club was sacred territory.

"Alone?"

She nodded.

"Would you mind taking a ride with us, Miss Warring?"

"To the police station? Am I under arrest?"

"What reason would we have to arrest you?" Sergeant Packer said, speaking for the first time.

"None whatsoever."

"You're not under arrest. There's just something we'd like you to see."

Ophelia hesitated. She was more curious than concerned, since she had not done anything illegal, at least not anything the two detectives were likely to care about.

"Okay," she said. "Let's go."

"Do you want to leave a note for your father?"

"No, that's okay."

Lieutenant Minelli looked at her with something close enough to concern for Ophelia to feel a spike of anger, but the moment broke as soon as the lieutenant turned and reached for the door.

Sergeant Packer opened the back door of the car for Ophelia and shut it after her before climbing behind the wheel and starting the motor.

"How long have you been a Goth?" Lieutenant Minelli was sitting sideways in the front seat, looking back at her.

"I don't know."

"I understand that you and your friends like to play at being vampires."

"Shouldn't you put your seat belt on?" Ophelia said. "It's the law."

"Do you believe in vampires?"

"What we choose to believe or disbelieve is irrelevant to what is real."

"That's what I would call an ambiguous answer."

Ophelia shrugged. They were driving in the opposite direction of the Cage Club. A good thing. There was no telling what bits of this and that the police might find lying around if they decided to have a serious look at the Brood's party place.

"Is it all pretend?"

Ophelia glared at the detective.

"What I mean is: Do you just play at drinking blood, or do you ever really—well, you know."

"What is this about?"

"I think you know," Sergeant Packer said without taking his eyes off the road.

"I haven't the faintest idea," Ophelia said. She sat back, crossed her arms, and looked out the window. Out of the corner of her eye she could see Lieutenant Minelli watching her, but after a few minutes the policewoman turned around to the front of the car and left Ophelia alone, though she never did fasten her seat belt.

Ophelia guessed where they were heading when they were still nearly a mile away. The streets were familiar enough, and by the time Sergeant Packer turned the Crown Vic onto Magnolia Avenue, it was obvious they were heading for the cemetery. The car slowed to a crawl and Lieutenant Minelli turned around again and gave Ophelia a close, appraising stare. Ophelia could see Sergeant Packer's eyes on her in the mirror.

"What are we doing here?" The officers did not answer. They drove into the old part of the cemetery on a road that ran along the base of a hill that had a memorial to World War I at its crest. A dozen or more police cars and other vehicles, including an ambulance, came into view only when they got to a little valley that fell away from the hill on its back side.

"You like to hang out in this cemetery."

"It's not a crime to visit my mother's grave, Lieutenant Minelli," Ophelia said, her eyes on the group of people gathered around a waist-high sarcophaguslike monument, one of the many ornate nineteenth-century oddities in the graveyard. The bone white marble seemed to have been defaced with black paint, but Ophelia realized in the next moment that it was in fact covered with dried blood. As they drove nearer, the inchoate pile perched on the bier turned out to be two bodies, limbs hanging at odd, uncomfortable-looking angles, slack in death.

Sergeant Packer stopped and shifted the Ford into park. He was looking at her in the rearview mirror, Lieutenant Minelli again turned sideways, as Ophelia stared at the macabre tableau. The fascination on her face transformed the moment she recognized the half-hidden, blood-matted faces on the corpses. It was Damien and Pendragon, the fledgling vampires from the Cage Club.

"There's a third victim you can't see from here. Rebecca Miller." Lieutenant Minelli glanced down, evidently consulting her notebook. "Although her vampire name is Letitia. She's behind the tomb thing where the other two are. At least her naked body is." The lieutenant's eyes met Ophelia's again. "We haven't found the rest of her head. We thought maybe you could help us out with that, Ophelia."

33

The Truth

OPHELIA WAS LATE getting home, delayed first by her appointment with Dr. Glass, and later the side trip to the San Francisco Public Library.

She had to put her shoulder into the door to push the day's mail out of the way. The foyer was getting out of hand. It was past the time to step in, even if it was to throw away the newspapers and junk mail. That much was plain from the way the police officers had reacted to the embarrassing chaos inside the house. But Ophelia had far more important things to think about.

The house across the street was dark. She checked this again as she locked the door behind her. Lights in the old Peregrine mansion were the first thing she looked for when the taxi turned up her street. But there was no one home.

Ophelia went upstairs without checking on her father. She turned on the shower and stripped off her clothes, leaving them where they fell in a pile on the white tile floor in her bathroom. Her sessions with Dr. Glass always made her feel dirty. It was not so much his questions about how often she masturbated and had she ever experimented with lesbian sex—Ophelia didn't mind talking about these things—but rather the way he *looked* at her. Dr. Glass was the one who needed a therapist to pry into his dark, damp fantasies. She had thought about throwing back in his face the fact that she knew he was prescribing Vicodin to Zeke, who was selling it at the Cage Club.

Dr. Glass had demanded that she tell him everything about the gruesome scene in the cemetery. Ophelia was a connoisseur of the macabre, but it gave her the creeps to see the delight he took in hearing about the way Damien's intestines had been wound around his neck like a bloody scarf. He admitted the police had been there to question him about Ophelia. He claimed that he'd told them he sincerely doubted she had anything to do with the triple murder.

There were two things he said that ate at Ophelia. The first was whether she thought the homicides had anything to do with the Ravening, since Letitia, Damien, and Pendragon had all been involved in the role-playing game. The second irritant was the question of where the blood had gone. Each of the trio had bled to death, and though there was plenty of blood at the scene, there wasn't enough.

The police had asked Ophelia the same two questions. Her answer to them, and to Dr. Glass, had been the same: no and no. But the truth was she knew—as everyone certainly did—that vampires had *everything* to do with the deaths and the missing blood.

And now she knew it for certain.

Ophelia stood looking up into the shower's steaming water, letting it beat down, driving the tension out of her. The old house had a huge water heater, and there was enough hot water for Ophelia to stand there until she couldn't stand it anymore.

She walked across the bedroom in the dark, drying herself with her towel, and looked out the window. He was still not home. It took a while to get her long hair dry. She brushed it out and left it to hang loose.

The bras and panties in her underwear drawer were all

black silk. Instead of her usual long skirt, Ophelia found a black leather micromini to wear. She put on a black blouse that was cut in front in a way that nicely displayed her breasts, which were of a size and shape that tended to make men stare. She retrieved her ankh and crosses from the bathroom, pulling her long hair out over the chains as she put them on.

There still was no light on across the street when she checked again, but then she noticed the faint golden light flickering on the floor. Someone had lit a fire in the fireplace in the front parlor.

Ophelia pulled on a pair of knee-high boots that zipped up the back, grabbed the Prada backpack containing the crimson file folder, and ran down the stairs.

"I know you're in there," Ophelia yelled through the brass letterbox opening.

The door swung open, and there she was, on her knees, looking up at him.

He stood looking down at her for a moment, his face unreadable. He offered her his hand, which felt warm, even feverish, when she accepted it and got back on her feet.

"May I help you, Miss Warring?"

"I would like to . . . ." She paused. "You know my name."

"I may not be very social, Miss Warring, but I do know my neighbors."

Ophelia took a deep breath before plunging on. "And I know who you are."

One of his dark eyebrows shot up.

"Would you like to come inside, Miss Warring? I was just about to make myself a cup of tea."

He stood aside for her, not waiting for her answer, as if he already knew that she would accept his invitation. And she did.

*　　*　　*

After looking through the contents, he closed the folder on his lap and sat looking down on it.

"You're not even going to bother denying you're Nathaniel Peregrine, are you," Ophelia said.

He looked up at her, and she could see danger in his dark eyes. But that did not matter to her. One way or the other, she would get something she wanted from him, even if it was death.

"Of course I am Nathaniel Peregrine. But I'm not that Nathaniel."

"Don't embarrass yourself. You saw the copy of the Matthew Brady portrait from the Civil War. And the time you came back after World War One—it is obvious that it's you under that beard. I know who you are, and I know what you are."

"No, my dear, you do not. You are mistaken."

"I think I've always known that vampires exist, in one form or the other. I've always been fascinated with them. They are sensual monsters. They don't kill their victims so much as seduce them. And, of course, they do not always kill the humans who give them what they need. If they choose to, they can change them, bring them across, make them immortal."

"I have more than a passing awareness of this group you are associated with, the Ravening," Peregrine said. He shook his head more with sadness than disapproval, she thought. "It is not healthy to be preoccupied with darkness and death."

"And why not? We're all dying from the moment we're born. Happiness, life, a future—those are all illusions for mortals, comforting lies we tell ourselves to help us pretend we do not see the rot and decay that is our true fate."

Peregrine looked at Ophelia in a way that made her feel

like squirming. It was as if he was looking directly into her soul.

"The day you saw me at the cemetery."

"I didn't think you noticed me," she said.

"I notice *everything*," he said, and smiled. "You were visiting your mother's grave."

"So?"

"It is hard to suffer the loss of a mother. I know what it is like to lose those closest to you. It can warp you. It can make you hate the world. If you're not careful, it can destroy you."

"When?"

Peregrine's eyes narrowed. "Your flippant attitude tries my patience."

"What are you going to do about it?"

He glared back at her but said nothing.

"You could kill me," she said. She knew that touched something, because he had to look away. They were sitting in the parlor in wing-backed chairs facing the fireplace. Even if she tried to run, she knew she couldn't get more than a few feet from him before he would have her.

"Or you could make me like you."

"I don't know what you're talking about."

"You could turn me into a vampire."

"I am not a vampire."

"Nathaniel, you're nearly one hundred and seventy years old. You are not as invisible to history as you think. I found some of the old newspaper accounts from New Orleans in 1863, where you were in the hospital before supposedly dying at Gettysburg. And that bloody spree in Haiti in 1914."

The look he gave Ophelia filled her with satisfaction.

"You didn't even know they wrote about that, did you? It was in the Port-au-Prince newspaper. And yes, I do read French. I read and speak it rather well. My mother went to a great deal of trouble, when she was alive, to ensure that I had a first-rate education."

"And now it is nearly time for you to go away to school."

She felt herself sag and tried to hide it by sitting up straight and looking the vampire directly in the eye. "I was going to go to Smith."

"To study poetry."

She gave him a curious look. "How do you know such things? Did you read my mind?"

He smiled for the first time, and the expression gave an entirely different dimension to his personality.

"You look like a poet, Miss Warring." His smile broadened. "And I read your poem about poppies in the *Western Review*."

Now it was Ophelia who smiled. "You read the *Review*?"

"I have to confess that poetry is one of my passions. Poetry and music."

He handed the folder back to her and stood.

"I would like to offer you another cup of tea, but I'm afraid I have a previous engagement. Perhaps another time."

She stood and looked up at him.

"Will you help me?"

"Help you how?" he said.

"Will you change me?"

"You are playing a very dangerous game, my dear. Besides, you're completely mistaken. The Nathaniel Peregrine you take me for has been dead for more than a century. But I would like to talk to you again. We could discuss poetry."

"That would be nice," Ophelia said, trying to decide

whether or not to believe him. The research, hasty as it was, seemed obvious enough. She was very good with a computer, and the work she'd done on her Hauntings San Francisco Web site had taught her the tricks she needed to know to be a good historical researcher.

"I would only ask that you do one small thing for me," he said, leaning forward a bit.

They were standing very close to each other. Ophelia could feel the heat coming off Peregrine's body. The way he was standing over her, he looking down, she up, their faces near, she thought he would kiss her—either that or sink his teeth into her neck. She had the sense that they were sharing the same moment, each wondering what the next move would be, when he spoke in his low, patrician voice.

"Promise me you will not tell others you think a Civil War general has come to live across the street from you."

Ophelia could almost see herself reflected in his dark eyes. It was as if she were dreaming. She felt lightheaded, even high. It was the effect he had on her. She suspected he could get women to say or do anything he wanted.

"I promise. But think about giving me the help I need."

He looked down on her, nothing changing in his expression, betraying not a hint of what his intentions were about his Gothic visitor.

34
Therapy

Dr. Glass leaned back in his Aeron chair and shut his eyes. The young woman buried her face in his lap, making pleasure sounds deep in her throat.

"This is the best therapy for you. The only way you will ever learn to coexist with your libido."

The word Candy had used to describe herself—*nymphomaniac*—referred to a diagnosis the psychiatric community had judged obsolete. Rather, the *DSM-IV* had substituted the term *hypersexuality* to describe individuals exhibiting an abnormally heightened level of sexuality. Dr. Glass had trouble with the new term, for who was to say what degree of sexuality was excessive? There was no ultimately useful scale to measure so-called normal desire in human beings. Dr. Glass was highly sexed himself, and there was nothing wrong with him.

"You must explore the boundaries of desire and see where your impulses lead if you ever hope to control them."

"Why don't you shut up and enjoy it?" Candy said without lifting her head out of his lap.

Dr. Glass was not in the habit of taking advice from patients, but for once he decided to make an exception.

He watched Ophelia get comfortable in her usual position on the couch, wishing he could join her there.

"You are much more relaxed than you were when we started these sessions."

"I suppose people like to talk about themselves and their problems. Even me, though I wouldn't have imagined it."

"You haven't exactly thrown inhibition to the wind and told me everything."

"No," she said, smiling to herself, "but I've told you a lot more than I ever expected to."

"And I have, much to my own surprise, been impressed with your worldview. No doubt you've noticed I've taken to wearing black."

Ophelia turned her head toward him and ran her big dark eyes over him in a way that excited him on a level that a slut like Candy never could. Had she noticed his altered taste in clothing? She did not say and Glass couldn't tell. He could usually read his patients, but Ophelia remained as mysterious and inscrutable as the day they first met.

"Western society has, as you've said, developed a pathological aversion to facing death. Aversion is an outward manifestation of fear, and fear indicates subconscious issues that should be addressed. I'm planning a major monograph on the subject for the next APA national convention.

"The sharply focused interest in vampires you share with your friends is noteworthy and has a sociological and psychological significance beyond what most people realize. The force that Jung called the will to power is powerful and openly acknowledged in your darkling coven of a social group. I'm sure I don't need to tell you that this runs counter to the despicable milquetoast character shared by the simpering cowards and politically correct weaklings who have taken over society."

Ophelia laughed quietly. Dr. Glass took it as a sign of approval. She had never before laughed in his presence. There was a delicious velvet quality to the sound, like moths fluttering against silk.

"But most significant of all is your choice to make blood an object of adoration," Dr. Glass went on. "Blood has always been a taboo substance. In primitive societies, women are considered unclean during menstruation. They are banished to seclusion in huts set apart from the rest of the clan, the blood making them unclean. The Jews have elaborate rituals to avoid the contamination of blood. But your circle has done something entirely new and unprecedented. You have taken blood, the substance of defilement and contamination, and elevated it to serve as your tribal totem."

"The blood is the life," Ophelia said.

"Yes!" Dr. Glass exclaimed. "You are precisely right and the rest of the world wrong. Whether we know it or not, we are all controlled by the language of the unconscious. The things we fear and the things we lust after exist beneath the level of our conscious understanding as symbols and images. It is the aim of psychiatry to study and analyze the unconscious, to learn the vocabulary of the dream mind that controls our waking action, not only to keep us from reenacting psychic trauma in disguised ways, but to unlock our secret hidden powers."

Glass was leaning forward, his eyes bright, his hands alive with gestures.

"I can hear the message in *here*." He touched his forehead. "We all can. The messages of the unconscious just keep coming, like a radio signal transmitted over and over again, until finally one day we tune it in and receive the message.

"In olden times, we would go to a priest or a shaman to divine the meaning. Now we turn to psychiatrists, but our job seems to be not so much to free the beast as to drug it into impotent numbness. But I see possibilities in you,

Ophelia, possibilities of a knowing I'd scarcely imagined existed."

Dr. Glass stopped, feeling for a moment a rare hint of uncertainty.

"Why are you smiling?"

"You're doing all the talking, Dr. Glass. This is supposed to be my therapy session. Did you have espresso at lunch?"

"I suppose it's because it's your last session. The insurance companies put a limit on the number of visits they'll pay for. After that, they expect psychiatrists to do their work with drugs and a few brief, well-spaced maintenance visits."

"I refuse to take drugs," the girl said.

"I understand and respect that. I endorse your position. I don't want to mute what's inside you. That's all the more reason for you to continue your therapy. We're just beginning to make progress. Your insurance wouldn't cover the cost, but your father can easily afford it."

"I don't think I want to continue."

"Don't you think you're benefiting from our sessions?"

"What I think is that I'm mainly indulging myself and entertaining you. I can tell how amused you are at some of my stories. I only agreed to see you because my counselor and the headmistress at my school insisted on it as a condition of graduation."

"Most schools would have expelled you for keeping an enemies list, Ophelia. School authorities are extremely sensitive to that sort of thing after Columbine, and rightly so."

"It wasn't an enemies list. At least not in that way."

"Keeping a list of people you hate isn't a good thing to do, given today's political climate."

"I know that now. But it seems ridiculous that they overreacted to something like that. It's not as if I threatened anybody. Those people all made it plain that they hate me. What difference does it make whether I hate them in my mind or write it down in my journal?"

"On top of the whole Goth thing and the way you withdrew from social activities at the school after your mother died, they took it as a warning sign."

"Let's not talk about my mom."

"Now who is avoiding the subject of death?"

"It's what I deserve for going to an exclusive private school for the children of San Francisco's ruling elite. At a regular high school, nobody would have given me a second look. They don't know what real freaks are at my school."

"So graduating does matter?"

Ophelia's shoulders rose off the couch in a slight shrug.

"How did you make out with the admissions people at Smith College?"

"Did my counselor tell you everything?"

Dr. Glass nodded.

"Some things ought to be confidential."

"And they are, when we talk about them in this office. I'm your doctor, Ophelia. There can't be secrets between us."

She had nothing to say to that. He hadn't begun to penetrate the layers of secrets hiding the real Ophelia, immortal black pearl, from being seen by the world.

"So?" he said.

"So what?"

"So did you get in to Smith?"

"Yes."

"That's quite an accomplishment."

Ophelia had no reply to that.

"It's something to look forward to, something to plan

for, going off to an upper-crust Ivy League college in the East."

"I don't think I'm going."

"Why not? Do you intend to stay here and care for your father? I daresay the only thing that can help him is a detox facility."

"I have everything I need here in San Francisco."

"Most young people your age would be looking forward to going away to college and making a life for themselves."

"Life is overrated. I've already told you: It's death that interests me."

Dr. Glass smiled to himself. He was hoping she would say something like that.

"You know you need more therapy sessions with me. I can help."

"I'll think about it," she said.

"And if you continue your therapy—indeed, even if you don't—it would mean very much to me if you would do one small favor for me."

"Such as?"

"Teach me to drink blood," Dr. Glass said.

Ophelia turned and gave him an opaque look, her eyes dark and heavily made up with mascara, that filled him with a mad desire almost beyond what he could control.

35

Temptation

"YOU UNDERSTAND THAT he is a *real* vampire?" Ophelia said.

Scarlet seemed to be having trouble focusing her eyes. "A real vampire," she said. "Fucking fantastic. Because I want to become a vampire. I'm tired of this fledgling shit, having to kiss everybody's ass—not to mention other parts of their anatomy."

"What the hell," Ophelia said, and rang the doorbell. It was a calculated risk, but maybe it would work. She had to do something to get Nathaniel Peregrine's attention.

The porch light came on, followed by the sound of the dead bolt being unlocked and the latch turned. The door opened.

"Good evening, Ophelia."

Peregrine looked as if he'd been expecting her, although that would have been impossible since she had only settled on her plan when she got to the Cage Club and found Scarlet there, stoned out of her mind on Vicodin, making out with Zeke in the Bondage Room.

"And good evening to you," Peregrine said, looking down at Scarlet.

The Ravening fledgling giggled and began to teeter on her stiletto heels. Ophelia put an arm around her, to keep her from losing her balance and falling.

"I brought you a present," Ophelia said, indicating the other girl.

Peregrine's eyes shifted back to Scarlet for a few moments. Ophelia had seen men look at Scarlet—her real name was Laurel—with open lust or revulsion, for she made a special point of being outrageous. Peregrine, however, did not react to her in any particular way. Ophelia had almost decided he would reject her bait when he invited them into his house.

"The night air is cool," he said, "and your friend looks chilly."

The only light in the main salon of the nineteenth-century home came from the fireplace and a single lamp beside a leather armchair. Apparently Peregrine had been reading Shakespeare. The book was left open, spine up, on one arm of the chair. Ophelia wondered what play or poem he was reading.

"Please excuse me," their host said, and disappeared without explanation.

Scarlet sprawled out on the couch, legs lewdly splayed, playing her role of überslut without even having to try. The black bustier was cut low enough to expose fully half of the dragon tattoo on her breast over her heart. Her bright red hair was all a-fly. She wore a silver ring in the side of her nose and a studded dog collar around her throat. Her skirt did not quite reach to the top of torn fishnet stockings held in place by an old-fashioned black garter belt, like a 1940s pinup model.

Peregrine brought back a silver tray. On it were a carafe of coffee, three cups, and matching silver bowls of milk and sugar.

"I hope you like French roast coffee," he said as he filled the cups.

"I like French everything," Scarlet said, her words slurred.

"Scarlet is a fledgling," Ophelia said to Peregrine. "I told her the quickest way to earn bones in the Ravening is with the help of an experienced vampire like you."

Peregrine glanced up at Scarlet. "Would you care for cream or sugar, Scarlet?"

"Both," she said.

"I know you must be hungry, Nathaniel," Ophelia said. "Even in a city like San Francisco, you have to be careful hunting. It must have been so much easier back in the 1800s, before video surveillance cameras and FBI crime databases. Back then, I would imagine it would be an easy matter for people to simply disappear."

"I admit that I sometimes wish I could return to an earlier, simpler time."

Peregrine put the cup and saucer on the table in front of Scarlet. She had settled back into the corner of the couch and closed her eyes.

"There you are, Scarlet."

The young woman did not move.

"She needs to take better care of herself, Ophelia."

"She took too many downers," Ophelia said. "I hope it doesn't make her blood too tainted for you to drink. Does that sort of thing bother you? If you wait a few hours, her system will start to clean itself out. There's no hurry. Nobody will be the least surprised if Scarlet doesn't show up at the house where she's been staying. They'll probably be relieved. She's a real piece of work. But then you can see that for yourself."

But Ophelia was the one Peregrine was staring at intently. He drew in a slow breath through his nose, almost as if he was savoring the scent of her, smelling things no ordinary mortal could detect.

"There's certainly nothing contaminating *your* blood, Ophelia," he said.

"I don't believe in drugs. Life is bad enough as it is."

"Nor do I," he said, sitting sideways on the couch beside Scarlet but not giving any indication he was going to ravish the girl. Indeed, it looked quite the reverse. He reached for an afghan throw draped over the corner of the couch and covered her, the way he might a sleeping child. "Although there was a time when it was different for me. I was given morphine after an injury and became addicted. It was a difficult time. Drugs are to be avoided."

"Especially when the ultimate drug, blood, is there for the taking."

"You don't know what you're talking about, Ophelia."

"I know who you are. I know your story. I told you, Nathaniel, I've got you dead to rights."

"And I've told you, Ophelia, you're mistaken. What you suggest is impossible."

Ophelia got up from her chair and unfastened the dog collar around Scarlet's neck.

"Look at her, Nathaniel. So young, so warm, so succulent. And perfectly helpless. There are more like her in San Francisco. I can keep you supplied and help clean up afterward, if you'll do just one small favor for me."

Peregrine was already shaking his head.

"Make me like you," Ophelia said. "Turn me into a vampire."

"Impossible."

"Free me from my pain."

"I can't do that. No one can."

"Do I ache any less for my mother than you did for your wife and children, after the Confederate raiders burned them to death in your father-in-law's house in

Kansas, where you thought they would be safe while you were off fighting for the Union?"

Peregrine looked stunned, like a bird that had flown into a window, Ophelia thought.

"Of course I know about it. It's all on microfilm from the old papers. You will never be able to blot out your past. The evidence exists in too many places. If you know where to go and what to look for—why, there it is, Nathaniel Peregrine, believed killed at the Battle of Gettysburg, still alive today. Although I doubt many people would recognize you for what you are. But you can't hide it from me. I am gifted—or cursed—in that way."

"Prescient," Peregrine said dully.

"The very word I prefer. The term *psychic* is demeaning. That word has been ruined by charlatans. I knew what you were the first time I saw you, the same way I knew my mother was going to die even before she realized she was sick."

"And what do your powers tell you about yourself?"

Ophelia gave the vampire a pained look. "I don't know everything."

"I know."

"I suppose what happens to me depends on you. I'm asking you, begging you, Nathaniel, change me. And if not that, kill me. For a long time I have been half in love with death."

"That was Keats's line."

"A vampire who loves poetry—could anything be better?"

"You have no idea what you ask of me."

Ophelia was exultant. "You've quit denying it. That is progress."

"Do not taunt me," Peregrine said, becoming angry. "And do not tempt me. I am not the solution to your problems. I did not come to San Francisco to take up your cross and bear it for you. There is no relief in the thing you ask me to do."

"I don't care."

"Not now, but you would. The only gifts the Change would bring you are loneliness, longing, endless wandering, and more pain. It is not at all what you think."

"Then drain me dry and save me the trouble of taking my own life." Ophelia unfastened the top buttons of her antique Victorian blouse and pulled it open and away from her neck. "Surely you cannot refuse such an offer. You must be hungry. Take my blood. Take as much of it as you need. Drink your fill, and free me from the hell I drag with me on this meaningless slog through life."

Though Peregrine did not move, she saw a strange glimmering light in his eyes. She knew that look. It was the same look she had seen in her father's eyes the nights he would come from the hospice where her mother was dying and look upon the bottles of whiskey, gin, vodka, and brandy kept on the sideboard in the dining room.

"I offer you my blood, fresh and pure from the body of a healthy female who doesn't smoke, drink, or take drugs. There are no contaminants in me. Imagine what it will be like to taste me, sweet and intoxicating, the first wine of summer. Is there anything that could bring you more pleasure? And if there is, take that, too. Take whatever you want, Nathaniel. You have the power. I can feel the strength radiating from you—and your desire."

Peregrine's lips drew back in a grimace, the blood teeth coming down from their recesses in his upper jaw. Even the best orthodontic fangs some Ravening players wore were but pathetic imitations of Nathaniel Peregrine's. His fangs were far narrower than mock movie canines, more like those found in a viper than anything mammalian.

Peregrine's arm shot out but not toward Ophelia. He grabbed Scarlet by the red hair and dragged her to him in a quick, cruel embrace. Her head rolled back as he buried his mouth in her neck. She gasped in pain, in pleasure, and threw her arms around the vampire, pulling him closer.

Ophelia sat there and watched, too fascinated to be enraged that it was Scarlet's blood he was drinking instead of her own.

36

To Be Like a God

"WOULD YOU LIKE to sign up for our e-mail newsletter?"
Ophelia sighed. "I already get it."

The clerk smiled, oblivious to her irritation. The sort of people who worked at Ophelia's favorite bookstore—ponytailed, latte-sipping, wannabe literati—drove her up the wall. They tended to collect in San Francisco anyway, the city exerting its strange gravitational attraction to the self-consciously hip. But she didn't want to interact with them, except when circumstances left her no choice.

"You know, every time I come in here, you ask me that question."

"We get in trouble with the manager if we don't," the clerk said with a grin. He was wearing a Che Guevara T-shirt. Ophelia was willing to bet he had no more than a vague notion who Guevara was, at best.

"You have asked me on at least three other occasions if I want to sign up for the e-mail newsletter. I'm in here a couple of times a week."

"No, really. Sorry. I don't remember. And I'd have to ask you even if I did. It's, like, a rule."

"Then it's, like, a stupid rule," she said savagely, mocking him. "I have a suggestion for you to share with your manager. Every time I come in here, I have to wait in line while the other hippies who work here stand around talking to one another, pretending they don't notice the jam-up at the checkout counter, pretending they don't hear the pages for more assistance at the front desk. Why don't you do a time study to determine the amount of time the average customer spends standing in line, waiting to give you money to enrich your stockholders. Then set a goal to cut that time in half. Something like that would be of actual service to your customers. Asking people to sign up for an e-mail newsletter—again and again and again—is really just a self-serving attempt to get people on your advertising list so you can spam them mercilessly with pitches to buy the latest pathetically written book that some publisher is trying to turn into a best seller."

The next person in the line, a man in a blue blazer, cleared his throat impatiently. The clerk stood there, too terrified to react to the petite young woman decked out in her ankh and Gothic regalia.

"Oh, forget it," Ophelia said, snatching up Amy Clampitt's poetry collection and charging toward the door. The clerk stood holding her receipt, his mouth open. At least he had the presence of mind not to ask her if she wanted it.

"You missed your appointment."

It was Dr. Glass. Squeezing her eyes shut as if against a painful light, Ophelia turned around toward the voice. Glass was standing there, an insipid expression of concern on his face.

"I didn't have an appointment."

"I made one for you. I left messages on both your answering machine at home and your cell phone."

"I told you, Dr. Glass. I'm through with all of that."

The psychiatrist stared at her. "Are you absolutely sure? We were finally beginning to make progress."

"I am totally sure."

He nodded. "I understand."

"Good," she said.

"Can I give you a lift home? The streets aren't safe after dark."

Ophelia looked up at him. It was interesting how different he looked when he smiled. It was as if he could turn off being a doctor and just become someone ordinary.

"Sure," she said. "That would be nice."

Dr. Glass led her to a green Jaguar sedan and opened the door for her.

"What did you buy?"

"A book of poetry."

Glass nodded and pulled into traffic. "Any more thoughts on college?"

"I'm still thinking I'm not going to go."

"Maybe it's for the best," Dr. Glass said. "It's something you have to decide for yourself. Emily Dickinson never went to college."

"True. The quickest route to my house is if you take a right here."

"We're not going to your house."

"And where are we going?"

"It's a surprise."

"Dr. Glass."

"Trust me," he said, looking at her full in the face and smiling again.

Ophelia did not trust the psychiatrist, but there was something almost playful in his manner that made her curious about what he was doing. They drove down toward the bay without talking, Mozart playing quietly on the CD player in the Jaguar. After a short while they entered a down-in-the-heels neighborhood with which Ophelia was more than a little familiar.

"Are you going where I think you are going?"

"And where would that be?" Dr. Glass asked, his tone almost teasing.

They came around the corner and the psychiatrist pulled the car over to the curb across the street from the alley entrance to the Cage Club.

"How do you know about this place? I didn't tell you."

"I am your doctor, Ophelia. It is my job to know."

Ophelia felt her face begin to burn. "You followed me."

"Don't be silly. Professional ethics would prohibit that."

Ophelia regarded him closely in the quiet car. He no longer seemed free of the sort of danger women instinctively know to steer clear of, and at the same time the interior of the Jaguar seemed to grow smaller and more confined, an inviting space that only too late she suspected to be a trap.

She was sitting at an angle to Dr. Glass, so it was easy for her right hand to find the door handle without him seeming to notice. Showing no fear but also with perfect economy of time and motion, she opened the door and got out in a single quick movement. Dr. Glass made no attempt to stop her. She shut the door and stood there, wondering whether she should walk or run toward the Cage Club, when she realized she'd left her new book on the seat. Not that she would risk her safety for the sake of something she could easily replace, but it did make her hesitate a moment. The driver's door opened and Glass got out of the car, holding the book.

"You forgot this."

He held the book out to her. Ophelia did not move a muscle for a few moments, though it seemed like much longer to her. She couldn't make up her mind what to do—indeed she couldn't even manage to consider the options rationally, the thoughts frozen in her mind. Some combination of her upbringing, her uncertainty about the psychiatrist's motives, and the wish not to act like a timid girl made her step toward Glass. He met her at the front of the car still smiling, the book held out to her. When she took it from him he made no attempt to grab her, no threatening moves. He was, she thought, a completely baffling person.

"Thank you. I'll find my own way home from here."

"Whatever you wish, Ophelia."

"Good night."

She turned and started to walk. She could hear his footsteps coming after her, not hurrying, but there, just behind her. She kept going until she got to the door.

"You can't come in here."

"Of course I can," Dr. Glass said.

"The club is only for vampires and fledglings in the Ravening."

"So?"

"I'm not trying to be dramatic, Dr. Glass, but not all of my friends are as nice as I am. There are some boys down there you do not want to meet, especially not in the cellar of the Cage Club, where there isn't anybody who can help you if things get out of hand. It's a rough crew."

"I can take care of myself," the psychiatrist said. He made a motion with his hand to get Ophelia's attention. She looked down, and saw that he was holding a pistol, the streetlight glittering on its silver surface.

Dr. Glass's smile was bigger than ever. He put his hand on Ophelia's arm, and she didn't dare pull away.

"My friends will castrate you if you do anything to hurt me, Dr. Glass."

"Now you are being dramatic, Ophelia. But not to worry. This is only a precaution," he said, and waved the gun. "This is just for persuasive purposes. Turn around like a good girl now and in you go."

Ophelia opened the door, hoping someone would hear them coming. The sound of industrial metal music throbbed dully, the sound floating up the elevator shaft from the lower level. It was dark inside, almost impossible to see once the outside door closed behind them. But Dr. Glass kept his hand firmly on Ophelia's arm so that she couldn't pull away from him.

The single dim bulb shined through the slats in the grate over the freight elevator. Glass let go of her long enough to raise the gate so they could enter. He seemed familiar with the place, as if he'd been there before. Ophelia thought of Dr. Glass hiding in the shadows, watching her and the others. For the first time, she thought she might be in serious danger. This was followed by a realization that struck her with the force of an epiphany: She did not want to die, at least not at the hands of someone like Dr. Glass.

Glass pushed the elevator button with the barrel of his weapon. The elevator began to rise.

"I see surprise in your face," he said.

Ophelia didn't answer.

"I know perfectly well about the basement revels. Our business is upstairs."

She was suddenly wet with sweat, though it was chilly in the elevator. Ophelia tightened her hold on the slim volume of poetry. She could hit him in the head with it, but she doubted it would even stun him.

The elevator stopped.

"Here we are." He raised and lowered his eyebrows.

Through the slats in the elevator door came a flickering glow, but even when Dr. Glass raised the gate, the source was too diffused to make out. He took her by the arm and led her through the abandoned department store. Someone had stapled huge sheets of translucent plastic from the ceiling.

"Careful," Dr. Glass warned, stepping over a fallen light fixture. "This place is a real mess. But you know that."

Ophelia didn't know it, for the Ravening had confined its activities to the basement. Certainly some of the boys had explored the rest of the building, but Ophelia had never been on the upper floors.

"Our destination is just a bit farther."

Glass pulled open a slit in the plastic and went through, his hand firm around Ophelia's wrist, pulling her after him toward whatever awaited in the middle of the room, bathed in weak illumination. She could see it moving just beyond the folds of hanging plastic, something short, an animal, maybe even a child. She bit hard on her lower lip to keep her composure.

The tentlike enclosure occupied a small open area in the center of the room, a circular space roughly thirty feet across. In the middle of this area was an old-fashioned wooden office chair with arms, one of those stout, institutional-looking pieces of oak furniture that appear too uncomfortable for sitting. In the chair was a skinny blond woman in bra and panties. Her arms and legs were secured to the chair with thick wraps of silver duct tape. She had a ball gag in her mouth, the sort of thing Ophelia had seen on S&M Web sites she'd visited late at night when looking for diversions on the Web. The woman was about Ophelia's age, but that appeared to be the only thing they shared, besides an unfortunate association with Dr. Glass. There was something common about the girl. She had the wild eyes of someone who had been smoking crystal, but there was madness in her eyes, too, along with fear.

Behind Dr. Glass's prisoner, on either side of the chair, were two blue plastic fifty-gallon drums, set up like tables and each holding a candelabra. It wasn't until Ophelia saw the drums—the pair of them—that she guessed how bad it was really going to be. Not that the drums signified anything, but since each drum was the perfect size to hold a human body, nobody needed to paint a picture for Ophelia.

She looked around behind her, judging her chances to escape back through the slit in the plastic, when she saw what else the psychiatrist had brought to his snug and lethal lair. Folded neatly on the floor was a black plastic apron of the sort Ophelia had seen during autopsies on true-crime television programs, a pair of yellow dish-washing gloves, and a battery-operated lantern.

"I trust this meets with your approval."

She forced herself to turn back to Dr. Glass. He stood beside the girl in the chair, stroking her hair with his hand.

"I was very careful in my preparations, not knowing how you vampires prefer to do things. There won't be a trace of evidence, once I pull down the plastic sheeting. It'll all fit in one of the blue drums. There's a big inciner-ator at the hospital for disposing of medical waste. I know just the right time to come around, when there won't be anybody there, and pop it in. I think you're going to find it very convenient as we begin to explore the mutual bene-fits of our new association."

Ophelia made herself nod.

"And what about the girl?"

"Poor Candy." He gave the girl a sad smile, to which she recoiled with as much horror as her bounds would allow. "Miss Priddle is also one of my patients. Alas, she has not been one of my successes, although I really did believe the electroshock therapy would help her turn the corner. We can pop her into the second barrel and no one will be the wiser. I'll have to come back in my Navigator to get her, though. The barrels are too big for my Jag."

Ophelia tried to think of something to say, but her mind was spinning helplessly.

"Dr. Glass," she said finally, amazed at the control in her voice, "what are you doing?"

"Isn't it obvious?"

Ophelia shook her head.

"I want to become one of you. I have come to admire you very much, Ophelia. You have stripped away the lies and illusion and exposed the true inner core to everything—power and blood. They're really the two essences that it all comes down to, aren't they?"

"Dr. Glass . . ."

"I want to join you. I want to be one of you. I already made one sacrifice for you, but you chose to ignore it."

Ophelia felt as if she'd been slugged in the stomach. "I don't know what you're talking about."

"Don't tease me, Ophelia. It isn't nice. It was on all the television stations. The newspaper is still writing about it."

Ophelia took a stumbling step backward, covering her mouth with her hand to keep herself from screaming.

"You didn't care for those sniveling little bastards. I overheard you railing about them to your friend Zeke. Or didn't you know that I was the one who slaughtered Letitia, Damien, and Pendragon like pigs in the cemetery?"

Ophelia bit down hard on the fleshy place where her thumb met the palm.

"I brought you the sacrifice. We can share her blood together."

It was obvious from looking at him—why hadn't she seen it before? Dr. Glass was completely insane.

Ophelia hadn't seen Dr. Glass exchange his gun with the box cutter, for it was only now that she found it with her eyes. He held it loosely, in an almost offhand manner, in his right hand. The box cutter was opened, and Dr. Glass gestured at his sacrificial lamb with the exposed edge of a new razor blade as he talked.

"Tonight, I will become a vampire, like you," he said, his voice rising. "Tonight, I join you in sharing the sacrament of the blood, and at last I learn what it is like to be like a god."

"Don't!" Ophelia cried, and ran forward, reaching for Dr. Glass's arm. But she was not close enough to have any real chance of stopping him. She involuntarily shut her eyes as the blade arced through the air at the end of Dr. Glass's arm. Something warm and wet sprayed her full in the face.

"Ahhhh!"

Dr. Glass's orgasmic delight was more than Ophelia could stand. She felt her knees buckling and she fell to the floor and curled up as small as she could, wishing she could will herself into nonexistence. Her only chance was to play along with Glass, to pretend to revel in the poor woman's spilled blood, but that was further than she thought she could make herself go. And so she would join Dr. Glass's other patient, stuffed into the blue plastic drum—the drum that he would push into a roaring inferno designed to consume severed limbs and infectious garbage—a fitting enough end. Only Ophelia hoped the end would come before that. She hadn't seen how long it took the other woman to die, once her throat was slashed. Ophelia hoped she didn't suffer much. She hoped—she prayed—death would come equally quick to her.

What felt like a body collapsed beside her on the plastic-draped floor.

Ophelia opened her eyes, expecting it to be Candy Priddle, freed by slashes of the razor from the duct tape holding her body to the chair.

It was Dr. Glass.

Ophelia screamed and jerked herself away from him as if jolted with a powerful electrical current. Glass stared at her sightlessly. He was dead.

"And so you see where all of this has led you?"

Ophelia raised herself up on an arm and looked over her shoulder. Nathaniel Peregrine was standing there, looking a little unsteady on his feet, no doubt intoxicated from the rich wash of blood sprayed over the plastic sheeting behind Candy Priddle and pooling under her on the floor.

Ophelia looked back at Dr. Glass and realized the odd angle of his head. Peregrine had snapped Dr. Glass's neck.

Ophelia pushed herself into a sitting position. Her eyes never left Peregrine's. She could sense his desire, and his hunger, so many times more powerful than the pathetic Dr. Glass's. It was like the sun's brightness compared to the light of the candles burning on the blue plastic drums.

"Now what?" she said.

To which the vampire answered, "Now what indeed."

37

City Lights

THOUGH THE VAMPIRE Nathaniel Peregrine was well into his second century on the planet, he seemed entirely comfortable with the present. Aside from a melancholy that crept into his eyes upon occasion, Peregrine appeared as at home in the world as anybody Ophelia had ever known. Still, she was startled when he picked her up in a car—a forest green Volvo station wagon—as if he were a prosperous San Francisco advertising agent instead of an exotic, immortal creature who, long before automobiles were invented, had ridden a horse into battle during the Civil War.

Peregrine slid a CD into the player and adjusted the volume. The vampire's taste in music was at least a little more than what Ophelia expected. The instrumental pieces were soft and bluegrassy, though in a sophisticated way, no hillbilly twang to the intricately arranged music for acoustic guitar, mandolin, and fiddle. And Ophelia actually liked the music, much to her surprise, though it was worlds apart from industrial Goth.

He didn't say where he was taking her, and she didn't ask. The Volvo headed across the Golden Gate Bridge. He pulled off the road in Sausalito, parking outside a restaurant overlooking the water. The hostess showed them to a table on the deck facing the harbor. The city lights across the bay glittered on the water, adding to the lights of Sausalito, and Alcatraz Island, and the stars overhead. The tide was running, creating the impression of something vast and powerful flowing beyond them as they watched. There was something there—an image still unformed in Ophelia's mind—a metaphor for something. She made a note of it. She could use it in her poetry, if she ever wrote any again.

"It is like life," Peregrine said, as if reading her thoughts. When she looked across at him, he indicated the bay with a nod. "Always in motion, sometimes this way, sometimes that, a force that cannot be controlled or reckoned with. The most you can hope to do is learn its rhythms and sail with them the best you can, because you certainly can't sail against them, not for very long."

"What do you know about sailing?"

"That's my boat." Peregrine pointed at the sleek outline of a three-masted yacht riding at anchor off the marina across the point from the restaurant. "I sailed here on her. And I will sail away on her, too, when I have seen enough of my old haunts."

"When?"

"Soon."

"Take me with you."

The vampire looked away from her and back out toward the sailboats, a few with lights burning inside or on deck, but most of them dark.

A waitress came to the table and Peregrine said they both needed cognac. Ophelia knew there was no way they were going to serve her without seeing her ID, and maybe not even after she showed them the fake one that claimed she was twenty-two. But the waitress smiled and went away for the drinks. Peregrine always got what he wanted, so far as Ophelia had seen. He seemed to have the power to make people obey him. He didn't stare at them, mesmerizing them with beady eyes, like Bela Lugosi in an old *Dracula* movie. Rather, Peregrine just said what he wanted and people gave it to him. At least everybody except Ophelia did. She was the only one who seemed to be able to defy him, though whether this was because of her own power or the vampire's sufferance was unclear to her.

"My wife wrote poetry."

"Did she really?" Ophelia asked with real interest.

"Ah. So it seems there is something about me you don't know."

"I'm sure there are a great many things about you I don't know."

"True," he said as the waitress returned with their drinks. "It was a long time ago—my wife, I mean. I miss her still. But you know the old saying?"

Ophelia raised her eyebrows.

"Life goes on," the vampire said. "Through happiness and sorrow, through good times and bad, life goes on." He held his glass up in toast. "To a long and successful life for you as a poet, Ophelia."

She touched her glass to his and took a small sip. The cognac burned her throat, but after a moment she felt it relaxing her. Peregrine was right; she had needed a drink.

"But only one," he said, completing her thought. "You have seen what too much drink can do to a person."

"My father," she said simply.

"I once was very much like him," Peregrine said. "I had a hard time of it when my family died. I took my relief where I could find it."

"No need to apologize."

"No, but losing yourself in a stupor of drink and

drugs—you're just numbing yourself to the pain; it isn't any kind of answer."

Peregrine drank his cognac in a single swallow, looking up to see Ophelia closely watching him.

"I have been beyond the consolation of such palliatives since the great Change. My system processes drink faster than I can put it down my throat. It's a different story with your father."

Ophelia sighed. "My father is hopeless."

"Yes, unfortunately I think he is."

"He is haunted by his past. He can't bear to be reminded of it. And of course, he does nothing but sit in that house and drink, where his past is all around him. I'm partly to blame for that."

"No."

"Yes, I am," Ophelia said. "He wanted to walk out of the house and never go back after my mother died. But I refused to go. It was my home. My life. I wanted to stay there and be surrounded with all the things I knew as a little girl. He tried to throw away her clothes and things— not put them into the garbage, but give them to Goodwill, to relatives, to anybody who would take them. I wouldn't let him. We had some terrific fights over it all. The only time he sets foot in their bedroom is when he changes clothes. He sleeps on the couch in the den."

"He's dying."

The breath caught in Ophelia's throat. She could see from the way Peregrine was looking at her that it was true.

"I smelled death all the way from my house across the street when I returned. It was almost more than I could bear. You can smell it, too, Ophelia. You just don't know it."

"Because I'm psychic?"

"Partly. All sentient beings, even ordinary humans, are

psychic. It is a latent sense. It frightens most people. They refuse to acknowledge what they don't understand and can't explain. It's like Shakespeare wrote. There are more things under heaven and earth than are dreamt of by most people."

"But my father."

"There is nothing anyone can do. He's destroyed himself. His liver and kidneys are gone. There's something growing in his lungs. I can hear it in his breathing. The years of cigarette smoking, you understand."

"You could help him."

"It is too late for him."

"As a mortal maybe, but you could change that."

Peregrine smiled but without joy. "That is your solution to everything. Do you really think it will solve your father's problems if I turn him into a vampire? Do you think it will solve your problems and make you happy? Do you really?"

Ophelia looked down at the table.

"I have lived a long life—a very long life. If there is one thing I have learned through all my experiences, it is that at the very deepest level what we crave most with all our hearts and souls is love. Unless you learn to embrace this one truth, Ophelia, you will never be happy, not as a human and certainly not as a vampire. Religious teachers tell us love is the secret force binding all of Creation. I have no doubt that someday some physicists will devise an equation proving that love is the force controlling and powering the universe and all of life."

The vampire took Ophelia's right hand and held it between his own, which felt almost hot to the touch.

"I had love and lost it," he said. "This is the way of the world. Anything we acquire we are destined to lose. One of the most important lessons life has to teach you is to let people go when it is time. Because, trust me, my dear, for so long as you live, you will be saying good-bye to people you love. If you have trouble grasping this, the destructive powers of the universe will attach themselves to you like a leech and drag you down into the depths of darkness . . ."

The vampire's voice trailed off, but Ophelia could see that he was lost in his thoughts and did not interrupt them.

"In my own time of darkness, the devil sent a demoness in the form of a beautiful young woman to torment me," Peregrine said. "She gave me the Change, turning me into the creature I am today. For nearly a century I followed her, and when I was finished with her, she followed me. We lived together in Rome, Venice, Paris. I tried to make a new start without her in Haiti, but she followed me to the islands just before the start of World War One, ruining one of the few chances for happiness I have had during the course of a very tedious life."

The vampire's faraway look shifted his focus until it was trained solely on Ophelia, and she could tell he was waiting for her to ask a question.

"Where is she now?"

The vampire shrugged. "I do not know. Perhaps she is out there, watching from a boat in the harbor."

A chill passed through Ophelia, making her reach for her brandy. "Really?"

Peregrine shook his head. "She is very clever, but she no longer has the upper hand. I would be able to sense her out there, if she were there. She will leave me alone now, if she knows what is good for her. You have nothing to fear."

The vampire's expression softened and he began to lightly stroke her hand.

"You are an enigma, Ophelia. You dress like a Goth, like a refugee from another time, and yet you spend your spare time with your computers and the Internet. You carve freedom from the past, yet you brood over your mother's grave. You write poetry—rather good poetry, if I may say so—but on death and other macabre, dark subjects. You are as tortured by your past as is your poor father. If you don't learn to come to terms with your grief, you will end up like him. Or like the psychopathic Dr. Glass. Or even worse, like me—a vampire doomed to walk the earth forever in search of love to set me free."

Ophelia did not dispute what he said. There was no point pretending she disagreed. Peregrine was dead-on right.

"You know that I am fond of you, Ophelia," the vampire said. "My wife wrote poetry, though not as well as you do. You even dress like she used to; black was very much the fashion back in the 1860s."

He smiled.

"I want to help you, Ophelia."

His eyes held hers, looking deep into her, perhaps seeing things within her own mind that not even she could see.

"I want you to think about it very carefully, Ophelia, and then tell me what it is I can do to help you." He smiled. "It is not a commonplace occurrence—a vampire putting himself at one's service. So whatever you choose to ask me for in the way of assistance, think about it carefully and choose wisely."

38

Two Years Later

WHEN OPHELIA GOT home, the first thing she did was go through the big house on Mulberry Street and open the windows. She had thoroughly cleaned the house before leaving, throwing out the old mail, newspapers, and unread magazines, washing the walls and windows, waxing the floors and woodwork, which hadn't been touched since her mother died. She hired a retired woman in the neighborhood to come every two weeks to dust, but the house smelled closed and musty after being shut for so long. Ophelia had planned to return sooner, but one thing led to another, and she'd spent the previous summer in Paris, which had been more wonderful than she could ever have imagined.

It was a pleasant day in early summer. The Northern California sky was cornflower blue, a comfortable breeze blowing in off the Pacific.

Ophelia unpacked her suitcases and put away her things. The clothes she'd brought home with her looked a little odd hanging in the closet next to her old Gothic weeds. She tried to remember when she bought her first skirt or blouse that wasn't black or white. Ophelia hadn't made a conscious decision to put all that behind her, but somewhere early on, she had walked into Dillard's or The Gap and bought something that looked not unlike the sort of clothing any other young woman her age and place in society might buy. Ophelia no longer needed to look different; she *was* different, and she didn't use the way she dressed to either advertise or disguise the fact.

She went down to the kitchen and opened a new packet of dark-roasted Starbucks coffee, enjoying the rich, smoky aroma filling the air. She still expected to see her father sitting there at the kitchen table, either drinking or passed out. He had hardly budged from that spot all the time she was in high school, like some sort of living art installation, a sculpture depicting depression and dissolution. Ophelia lingered behind the chair where he used to sit. His presence was still in the house, as was her mother's. She could feel Mother with her as the breeze came in through the windows, lifting the antique lace curtains.

That was the good part of ghosts, she thought, the love they leave behind to comfort and reassure the living, even if we're not able to identify the source of the good feeling washing warmly over us when we visit a place where people were, if only for a brief time, happy.

The coffeemaker made a slurping noise as the last bit of coffee was forced through the strainer and into the carafe. Ophelia poured herself a cup and sat down with anticipation to read the letter that had been forwarded to her post office box in San Francisco.

The envelope was crinkled and water-stained, as if touched by the rain. The canceled stamps were from the Seychelles, an island group east of Africa, near Tanzania, north of the island of Madagascar. She tapped the envelope on the table and carefully tore it open along the narrow edge opposite the stamps. The writing on a dozen pieces of green-lined notepaper inside were in her father's distinctive block printing.

Ophelia greatly enjoyed her father's letters about his

adventures in the Galápagos, rounding Cape Horn, visiting the ruined Buddhist temples of Cambodia. Though she had never realized it before this correspondence began, her father had talent as a writer. He had a good eye for detail, and a philosopher's insight into the things that made the people he met in faraway lands different, and the things that made them all the same. She kept his letters, and not just for sentimental reasons. Ophelia planned to one day excerpt them in a collection of travel stories.

But she would not share with the world, or with anybody, the early letters, which were filled with pain, regret, and sickness. Her father had gone first to Tahiti, the long crossing without alcohol on the boat a chance at least to begin to get drinking out of his system. The first letter made it plain to her just how sick he was. By the time the letter arrived from Fiji, her father wrote that he was coughing up blood. Ophelia knew that the next letter she got from the South Pacific probably wouldn't be from her father, but a letter of condolence to tell her he had died.

Her father's letter from New Zealand reported that he'd gotten through the bad spell and felt good enough to do some snorkeling. In the letters she'd gotten after that, one every month, her father never mentioned his health except to say he was well, and detailing trips up mountains, down white-water rivers, and through jungles that only a strong man in robust health could have endured.

One day, the letters would stop. Nobody had told her that. Nobody needed to tell her. Notice would come that the boat had sunk in a typhoon, or something along those lines, claiming the lives of her father and his friend, the captain, Nathaniel Peregrine. That wouldn't happen for a few years, and until then, there would be the letters, which had become one of the things Ophelia enjoyed most in life, and looked forward to with great anticipation. And even when the time came, she would know they were out there, watching over her from afar. It was hard to imagine that they would not all meet again someday, perhaps when she was old and gray, though her father and Nathaniel Peregrine would look as if they hadn't aged a day. Yet for the most part, they had gone different ways, and that made her a little sad.

Ophelia had been so certain that she was destined to become like Peregrine, but she knew now she had been wrong. Ahead of her were two more years of undergraduate classes, a master-of-fine-arts degree, and probably a doctorate, all leading to a professorship at Smith or a similar college, and a career divided between writing poetry and teaching other bright young minds to love verse as much as she did. Maybe there would even be a family in her future. She had met a boy the summer before, in Paris, and he was coming to visit her in San Francisco in July.

Ophelia read slowly, savoring every word, wanting it to last.

The note at the end was in Nathaniel's hand, an old-fashioned script that always made Ophelia think of the writing on the Declaration of Independence. She would never be able to thank Peregrine for everything he had done for her. He had given her back her life and saved her father's as well. Beyond protecting her from the insane Dr. Glass—who almost certainly would have killed her— the vampire had stood by her throughout the awful week when police were interrogating her and everybody else involved in the Cage Club scene about their investigation into the double murder. The fact that Ophelia had been one of Glass's patients made them suspicious about her, but the police were never able to prove she was in the building the night Glass and the other girl died. And when it turned out that Zeke and a handful of other Ravening players were also Dr. Glass's psychiatric patients—all of them from wealthy San Francisco families—the investigators stopped paying so much attention to Ophelia. After an investigative reporter at the newspaper discovered that Glass was supplying Zeke and some of the others with prescriptions for powerful drugs, sharing in the profits when the drugs were resold on the street, the police seemed to lose interest in finding Dr. Glass's killer. Then a coroner's jury agreed with the crime-scene investigators' report that Dr. Glass was the one who had slit Candy Priddle's throat. In the end, no one was ever charged with killing Dr. Glass. The last detective who talked to Ophelia made it obvious that the police thought Dr. Glass had gotten what he deserved.

Congratulations on completing your sophomore year at Smith, Peregrine wrote in his brief note to Ophelia. *Keep posting your new poems on your Web site. The first thing I do when we get somewhere that has Internet access is read your latest work. (Your poem about twilight was sublime!)*

Ophelia poured another cup of coffee and went upstairs and turned on her computer. A new poem about homecomings was taking shape in her mind. She would write it directly into an HTML file and post it for her vampire friend and her father to read in an Internet café in Mozambique or Sri Lanka. She'd long since stripped her Web site of the photos and other information about haunted places; they were no longer an interest of hers. But she still used the same Web domain name, which seemed appropriate enough, given the unusual circumstances surrounding Ophelia's house, and the house directly across the street, where Nathaniel Peregrine and his family had once lived: *www.hauntedsanfrancisco.com.*